"Do you know how to fire a gun?" Gabe asked.

"I've never even touched a gun," Amelia replied. "Much less fired one. And I haven't the slightest desire to do so."

His fingers slid down her cheek to trace the fine line of her jaw. "You're in the Wild West now, Amelia. Things out here aren't resolved at tea parties."

She drew in a breath and waited for his fingers to leave her skin so that she could swallow the liquid that had pooled in her mouth.

He dropped his hand. The sun glinted highlights in his hair and mustache. Amelia tried to concentrate on what she was saying. "I...don't think I could fire a gun."

"Then I'll teach you," he said. His deep voice had taken on that husky tone again. Something was definitely happening between them, and Amelia had absolutely no idea what to do about it!

Dear Reader,

Ana Seymour has set her sixth book for Harlequin Historicals in a gold-mining town in the Dakota Territory. *Gabriel's Lady* is the story of an eastern do-gooder who heads west to rescue her wayward brother and finds herself falling in love with his disreputable mining partner. This delightful Western is the first of two connected stories, so keep an eye out for the brother's story, *Lucky Bride,* coming in January.

For those of you whose tastes run to medieval novels, *Knight's Ransom* is the next book in Suzanne Barclay's dramatic ongoing series, The Sommerville Brothers. This story of a French knight who captures the daughter of his enemy to avenge the murder of his family marks the author's exciting return to the series that won her several awards and terrific reviews.

RITA Award finalist Laurel Ames is back with *Tempted,* her new novel that *Affaire de Coeur* calls an "exciting, unusual, and delightfully quirky Regency." And Emily French rounds out the month with her emotional tale, *The Wedding Bargain,* about a Puritan woman who defies her community to marry a bondsman with a tortured past.

We hope you'll keep a lookout for all four titles wherever Harlequin Historicals are sold.

Sincerely,

Tracy Farrell
Senior Editor

Please address questions and book requests to:
Harlequin Reader Service
U.S.: 3010 Walden Ave., P.O. Box 1325, Buffalo, NY 14269
Canadian: P.O. Box 609, Fort Erie, Ont. L2A 5X3

GABRIEL'S LADY

ANA SEYMOUR

Harlequin Books

TORONTO • NEW YORK • LONDON
AMSTERDAM • PARIS • SYDNEY • HAMBURG
STOCKHOLM • ATHENS • TOKYO • MILAN
MADRID • WARSAW • BUDAPEST • AUCKLAND

ISBN 0-373-28937-5

GABRIEL'S LADY

Copyright © 1996 by Mary Bracho

Books by Ana Seymour

Harlequin Historicals

The Bandit's Bride #116
Angel of the Lake #173
Brides for Sale #238
Moonrise #290
Frontier Bride #318
Gabriel's Lady #337

ANA SEYMOUR

has been a Western fan since her childhood—the days of the shoot-'em-up movie matinees and television programs. She has followed the course of the Western myth in books and films ever since, and says she was delighted when cowboys started going off into the sunset with their ladies rather than their horses. Ms. Seymour lives with her two daughters near one of Minnesota's ten thousand lakes.

To Midwest Fiction Writers "veterans":
Kathleen Eagle, Tami Hoag, Betina Krahn,
Pam Muelhbauer

I was so lucky to have you as mentors…
and I am now even luckier to have you as friends.

Chapter One

Amelia Jenks Prescott sat up straight in her seat and gave a deliberately loud sigh. If the disreputable-looking fellow sitting across from her had any trace of the gentleman, he would wake up and move his long legs aside to give her cramped body a bit of room.

It seemed weeks since she had left the relative comfort of the train back in eastern Dakota Territory to climb into the tiny confines of a traveling coach. At first it had been just Morgan and herself, which had been tolerable, but in Rapid City a man and a woman had joined them. The woman had introduced herself rather vaguely as a Mrs. Smith. The man had not said so much as a hello. Then both had gone to sleep, a feat Amelia had found utterly impossible during the long, jarring ride.

She moved one foot to the other side of the man's boot and tried to stretch out her legs. At least they would arrive in Deadwood that night. She could find Parker, rest up a couple of days and, with any luck at all, be back in New York within a fortnight.

She nudged the man's leg with her knee. Through the thin muslin of her dress the muscles of his thigh felt rock hard. To her surprise, her cheeks grew warm. She wasn't accustomed to blushes. But then, neither was she accustomed to having her legs entwined with those of a strange man—a very *masculine*-looking man. And handsome. With carelessly curly, long blond hair, side-burns and an unruly mustache. Blue eyes. She'd seen just a glimpse of them before he dozed off, his head cocked to one side on the horsehair seat. Amelia had had plenty of time to study him and to come to the conclusion that he was a lout. Though his clothes were of good quality, they were disheveled. His white shirt was open at the neck with no sign of a tie. It had been a good three days since his face had seen the edge of a blade.

Her nudge had produced no effect. She cleared the dust from her dry throat and said, "Sir, might I re-quest you to sit up in the seat?"

The blue eyes opened. "I beg your pardon?" the man asked sleepily.

Amelia pointed to their nearly joined legs. "I don't believe these coaches were designed to provide their passengers with *beds*," she said frostily. "I need a bit more room."

Gabe Hatch ran a hand across his whiskery chin. Slowly he pushed himself backward against the straight seat. The hours of sleep had not gotten rid of the ham-mers pounding inside his head. He had an acid taste at the back of his throat. When had he eaten last? Cer-tainly not since he'd started in on the Mad Mule Sa-loon's finest rotgut.

When he had climbed into the coach that morning his head had been clear enough to take notice of his trav-eling companions, especially the slender beauty seated across from him. From the fancy cut of her blue taf-feta dress, her fashionable feathered bonnet and the haughty way her pretty nose had turned up when he and Mattie had climbed on board, he'd decided that she was probably a Southern belle. But now, taking a better look, Gabe reckoned he'd have to reconsider. A Southern belle would endure excruciating pain before she would press her legs against his as if they were at the Saturday-night wrestling competition at Chauncey's. And no Southern belle would stab him with such a direct gaze. The stabbing eyes were brown, he noted idly—dark, velvety brown.

"I didn't mean to wake you, but I've been quite cramped most of the day, Mr., er . . . ?"

Gabe shifted once more to allow the woman more space. There was a wave of pain behind his eyes and he felt sick to his stomach. "Gabriel Hatch, ma'am—or should I say miss?"

Amelia moved her knees to take advantage of the additional room and answered in a less hostile tone. "Miss Amelia Jenks Prescott."

His eyes widened in surprise. For a moment he looked as if he were going to say something, but finally he simply nodded his head and murmured, "How d'ye do." Then he smiled at her.

Amelia felt the breath catch at the back of her throat. Mr. Gabriel Hatch was not at all the kind of gentleman she was used to associating with, but she imagined that even back in the finest parlors in New York City that smile would cause a stir. Cynthia Wellington, for one, would have set her cap for him in the blink of an eye.

She gave a tentative answering smile. "I'm sorry I had to awaken you," she said again.

Gabe leaned forward until his face was just inches from hers and said softly, "You can awaken me any time you like, Miss Prescott."

The words carried a suggestive undertone that left Amelia speechless. And it wasn't only the words that shocked. When Gabriel Hatch moved close, she could smell the distinct odor of liquor. Dear Lord, the man was a drunk! The hands that had been folded demurely in her lap tightened. She leaned back as far as she could and closed her eyes. This was exactly the type of character she had anticipated meeting when she had started out on this onerous journey. She would simply ignore the comment . . . and the man himself.

"Are you feeling all right, Missy?" Morgan's resonant voice had an edge of concern.

Amelia debated the wisdom of opening her eyes. She did not want any further exchanges with the inebriate Mr. Hatch. "I'm fine, Morgan," she said finally, opening her eyes but keeping her head turned toward the side to look directly at the big man who had been her family's retainer for as long as she could remember.

She reached out to give his hand a squeeze. "I think we must be almost there, don't you?"

Morgan shook his head doubtfully. "It doesn't seem to me that this trip's *ever* going to end."

She gave him a look of sympathy. Morgan didn't like to travel. He always said that his six-week passage across the Atlantic in the hold of an immigrant steamer had been all the traveling one man needed for a lifetime. It was only his loyalty to Caroline Prescott that had made him agree to accompany Amelia halfway across the country into the savage West. On a temperance crusade back in '58 Amelia's mother had plucked Morgan from the gutters of New York City and had convinced him to start a new life as a sober man. He'd been employed by the Prescotts ever since.

"The driver said we'd be pulling in by suppertime," Amelia reassured him.

The talking had now awakened their other traveling companion. Morgan's long legs allowed her little more room than Gabriel Hatch's slouching posture had allowed Amelia, but the gray-haired woman was so small that the two appeared to fit comfortably. "I wouldn't put too much faith in anything Charlie tells you, my dear," she said, sitting up and adjusting her tucked silk bonnet. "Back in Tennessee we would say that Charlie's one of those fellows who's mostly all vine and no taters."

Amelia laughed, even though the woman's words were not reassuring. "Are you just arriving from Tennessee?" she asked.

The woman shook her head. "Lordy, no. I haven't been back home in years. I live in Deadwood now...before that Colorado and before that Californy. I'm Mattie Smith." She gave a little nod. "Pleased to make your acquaintance."

Amelia felt herself relaxing. It was comforting to meet another woman in this godforsaken territory. Perhaps she and Mattie Smith could be friends during her short stay in the Black Hills. "The pleasure is mutual, Mrs. Smith. I'm Amelia Jenks Prescott. Is your husband a miner?"

Gabriel Hatch gave a half cough, which drew a sharp look from the woman sitting beside him. "Watch yourself, Gabe," she said crisply. "If you can't see that Miss Prescott here's a lady, then you ain't got the brains God gave a squirrel. Besides, I did have a husband once—Ezekiel Smith, God rest him. He said he was going to make a Christian out of me, but never got very far. The apoplexy took him one day when he had just started in on the Corinthians.''

Amelia's eyes went to Gabe, who shrugged. "I didn't say a word.''

"Mind that you don't," Mattie Smith said. She turned back to Amelia. "Don't let him bother you none, Miss Prescott. Gabe's usually not a bad sort, but today he's got a head on him, as you can see.''

Gabe glowered. "Which is why I should be back sleeping peacefully in my hotel room, where I would be, Mattie, if you hadn't insisted on hauling me out of there....''

Amelia blinked in confusion. Mrs. Smith gave every appearance of being a proper, decent woman. She rather reminded Amelia of her aunt Sophie, the one who brought her sweetmeats every Christmas. But the description of her marriage was certainly odd. And for the life of her, Amelia couldn't determine what could be the relationship between Mrs. Smith and the dissolute Mr. Hatch.

"Go back to sleep, Gabe, and let me talk with Miss Prescott in peace," Mrs. Smith interrupted him good-naturedly.

It looked as if Gabe was about to protest when the coach suddenly gave a lurch to the right, then bolted forward, throwing Amelia into his lap. His hands closed firmly around her arms and kept her from being thrown against the side of the coach. The cab gave four bounces, each slower than the last, and finally came to a stop, tilted crazily toward front right.

Amelia looked up at Gabe Hatch. His expression was one of annoyance, not alarm. His hands loosened their grip on her arms and slipped behind her back to pull her more securely on to his leg. Her left breast was pressed tightly up against his paisley silk vest. The smell of whiskey was overpowering.

"Are you all right?" he asked.

She twisted her body, her rear end sliding intimately along the smooth serge of his trousers. Finally with a shove against his chest, she pushed herself back to her own seat. "Let go of me!" she said belatedly.

Gabe held up his empty hands and gave her an amused smile.

"Is it a broken wheel?" Mrs. Smith asked without concern.

Gabe leaned his head out the tiny coach window. "Looks like we've gone off the road into a coulee." He pushed the coach door open with one booted foot, then, hanging on to the listing doorframe, swung himself to the ground. "You'll have to get out," he said to Amelia.

Amelia looked over the edge of the doorsill. The drop to the floor of the dry creek bed was a good four feet. There was no way Morgan could maneuver over her to get out first and give her a hand, and she would rather fall flat on her face than touch Hatch again. Carefully she gathered her skirts in one hand, then held on to the coach with the other and gingerly lowered herself. Gabe stood watching, arms folded.

Morgan followed Amelia, his legs reaching the ground with hardly a stretch. Mrs. Smith slid along the seat toward the door and reached toward Morgan with one tiny hand. He leaned into the coach and plucked her off the seat, then set her safely down on her feet outside.

"Oh, my," Mrs. Smith said with a little intake of breath. Her eyes went to the bulges underneath the sleeves of Morgan's linen shirt.

The driver, the man Mrs. Smith had called Charlie, had climbed down from his seat and was flat on his back looking at the underside of the carriage. "Don't look good," he said.

With a sigh of exasperation, Gabe dropped to the ground and pulled himself under the coach. Heedless of the smears of dust on his black suit, he slid back out again and sat up with a look of disgust. "The axle's cracked. This rig's not going anywhere."

Amelia's mouth dropped open. "What do you mean, 'not going anywhere'?"

Gabe stood and brushed off his hands. "I mean, Miss Prescott, that you might as well go and sit yourself down over in that soft buffalo grass, because we're going to be here a spell."

She looked around at the barren terrain in disbelief. "Can't you fix it?" she asked the driver, who was sitting on his haunches and shaking his head at the disabled coach. His greasy gray hair brushed the shoulders of his buckskin jacket.

"No, ma'am," he said mournfully without looking up.

"Well . . ." Amelia turned around in her tracks as if searching the horizon for a rescue party. "Someone will have to ride for help," she said finally, looking doubtfully at the four swaybacked horses hitched to the coach.

Gabe reached up to the luggage rack and pulled down a bedroll. "Feel free to give it a try, Miss Prescott. Through Candle Rock Canyon without a saddle or bridle—that would be some mighty fine riding."

"I didn't mean that *I* should go," she said to his back as he sauntered across the dry creek and climbed up the other side to a grassy bank.

Mattie Smith leaned over and patted her on the arm. "Don't worry, dear. Someone will come along before too long. In the meantime, we'll just make ourselves up a comfortable little campsite."

"Campsite!"

"It would be silly for us to keep sitting in that stuffy old cab."

"But..." Amelia's voice faltered. "How long will we be out here?"

Charlie stood and gave a frustrated kick to the broken vehicle. "The mail stage should be coming through about this time tomorrow," he said, punctuating the remark with a stream of brown tobacco juice that landed precariously close to Amelia's skirt.

"Tomorrow..." she repeated, her voice dazed.

Gabe forced himself to take another hot swallow of Charlie Wilson's coffee. He needed an antidote for his hangover. The sleep and fresh air had not been enough. He swatted idly at the insects that swarmed around his head. Pesky little creatures, but not vicious. Not like the blackflies farther out on the prairie that could engulf an animal in minutes and suck it dry. Kind of like some women he could name.

He looked across the campfire toward Amelia Prescott. She was a dyed-in-the wool New Yorker, not at all like her brother, who had taken to the West like a duck to water. When he'd tried to strike up a conversation with her, she'd backed away from him like a pup facing a rattler. It was just as well. He was in no mood for females, particularly not prickly Easterners with highfalutin ways. Even if this one did have hair the color of polished mahogany and a tantalizing figure that, under normal circumstances, would have caused more than his brain to come to attention.

"Are you feeling any better, Gabe?" Mattie's mellow, sympathetic voice broke into his reverie. She stood next to him, only a head taller than he was, sitting.

Gabe gave up on the coffee and poured the remainder into the ground at his side. "I'm all right," he said with a frown.

"You ought to be thanking me, you know."

"Is that right?"

"That trollop was after your money. I saw her watching you all night at the tables. And when you started in drinking like a damned fool, she went over to have a cozy little chat with the bartender. They might even have slipped something in your drink."

"Trollop?" Gabe asked with a lazy smile.

"Darn right. I saved your purse, dragging you out of there. Your worthless hide, too, likely. And I ask myself, why did I even bother?"

"'Cause I'm the only tinhorn in Deadwood you can trust, Mattie, m'love. And without me you'd never be able to get your accounts straight."

Mattie sighed and dropped to sit beside him. "What were you trying to do, anyway, Gabe? I never saw you drink like that in Deadwood."

"If you must know, you interrupted my anniversary celebration."

"Anniversary of what?"

"What else? Of my wedding."

Mattie's jaw dropped. "You're married?"

"I was. My wife's dead."

Mattie shook her head. "Who'd have figured? I always took you for the confirmed-bachelor type."

"Yeah, well, we all make mistakes."

"Do you want to talk about it?"

Gabe flopped back on the grass and looked up at the stars that were growing brighter in the night sky. "No. But that probably won't stop your asking. Let's just say that once a year I make it a habit to get stinking drunk in tender memory of the idealistic fool I once was. If there's a friendly...'trollop' available, I might invite her to share my celebration. And that's the end of it. The other 364 days of the year I try to live a moral and up-standing life relieving cowboys and miners of their excess cash, which, if left in their hands, would in all probability lead them down the path of degradation and sin."

Mattie grinned. "I hadn't realized that your motives were so lofty, Gabe."

"Just shows how little you know of me, Mattie. I'm a prince of a fellow."

"I never said otherwise. But as to your marriage..."

Gabe rolled up to his feet. "What is it about women that makes them ask so gol-danged many questions?" he asked her, softening the query with one of his dazzling smiles.

Without another word he walked away into the dark.

Amelia dug in her carpetbag and pulled out the silk shawl her mother had given her on her twenty-first birthday. It had been the only bright moment in an otherwise miserable day. They had all known it was going to be hard getting through the celebration without Parker. Amelia and her brother were exactly one year and one week apart in age, and up to this year they had always celebrated their birthdays together. Now Parker had taken off with only a note to explain that he had joined the latest group of gold-crazed prospectors rushing to stake out new claims in the Black Hills. Amelia could hardly believe it, and her father had been so distraught that the strain on his fragile heart had sent him to bed for two days.

It had been on the very day of her birthday that the doctor had told them sternly that her father was simply in no condition to continue to work full-time at the bank he had founded and controlled like a fiefdom for the past twenty years.

Amelia ran the fine silk through her fingers, remembering. Then she twisted the shawl around her head, letting it drape over her shoulders. She might look odd, but the insects around her ears were making her crazy. If the shawl didn't work to keep them away, she intended to climb back into the listing coach and make her bed there.

"Is that the latest New York fashion?"

Amelia jumped at the sound of Gabe Hatch's voice coming out of the darkness behind her. She had managed to avoid talking to him most of the evening. She cranked her head to watch him emerging from the darkness. "How did you guess that I was from New York?"

He shrugged and crouched down next to her. "You have the stamp."

She turned back toward the fire. "I'm trying to get away from these miserable bugs. If I were in New York, I'd be wearing this shawl to the opera."

"They won't hurt you—the bugs, I mean. I'm not too sure about the opera."

Amelia ignored his gibe. "There must be *millions* of them. Is it always like this on the prairie?"

"Yup. This time of year." He leaned close to her head and sniffed. "Part of the problem is you smell too pretty."

Amelia pulled away. "I beg your pardon?"

Gabe went from his crouch to a sitting position and leaned back on his hands, stretching his long legs out in front of him. "Your hair. You've used some kind of fancy soap and the bugs like it. Not that I blame them," he added with a grin.

For the second time that day Amelia felt her cheeks growing warm with a blush. Not even her father had ever commented on anything so personal as the soap she used. All at once she remembered that Mr. Gabe Hatch was a reprobate. She should refuse to talk with him. But she found herself answering tartly, "I suppose they like it better than the odor of liquor."

Gabe's grin stretched wider under his golden mustache. "Now, that would make an interesting experiment, Miss Prescott. And I just happen to have some whiskey in my bags. Shall we try it out—for the sake of science?"

If it weren't for the man's remarkable smile, she would just refuse to speak to him entirely. But there was something so engaging . . .

"Shall I get us a bottle?" he asked again.

Amelia took a deep breath. "Mr. Hatch," she said primly. "Obviously you are one of the unfortunate souls who . . . imbibe. I feel it my duty to tell you, sir, that this practice is one which can only lead to a most dire fate."

"Ah." Gabe's expression became sober, but his blue eyes mocked her. "A temperance crusader. Is that why you've come to the Black Hills, Miss Prescott? You'll have plenty of fodder for your campaign here, I wager.''

"I'm no crusader, Mr. Hatch. I was merely giving you some friendly advice. I was not named after Amelia Jenks Bloomer for nothing.''

Amelia bit her lip. Her mother, Caroline, had been a friend of the noted crusader for temperance and women's suffrage when Amelia had been born, but in recent years Amelia had become a bit embarrassed at the name, particularly now that people had taken to applying it to a type of women's underclothes. Nevertheless, something in Mr. Gabe Hatch seemed to bring out the reformer in her.

"I suppose your brother is named John Brown,'' Gabe said with a look of amusement.

The remark took Amelia by surprise. Her brother had, in fact, been named after an abolitionist. Not the misguided firebrand John Brown, but the abolitionist preacher Theodore Parker, one of her father's idols. "How do you know I have a brother?''

Gabe reached to throw a small log into the campfire. "I'm just teasing you.'' His eyes came back to her. "Are you against teasing, too?''

Amelia shifted uncomfortably. The shawl had fallen to her shoulders. She had quite forgotten about the insects. "I'm not against teasing, Mr. Hatch, but you'll forgive me if I do not find it appropriate under the circumstances in which we find ourselves.''

Gabe leaned back again and looked up at the sky. "Nothing wrong with the circumstances as far as I'm concerned. It's a beautiful night.'' He waved a hand upward. "Tell me if you've ever seen a sky like that back East.''

Amelia tilted her head. The sky had turned black. As she continued to stare, more and more stars appeared, until the points of light seemed to be swirling around them. "No, I've never seen anything like this," she answered him finally.

Gabe nodded. "That's the West for you. We may be lacking some of the comforts you have back home, but there are sights here that will make your heart want to leap right out of your body."

His voice had softened. Amelia continued to stare at the spinning, star-spangled sky. A log fell in the campfire, sending up a shower of sparks that joined in the display. "There are more things in heaven and earth, Horatio . . ." she murmured sleepily.

"Than are dreamt of in your philosophy," Gabe finished quietly.

Amelia sat up straight. "You know Shakespeare, Mr. Hatch?"

Gabe grinned. "You're surprised that a lost soul such as I can appreciate the Bard?"

Amelia nodded slowly. His eyes in the firelight were really the most extraordinary blue.

"I find it useful," Gabe continued, moving closer to her. "I haven't found a woman yet who can resist a sonnet." He reached out and took her hand in his. "'Shall I compare thee to a summer's day,' Miss Prescott?"

She pulled her hand out of his grasp and leaned back on it. For the third time that day her cheeks began to burn. Perhaps she was coming down with some kind of prairie fever. She closed her eyes and pictured herself arriving in Deadwood just in time to expire in Parker's arms. It would, she thought, serve her foolish, bull-headed brother right.

Chapter Two

Tin-roofed shacks, brush houses, tents and wagons made into temporary sleeping quarters dotted the steep, wooded sides of Deadwood Gulch like debris scattered after a storm. It was only on the floor of the gulch, the single main street of Deadwood proper, that the structures became real buildings. Amelia stepped down from the lumbering mail coach and looked up and down the block in amazement. It was solid saloons.

"How many drinking establishments does this town have?" she asked Mattie Smith.

Mattie smiled. "Twenty-seven, at last count. You temperance workers have your work cut out for you here."

Amelia shook her head. "I told you—I'm not a temperance worker. I'm just here to find my brother."

"So how come you went off to sleep in that broken-down coach last night the minute Gabe took out his bottle?"

"I don't *approve* of spirits, Mrs. Smith. But I'm not a crusader."

"Well, I'm glad to hear that, Miss Prescott, because you'll find Deadwood a sight easier to take if you don't start in preaching. The truth is that most of these boys come here thinking they'll be rich in weeks. Instead they end up broke and homesick. I figure they deserve what little comfort they can get."

Amelia looked down at her pleasantly rounded companion. "You're a compassionate person, Mrs. Smith, I can see that. I promise you that I don't intend to set about reforming disappointed miners. I just want to find Parker."

Amelia felt a sinking sensation as she realized that the task might prove more difficult than she had anticipated. It might even mean going into some of these... drinking establishments. She sighed. Perhaps Morgan would know what to do. He and Mr. Hatch had both left the coach at the edge of town in front of a tall, thin building with narrow letters that spelled out Telegraph squeezed across the front. Morgan was always proud when an occasion arose to show that he had book learning, a skill he had never had a chance to acquire during his childhood in the mines in Wales. He still worked with her father three nights a week after supper, though Morgan had mastered the basics years ago and their lessons had evolved into spirited discussions of various books they read together.

Mattie cocked her head to one side. "Parker Prescott. Now, that name sounds familiar."

Two cowboys with wide leather chaps over their dirty denims came crashing out of a swinging door just a few feet from where the women were standing. Mattie gave them a brief glance, then continued speaking. "Why, that's Claire's young man. Of course... *Parker.*"

One of the cowboys was holding up a hand of cards. His face was a mottled red, and he was sputtering like a crusted-up teakettle. The other man reached down into his pants and pulled out a revolver. Amelia felt a quick rush through her midsection. "Mrs. Smith, that man has a gun!"

Mattie Smith took Amelia's arm and drew her around the back of the stagecoach. "We'll just stay out of the way back here," she said as calmly as if she were discussing dress patterns.

Amelia leaned against a thick leather luggage rack. "That man pulled a gun," she repeated in a shaky voice.

"Lordy, child. You're pea green. We've got to toughen you up, I reckon. Everyone's got guns in Deadwood. But they don't do much harm. Most of these boys can't hit the side of a barn with their eyes open."

"Shouldn't we call the police?"

"We don't have any police. No sheriff, either. Why do you think Deadwood's so popular with every no-account west of the Mississippi?"

Amelia gripped the edge of the stagecoach and peered cautiously around the corner. The cowboy who had pulled the gun was sprawled on the ground. The other man, cards still clutched in one hand, was sitting on top of him with his free hand pressed down on his opponent's neck. Several feet away, the revolver lay discarded in the dusty street, sun glinting off its steely barrel.

"Come on," Mattie urged. "Let's get out of here. Charlie will take care of your bag until you come back for it."

Amelia let herself be led down the street. "There's no law in Deadwood?" she asked, her head turned back to the scene behind them. A burly redhead was trying to separate the two combatants as the sidewalk filled up with onlookers.

"There's all kinds of law—the law of the gun, the law of the best hand, the law of the almighty dollar," Mattie continued. "But if you mean *real* law...nope. Not in Deadwood."

"I was hoping to ask the police to help me find Parker."

Mattie gave a snort. "That's what I was trying to tell you, child. I can take you to your brother. Come on with me to my place."

Amelia's eyes followed Mattie Smith's hand as she pointed across the street and down a short distance. Nestled between two rough board saloons was a neatly painted clapboard house, looking for all the world like a little piece of New England. A trimmed row of bushes dotted with pink primroses edged the railing of a small front porch. Pink curtains showed at each of the six real glass windows.

"You live right here in the middle of town?"

Mattie didn't answer. She waited until a buckboard had rattled past them, then took Amelia's hand and led her across the street.

Amelia followed along, asking in some confusion, "How do you know my brother, Mrs. Smith?"

It wasn't until they stood directly in front of the tidy yellow house that Amelia saw the discreet sign. Female Companions. Cleanliness Guaranteed. Mattie Smith, Proprietor.

Amelia pulled back with a kind of horror as Mrs. Smith said cheerfully, "Here we are."

"I can't go in there," Amelia said stiffly.

A gleam of sympathy appeared in Mattie Smith's soft gray eyes. "I don't mean to go against your sensibilities, Miss Prescott, but you did say you wanted to locate your brother, right?"

"Yes, but—"

"Then you'd better follow me. Because the odds are ten to one that this is where you'll find him."

Amelia settled into the feathery softness of the rose damask sofa and closed her eyes. In her wildest dreams she would never have imagined that she would find herself in such a place. Although, except for a cloying scent that was fast bringing on a megrim, the little parlor of Mattie Smith's . . . house . . . was not really much different than the sitting rooms back home where she and her mother would take tea with the other ladies of middle-echelon New York society. But when she had entered the front door she had had a direct view up the stairs to a room bathed in red light. Glowing red. She didn't even dare think about the type of activity that might take place in such a room.

"Hey, sis." The soft voice coming from the doorway popped her eyes open.

In an instant she had jumped to her feet and was caught up in her brother's arms. "I could kill you," she said, laughing and hugging him as great tears rolled down her cheeks.

Parker lifted her off her feet and spun her around. "I'd deserve it," he said, giving her a sound kiss.

Amelia put her hands on her brother's shoulders and pushed herself out of his grasp. "I mean it," she said through subsiding sniffles.

Parker's grin faded. "I do, too. I deserve anything you want to do to me, my darling little sister. But it's *damn* good to see you."

Amelia's outburst of tears ended with a final jerky breath. "Don't swear," she said. The admonition was automatic. Though she was a year younger than her brother, she'd been giving him orders her whole life. Their parents had so often been away from home, involved in their own special causes, that Amelia and Parker sometimes felt that they had raised each other. Amelia mothered Parker, injecting some caution into his wild schemes, and Parker provided Amelia with a father's strength and protection. At least, he *had* until he had taken off without a word.

"It's *very* good to see you, sis," Parker amended, tenderly pinching her cheek with a callused hand that Amelia did not recognize as belonging to her brother. His appearance was different, too. His dark brown hair was longer and had reddened in the sun. His skin was tanned and leathery, making him look years older. "But what in blazes are you doing here?" he asked. "Surely you didn't come all this way by yourself?"

"Morgan's with me. He's down at the telegraph office sending a wire to Mother and Father."

"How are they? And Matilda? I bet she misses having her pies stolen right off the cooling rack now that I'm gone. And Chops?"

Amelia smiled and motioned to Parker to slow down his questions. "Matilda says she always knew you were a scoundrel, and when you come home she's going to give you a piece of her mind, if not a licking with her wooden spoon. And Chops wouldn't eat for a week after you left until we finally took to mixing his food with liver paste. So now we call him Golden Chops. As to Mother and Father..." She bit her lip. "They were terribly hurt, Parker."

Parker looked down at Mattie's rose-patterned carpet. "I know. It was the one bad thing about this whole plan. I never wanted to hurt them." He blinked and swallowed hard. "Or you, either, sis."

Amelia let out a deep breath and asked the question that she had been waiting to ask for the past six months. "How could you do it, Parker? How could you leave us that way?"

Their identical brown eyes met, hers accusing, his guilty. "It seems a lifetime ago, you know. At the time I thought I was leaving because I was sick of Father trying to badger me into working at his precious bank. And I was miffed when Cindy Wellington threw me over for Jack Hastings...."

Amelia gave an incredulous huff. "Cynthia Wellington goes through men faster than she does hankies. She's had at least a half a dozen since Jack Hastings, and besides—"

Parker stopped her with a wave of his hand. "Come on and sit down. Just listen to me for a minute," he said, leading her to the rose sofa. "I said I *thought* I was leaving for those reasons. But as soon as I hit the prairie west of St. Paul, I knew that none of those things were important."

"Then what—"

Parker put a finger on her lips. "If you can keep still long enough, I'll try to explain, though it's all beyond words, really."

He shifted his gaze from her to look out beyond the pink curtains to the view of the canyon rising above the buildings across the street. "I've never seen anything like the West, sis," he continued in an almost reverent tone. "It's fresh and majestic, wild and exciting. It..." He turned back to her as he searched for the words. "It fills me up. I don't know any other way to say it. It fills all those places in me that were so empty back in New York."

For once Amelia had no reply. It was as if her brother, the person she had always known better than anyone else in the world, had passed a boundary into a place she couldn't follow. She had been prepared to demand that they return to New York immediately. Their father needed them, needed Parker. But as she watched this totally unfamiliar expression on her brother's dear, familiar face, the words wouldn't come out.

"Listen," Parker said in a brisk tone designed to squelch the emotion that had crept into his voice, "I can show you what I mean better than telling you. Let me take you out to my place to see the mine."

Amelia looked around once again at Mattie Smith's parlor. "Well, at least let's get out of *here.*"

Parker followed her gaze with amusement. "What do you suppose Mother would say if she knew we were sitting in a bawdy house parlor?"

The notion did not seem so shocking to Amelia now that Parker was beside her. In fact, nothing did. Not the broken-down stagecoach nor the fight out on the street. Parker would take care of her now. And she would take care of him. She gave a happy giggle. "She'd haul us up in front of one of her crusading friends—The New York Ladies' League for the Rehabilitation of Fallen Doves, or some such."

Parker stood with a grin and reached for Amelia's hands. "Mother and her colleagues would have a field day in this town."

Amelia had to admit that the scenery as Parker led them up the trail toward his mine was breathtaking. When they had left Mattie Smith's parlor, the little proprietor had been nowhere in sight, so without taking their leave they had made their way back to the stagecoach to find Morgan and retrieve their bags. Then they had gone to the livery where Amelia and Morgan had rented horses over Morgan's protest that there wasn't anywhere he couldn't go on the two good feet that God had given him.

Amelia's mount was a trim brown mare that had taken to her new rider immediately. The stableboy had said her name was Whiskey, which had caused Amelia and Parker to burst into one of the laughs they had shared so often through the years.

"I've been in Deadwood less than a day and I've already visited a brothel and acquired a horse named Whiskey," Amelia said, choked with mirth. It was remarkable how just a short time in her brother's company had restored her good humor.

"You shouldn't have gone into that place, Missy," Morgan called from behind them. "Your mama's going to say I didn't take proper care of you."

Amelia turned around in her saddle. "I suspect there are a few things about this trip that Mother will never know, Morgan."

Parker threw back his head and laughed as he spurred his horse up a sudden incline in the trail. "It's called independence, Morgan. Isn't that what you left the coal mines of Wales to find?"

Morgan shook his head. "Independence is not about doing things your mama and papa wouldn't approve of."

Parker's smile stayed in place. "I know. Maybe after a few days in the West you'll start to understand the kind of independence I'm talking about."

Amelia looked affectionately from her brother to Morgan, who appeared gangly and uncomfortable on the small gelding they'd rented. "You need a bigger horse, Morgan," she shouted back.

"This one's plenty far off the ground for me, Missy. I don't need to go breaking any bones in my old age."

Morgan still had the strength of men half his age, and there was not a gray strand in his thick black hair, but once he'd passed what he had figured was his fiftieth birthday last year, he'd started talking about being old.

Amelia smiled and turned to the front again. The trail had leveled off and they emerged from the piney woods into a small valley. She'd seen such a vista once on the stereopticon at a party at the Hastings', but it couldn't prepare her for the real thing. Long grasses swayed green and golden in the sunlight, sloping down to a sparkling blue-gray stream where a group of deer drank and grazed. On every side pine-covered hills formed a dark majestic backdrop against the bluest sky she'd ever seen.

"Here we are," Parker said, stopping his horse and throwing his arms wide like a circus ringmaster. "Pronghorn Valley."

"Look at the deer!" Amelia said with a little squeal of delight.

"They're not deer. They're pronghorn antelope—the sweetest critters you'd ever want to meet."

"It's a beautiful place, Parker," she said, her voice dropping.

Her brother nodded. "The mine's right across the valley, upriver. Come on. I'll race you."

His horse took off gracefully in response to his signal. Amelia spurred hers to follow him, shouting back to a frowning Morgan, "We'll wait for you."

They raced along through the grasses, sending the herd of antelope bounding away into the trees. Fox hunting had been one of the few activities the brother and sister had shared with their busy parents, and they'd been well schooled in equestrian arts. Neither Amelia nor Parker had ever cared much for the actual kill, but both had enjoyed riding and the freedom of being out in the countryside, away from the cluttered streets and foul air of the city.

Parker slowed as they approached the end of the open grass. Amelia was by his side almost instantly. "Not fair," she said, out of breath. "I've a new mount and don't know the way yet."

"You always did manage to find some excuse for losing," he taunted.

Amelia pulled herself up in the saddle and adjusted the flat silk hat that had tilted crazily along with the chignon it was perched upon. "Mercy, that felt good," she said with a grin.

Parker beamed at her as they took a minute to enjoy being together again. Morgan and his horse were still halfway across the meadow, heading toward them at a sedate walk. From this vantage point Amelia could look up the end of the valley and see a series of odd-looking wooden contraptions built next to and partly in the river. A rough bridge crossed the water and led to a small house built from unfinished pine logs.

They walked their horses up the hill toward the structures. "Home sweet home," Parker said.

Amelia's gaze had fixed on a tall blond man emerging from the door of the cabin.

"Oh, good," Parker said. "You can meet my new partner."

The smile faded from Amelia's face as she let her horse take its lead from Parker's. They picked their way through scattered mining equipment and what looked like mazes built of wood. When they reached their end of the little bridge Parker stopped and waved to the man across the river. "Gabe," he yelled. "Come meet my sister."

Gabriel Hatch sauntered across the log bridge. He'd bathed and shaved and changed his clothes. His dark suit was impeccable. His shirt was snowy white punctuated with a dark purple waistcoat and matching silk tie. He could have passed for one of the dandies from London who visited their father now and then on transatlantic business.

"We've met," he said, approaching their horses. He turned to Amelia. She could see the sunlight actually glinting off his long blond eyelashes as he winked at her and drawled, "I had the honor of spending the night with your sister, Parker."

Parker's eyes widened. He snapped his head around toward Amelia.

She unconsciously tightened her fingers around the pommel of her saddle as her knees suddenly refused to hold her on the horse.

Gabe took a step forward and offered his hand. "May I assist you?" The formal politeness of his tone was contradicted by a smug smile.

Amelia ignored his proffered hand and slid off her mount as gracefully as her weakened legs would allow.

"It's nice to see you again, Miss Prescott," he persisted.

"The feeling is not mutual, Mr. Hatch," she said stiffly. Then she grasped her horse's reins and pushed her way past Gabe on to the wooden bridge, leaving Parker staring after her in amazement.

Chapter Three

Amelia couldn't remember when she had been so tired. She had hardly slept the previous night after she had chosen to spend it in the broken-down stagecoach. Every time she had dozed off she would start to slide down the seat cushion until she ended up crumpled against one wall. She had finally turned around and ended up sleeping with her head downward and her feet stretched above her, a position that had left her ankles quite numb.

Tonight might not prove to be much better, she thought, looking over at the one wooden cot in Parker's tiny cabin. There were two blankets folded on it haphazardly, but no sign of either a mattress or sheets. Tears of exhaustion burned in her eyes.

The final frustration was that "partner" Gabe Hatch had stayed the entire evening, preventing her from having the serious conversation with Parker that she had rehearsed through all those long miles of weary travel between New York and Deadwood. Couldn't the man tell when he wasn't wanted? Evidently not.

Of course, Parker and Morgan had provided an appreciative audience for his stories about his gambling adventures on the great steamers that plied the waters up from New Orleans. And his tour of the Colorado camps, where he had spent several weeks as an *escort* to the famous actress, Lotta Crabtree.

The whole display had given Amelia the headache that had threatened since she had awakened in the stagecoach that morning. Most of the questions she had for Parker had remained unanswered. She still did not know how he had ended up with Gabriel Hatch as a partner. And she had not been able to pin him down about returning home with her.

She stood up from the cane rocker that was the only civilized piece of furniture in the room. "It's getting late, gentlemen," she said.

Morgan, Parker and Gabe turned their heads toward her in unison. Parker jumped up and went to put his arm around her shoulders. "I'm sorry, Amelia. I should have realized you'd be tired after your long trip. Gabe and Morgan and I can go on down into town, unless..." He looked suddenly uncertain. "You're not afraid to be out here by yourself, are you, sis?"

Morgan uncrossed his long legs and stood with a stretch. "I'm not leaving Missy up here by herself. No way. You and Mr. Hatch go on ahead if you like."

Gabe was the last to his feet. "Gabe," he said to Morgan. "It's just plain Gabe."

Morgan nodded and repeated to Parker. "You and Gabe can go to town if you like."

Parker's tanned forehead furrowed with lines Amelia had never seen. "I...I guess I shouldn't be leaving you by yourself," he said slowly.

Amelia had the impression that her brother was seeing the independence he had found so intoxicating being abruptly curtailed, an assessment she felt was unfair. She hadn't come to Deadwood to become his warden.

But in spite of herself, she asked, "Where do you go in town?"

Parker flushed. "The Lucky Horseshoe usually... if I'm thirsty."

"And the Lucky Horseshoe is ..."

Parker dropped his arm from her shoulders and stepped back. "Well, it's... a saloon. Ah, shucks, sis. There aren't any other places in Deadwood to go."

"Except for Mrs. Smith's?"

The flush deepened. "You looked just like Mother when you said that. And you don't really know what you're talking about. The girls at Mattie's are... Well, let me put it this way. I've learned a thing or two about the wicked ways of the world that Mother preached about. And not everything is the way she painted it."

Amelia felt the pressure of her headache behind her eyes. She did not want to argue with Parker tonight, but she felt compelled to ask, "So after a few months in the West you now think it's perfectly all right to drink spirits and consort with loose women?"

Gabe was watching the exchange without amusement. He could see the hurt in Amelia's eyes. But he could also understand Parker's chafing under her scrutiny. A young man who had just discovered the wide world did not want to be cross-examined like an errant schoolboy.

"Your sister's right, Parker. It's too late for more socializing. I've overstayed my welcome. How about if I invite you all to supper tomorrow?" He gave a little bow in Amelia's direction. "At the Willard Hotel, *not* the Lucky Horseshoe."

But Parker's attention stayed focused on his sister. "If you've come out here to light into me like one of

Mother's holier-than-thou reformer friends, you might as well just get right back on the stagecoach east.''

Drums sounded in the back of Amelia's ears. ''Parker Prescott! How can you say such a thing after I've come all this way—''

''I didn't ask you to come—''

''With our father practically at death's door all for worry over you?''

''Since when has Father worried over me?''

''He worries about both of us. He loves us.....''

''Father never worries about anything but his noble causes and his beloved bank!''

''Stop it!'' Morgan's deep voice interrupted. Amelia and Parker stopped talking, but continued to glare at one another.

Morgan walked slowly across the room. As he had done all their lives when he wanted to make a point, he spoke very slowly and his Welsh inflection became more noticeable. ''I'm too old to be a referee to fighting children. And these old bones are too weary to stand here and listen to you two caterwauling all night long.''

Parker's expression remained hard, but Amelia looked contrite. ''You probably didn't get any more sleep than I did last night, Morgan,'' she said. ''Let's call it a day and see what kind of sleeping arrangements we can figure out.''

Parker's lips were set in that way Amelia knew so well. He said stiffly, ''You'll take the bed in here, Amelia. Morgan can sleep out in the lean-to. I'll join him there when I get back.''

''Back from where?''

''Back from Mattie's!'' he shouted. He turned sharply on his boot heel and stalked out the door, ripping his hat from the peg along the way.

Amelia watched him go in disbelief. She had known
that there would be unpleasant moments as she per-
suaded Parker that he had to return with her to New
York, but she hadn't imagined a raw shouting match
their first evening together. Her head throbbed and she
felt a little sick to her stomach. She turned her anger on
their guest. "I suppose he's trying to live up to you, Mr.
Hatch. All those exploits you make sound so attractive."

Gabe gave her a sympathetic smile. "How old's your
brother, Miss Prescott?"

Amelia rubbed her sore eyes. "Twenty-two."

"Well, there you have it. Any lad worth his salt is
going to be out trying to get a taste of life at twenty-
two."

Amelia sighed and stretched her neck. Morgan bent
over her. "You got one of your headaches, Missy? You
need to get to bed."

Amelia nodded tiredly as Gabe said, "You need fresh
air more than you do sleep."

Amelia looked puzzled. "Believe me," Gabe continued. "There was a period in my life when I became an
expert on headaches—both causin' them and curin'
them. You need to clear all this smoke out of your head
before you settle down to sleep." He gestured toward
the fire, which they'd kept burning all night in deference to the approach of autumn chill.

Gabe reached carefully around Morgan's big shoulder and took Amelia's arm. "Come on. Just walk outside a few minutes."

Too tired to protest, she let him lead her out the door
as Morgan watched with a doubtful expression.

"Why didn't you tell me you were my brother's partner?" she asked as he slowly led the way down to the log bridge.

"I thought it was Parker's place to explain the situation to you."

"Well, it would have been more...gentlemanly to tell me that you knew who I was."

"Yes, ma'am. It would."

"So you owe me an apology."

They reached the bridge. "The problem is that being a gentleman doesn't happen to be one of my favorite occupations."

"Favorite occupations such as drinking?"

Gabe leaned his arms on the log railing. "Well, no. You've been misled on that account, Miss Prescott. Drinking's not exactly a favorite, either."

The cool air, just barely scented with pine, did feel good inside her nostrils. Amelia took a deep breath. Beneath them the rush of water sounded comforting, like an odd lullaby. Gradually other night sounds seeped into her consciousness. The insects that had bothered her so out on the trail were nowhere around, though she heard their rhythmic chirping out in the woods. And from just across the river there was an eerie hooting sound.

"Is that a real owl?" she asked in amazement. Owls had always been something out of a children's storybook. She'd never seen one or even heard one back in New York.

Gabe laughed. "That's a real one, all right. A lusty hoot owl, calling out for a mate. Not too much different from your brother."

They had reached the middle of the bridge, and Amelia looked down at the water. She had the feeling that Gabriel Hatch was flirting with her by making such improper comments, but it was not a kind of flirting with which she was familiar.

"Back home Parker would never have dreamed of going to a place like Mrs. Smith's."

"Oh, he dreamed it, all right. All young men do. It just wasn't the kind of dream you share with your family."

Amelia shook her head. The water underneath her danced along in a moonlit ballet. "I'm starting to feel that New York is very, very far away," she said softly.

Gabe fought back an impulse to put an arm around her. In fact, he realized with surprise, he wanted to do more than that. Last night at the campsite he had been ready to dismiss her as a snobbish Eastern prude who was not worth more of his attention. But once he'd left her at the stagecoach this morning, he'd been unable to get her out of his mind. Instead of heading for the game at the Lucky Horseshoe, he'd found himself riding out to Parker's place. And staying all evening. And now he was standing with her in the cool night air, thinking about young men's fancies and hoot owls and imagining how it would feel to wrap her up in his arms.

Amelia had been at first anxious, then furious when she awoke the next morning to hear from Morgan that Parker had not returned home. Morgan tried to tell her, as Gabe had the night before, that it was not such a strange thing for a young man to spend the night away from his home. "Like some sort of tomcat, you mean," Amelia had snapped. And Morgan had looked embarrassed and headed down to the river to fetch water.

Parker had shown up midmorning, whistling and ready to charm his sister into forgetting their quarrel.

He apologized profusely for leaving her on her first night and called himself a scalawag and several other creative names that had Amelia laughing in spite of herself.

By lunchtime they were friends again. They sat on the banks of the little Pronghorn River and ate cold boiled potatoes and hard rolls. "I must say I'm not much impressed with the cuisine here in your fabulous West," Amelia said.

Parker reached for the jug of cider to wash down his dry lunch. "I just haven't had much time for figuring out things like cooking."

"You don't even have a stove."

"Every ounce of dust I find goes right back into the mine." He indicated all the mysterious equipment that surrounded them. "I've bought all this just from working the river with my own two hands and a washpan. Now with a sluice and a Long Tom and a cradle, pretty soon I'll be taking out twenty-five dollars a day or more. And if I find a vein in those cliffs over there, why, the sky's the limit. Twenty-five dollars will be my tip to the shoeshine boys back on Park Avenue."

A glow came into his eyes when he started to talk about his mine. It made Amelia uncomfortable. It was going to be harder to talk Parker into returning home than she had anticipated.

"Couldn't you come home for a couple of years, just to help Father get used to the idea that he can't run everything at the bank anymore? Then you could come back out here."

Parker looked at her as if she were crazy. "A couple of years? This could be *gone* by then. Look at California—the richest strike in history, they called it, and now it's mostly played out. I'm just damn lucky I was able to stake claim to this place. There aren't too many more prime spots left. Before long they'll all be taken.''

Amelia decided to ignore the strong language. In view of the obvious nature of Parker's disappearance last night, she decided that swearing was the least deleterious of Parker's new activities.

''He could die, Parker. That bank is his life, and he's simply not willing to turn over the reins to anyone else but you.''

''He's not willing to turn them over to me, either, sis.''

''At least you could try.''

Parker tore at a tuft of grass and threw it violently into the river. ''We've been warned about Father's heart condition for years now, Amelia. How come it suddenly gets so especially grave just when I'm trying to make a new life for myself?''

Amelia put her hand on her brother's knee. ''We owe them, Parker. They're our parents, and they've always taken care of us.''

Parker was silent, continuing to pull up blades of grass. Finally Amelia said, ''Couldn't your *partner* run the mine for a while? What's his stake in this, anyway? You say you bought this equipment yourself. What has he put into it?''

Parker flopped backward on the grass and closed his eyes. ''It was sort of a . . . mistake.''

''What does that mean?''

He winced and peered up at her through one half-open eye. ''You'll find out sometime, I guess. I lost half the mine to Gabe in a poker game.''

''A poker game!''

''When I first came out I didn't know what the heck I was doing, and I was hardly panning out enough to eat on, so I thought I'd try my luck with the cards. It worked out pretty well—for a while.''

Amelia turned around and sat back on her knees facing him. "I *knew* that that Gabriel Hatch was the one who had gotten you into trouble."

Parker opened his eyes. "It was my decision. Gabe had nothing to do with it. Besides, the pot I lost was worth more than my entire mine, but he refused to take more than half."

"How generous of him! He refuses to *steal* more than half the property of an innocent boy who doesn't know what he's doing."

"I knew perfectly well what I was doing, sis. In fact, you might be surprised to know that I was getting pretty good at the tables."

"Good enough to lose half your mine."

"Just forget it, all right? It's my business, not yours." He rolled to his feet. "I have to get to work."

Amelia watched as he crossed the bridge over to the long wooden trough that ran along the gravel bank of the river. He set his wide-brimmed hat back on his head and bent over to pick up a shovel.

So they had quarreled once again. Parker had changed in the few months they had been separated, and Amelia felt a stab of grief. She wanted her brother back. She wanted her family living all together harmoniously in their comfortable house in New York. But she had the sick feeling that those days were gone forever.

She stood and walked slowly up to the cabin. She felt the need to blame someone for the change in Parker, and the likely candidate was Gabriel Hatch. But when she tried to generate some anger against the attractive gambler, she found herself remembering how he'd helped cure her headache last night, how he'd tried to console her about Parker. Most of all she found herself remembering that when she'd stood next to him on the bridge in the moonlight, her heart had inexplicably started beating as wildly as the wings of a trapped bird.

Amelia knelt on the stone hearth of Parker's big fireplace and stirred a pot of stew that Morgan had helped her fashion from a squirrel he had caught that afternoon. The concoction smelled gamey to her, but she was hungry enough to be willing to give it a try.

She had utterly refused to consider going to town to dine with Gabriel Hatch at the Willard Hotel. Morgan had reminded her of the invitation just after Parker had confessed the manner in which Hatch had obtained half the mine. Though Morgan felt it would be rude to turn the man down, Amelia had decided that, considering the strange feelings the gambler had engendered in her, the less she had to do with him, the better.

The door opened and Parker's lanky frame filled the doorway. They hadn't spoken since their quarrel at lunch. "I have a proposition," he said.

His voice sounded hesitant, but hopeful. She looked up.

"I *know* I can make the mine work, Amelia. And I've just *got* to be able to give it a try."

It wasn't what she wanted to hear. Her shoulders sagged, and she went back to stirring the stew.

"Don't turn away, sis. Listen to me. As I said, I've a proposition. If I had Morgan to help me, I could really get this thing going. Give me six weeks—*six weeks*—to make the mine profitable. At the end of six weeks if I haven't either found my lode or built up our panning to at least twenty-five dollars a day, I'll go back home with you."

His face had that expression of satisfaction he'd always shown when he'd beaten her at a game of chess or two-handed whist. "And what if you do strike it rich, as you say, by the end of six weeks?" she asked.

He hunched down next to her, his eyes gleaming. "Then you and Morgan go on back to New York by yourselves. I'll send Mother and Father my love, and before long I'll send them enough money for that tour of Europe they've put off their entire lives. Father can't very well work at the bank if he's on the other side of the Atlantic Ocean."

Amelia considered her brother's words. She didn't believe there was any way he would be able to make the mine work in just six weeks, even with Morgan's help. It would mean a delay in their return, but perhaps this bargain would be a way to accomplish her mission without more fighting. "You'd need to ask Morgan if he'd be willing," she said.

Parker grinned. "I already did. He says he'll go along with whatever you decide."

Amelia gripped the handle of the stew pot with the makeshift apron she had fashioned that morning from one of her petticoats. "This is ready to eat," she said, standing.

Parker pulled out the flap of his shirt and used it to take the pot from her and carry it to the table he had built from two flour barrels and some planking. "So what do you say?" he persisted.

Six weeks. Six weeks of a wooden bed and squirrel stew and...

"I'd want you to stay away from that Mr. Hatch," she said. "I still think that he's responsible for getting you into trouble."

Parker seemed to sense her capitulation. He leaned over and gave her a kiss on the cheek. "I haven't gotten into any trouble. At least, not any I can't handle. But as to Gabe, he has as much right to be around here as I do. He owns half the place."

Amelia felt the strange flutter in her chest again. She looked up at her brother. "So Gabriel Hatch is part of the deal?"

Parker gave a firm nod. "He's part of the deal."

Chapter Four

It had been a discouraging day. The stew of the previous evening had not set well with her, and Amelia's stomach had rolled all morning. She had gotten on Parker's nerves again with her hovering presence. All she had wanted was to understand the workings of the mysterious equipment he had installed at his mine, but he had grown defensive at her questioning. By mid-afternoon he was fully out of sorts and had taken off again for an unspecified destination "in town."

Amelia sat on the hard cot and looked disconsolately around at the single room that would be her home for the next six weeks. There were two windows chopped in the logs, but they were covered by oil paper, so it was impossible to see outside. Besides the cot, the crude table and four barrel chairs, there was the cane rocker, a set of cupboards built up the wall and a large wood bin. That was the extent of the furniture. Amelia closed her eyes and pictured the elegant Prescott parlor back home with her mother's prize Biedermeier furniture. Independence certainly had its price, she thought wryly. But when tears began to prickle behind her eyelids, she gave herself a shake and stood. One of Caroline Prescott's favorite phrases was, "Never underestimate the power of the human spirit." Surely her mother's daughter could not let herself be daunted by an unasked-for stint of pioneering.

She brushed her hands together resolutely. The room was sparse and crude, but it didn't have to be dirty. Her first order of business would be to give this place a good, thorough cleaning. She marched across the room and flung open the door to call to Morgan, who was at the river's edge sifting a cradleful of sludge.

"Does my brother have any cleaning supplies in the lean-to?" she called.

Morgan laughed. "Cleaning supplies?"

"Brushes, brooms, buckets, soap."

With no apparent effort, the Welshman pulled on a thick rope and hoisted the heavy cradle into an idle position. Then he came over to her. "I don't think so, Missy. What do you want those things for?"

"To clean, of course. If this is to be our home for the next few weeks, the least I can do is try to make things a little more livable."

Morgan peered into the tiny cabin with a doubtful expression. "It would be quite a task, if you ask me."

"Well, it would give me something to do. Obviously Parker doesn't want me hanging over him while he's mining. So I've decided that I'll just take over the housework and the cooking."

"The cooking?" While money was not abundant in the Prescott household with all that was spent on their parents' respective crusades, the family had never been without a cook and a maid.

Amelia nodded firmly. "I don't know why not. I have two good hands and a brain in my head. It can't be that hard to learn. We'll start by going into town and picking up some supplies."

"Yes, ma'am," Morgan said, shaking his head.

There seemed to be no way to lock up the cabin, so they merely shut the door, saddled up their horses and rode away, leaving everything unprotected, as appeared to be the custom in this strange land. They headed back across the beautiful meadow, then followed the twisting path into town. Amelia's spirits rose as they went. It felt good to be doing something, to have a purpose. Parker would feel better, too, she decided, when she told him that she was going to leave him alone to his mining operations and that she would take care of having a clean house and a nice hot meal ready for him each day. Perhaps if she made him happy enough, he would agree to give up his trips to town.

When they reached the main street, she told Morgan, "I'm going to send a wire to Mother and Father letting them know that we'll be heading back in six weeks. I don't know exactly how I'll explain the delay, but I'll think of something. In the meantime, I'd like you to look for Parker."

Morgan frowned as he tied their mounts to the rail in front of the telegraph office. "I don't like leaving you alone, Missy. And, anyway, where am I supposed to find that wild brother of yours?"

Amelia shrugged. "I believe he mentioned an establishment called the Lucky Horseshoe."

Morgan's frown deepened. "Now, Missy, you know very well that I haven't been inside a saloon these past twenty years."

Amelia bit her lip. "I didn't say you had to *drink* anything, Morgan. Just fetch him out of there. Tell him I want to talk with him."

"I don't know...."

Amelia gave him a gentle shove. "Go on with you. I'll send my wire and then meet the two of you at the general store."

His big boots shuffling against the fine dust of the street, Morgan headed down the row of saloons toward a large building at one end that sported an awning and a shellacked sign painted with an upside-down horseshoe.

Tinny piano music drifted out through the saloon's wide-open door. Morgan took a deep breath, set his shoulders and walked in.

Gambling tables covered with green felt filled over half of the large, smoky room. Clustered next to the bar were a few smaller tables just for drinking. Most were empty. A busty woman with bright yellow hair sat on a stool next to the bar, her crossed legs revealing the grimy ruffles of at least three petticoats.

Morgan paused at the door and squinted through the smoke at the gambling tables.

"Hey, big fella," the woman at the bar called to him. "Wanna buy me a drink?"

He walked slowly toward her, politely removing his hat as he went. "I'm just here looking for a friend, ma'am."

"I can be right friendly when I want to be, Samson." Her eyelashes were crusted with kohl. Close up she looked much older than she had from the door. There was no welcome in her eyes to match her words.

"Ah...the name's Morgan, ma'am. Morgan Jones. But I really just came to find a fellow name of Parker Prescott. Would you know him, by any chance?"

She smiled. "Parker's a regular. And a right pretty boy he is, too." The thickened lashes fluttered up and down. "But I prefer the strong silent type, don't ya know. So how's about that drink?"

Morgan shifted his weight from one foot to the other. "Ah...have you seen Parker around here this afternoon?"

The woman leaned back against the bar and turned her head to call to the bartender at the far end. "Roscoe, this fellow here doesn't want to have a drink with me."

The words were slurred, and as she swung around she teetered for a moment at the edge of the stool. Morgan put out a hand to steady her.

"No sampling of the merchandise," said a voice behind him. "If you want Stella's company, you'd better buy a drink."

Morgan turned around. The man in back of him was a middle-aged man, elegantly dressed with a bright silk vest that stretched over a banker's paunch. His cheeks were slightly flabby and his hands looked soft. He had thinning hair that he'd greased and pulled over to one side. Normally Morgan would have brushed off such a man like a bread crumb on a tablecloth, but there was something in the fellow's expression that gave him pause. The man smiled and stood politely awaiting Morgan's answer. His steel-colored eyes held a deadly expression that matched the deadliness of the long-barreled Colt Special tucked into his belt.

"I don't drink, sir," Morgan said softly.

The man's smile grew broader. "Well, now. That's a strange thing to say for a man standing in the middle of a saloon. Or did you think this was the Ladies' Aid Society?"

Morgan held his temper. "I'm just looking for Parker Prescott."

The man hesitated for a minute, then seemed to make a decision. He clapped Morgan on the back and said heartily, "Any friend of Parker's is welcome here, my good fellow. I take it you're new in town."

Reluctantly Morgan introduced himself.

"I'm Jim Driscoll. Big Jim, most folks call me." He patted a hand on his stomach and laughed. He pushed the woman roughly off the stool. "Go on upstairs and get some coffee to sober up, Stella," he told her. "How're you supposed to last out the night when you're sotted before sunset?"

She stumbled away from the bar and headed toward the stairs at the end of the room. Driscoll indicated the seat she had vacated. "Sit down, Jones. The first one's on the house for a new customer."

Morgan didn't move. "Thank you for the offer, Mr. Driscoll, but as I said before, I don't drink. If Parker's not here, I'll just be moving along."

"Something wrong with our liquor, man?" Two cowboys, one with two Smith & Wessons holstered in a double gunbelt and one with a Colt Peacemaker stuffed into his pants, had quietly come up along either side of Driscoll. Morgan took a step backward but found himself up against the long bar. "I'm not here for trouble," he said, holding out his empty hands.

"It looks like Mr. Jones's backbone doesn't quite match up to the rest of his size," Driscoll said with a sneer.

Morgan dropped his hands and tried to move around the three men. Before he could take a second step, the man with the gunbelt had cleared leather. Slowly he pulled back the hammer of the big gun, cocked it and pointed it at Morgan's chest.

Morgan froze in place. A rivulet of sweat made its way along his temple. Driscoll was still smiling. Chairs scraped and the piano music across the room slowed, then stopped altogether.

A man at one of the gaming tables rose to his feet and sauntered toward the group at the bar. "What seems to be the problem here, Driscoll?" Gabe Hatch asked in an even voice.

The smile dropped off Driscoll's face as he turned toward the newcomer. "Go on back to your game, Hatch. This is a private matter."

Gabe ignored him and kept on coming, stopping just behind the cowboy with the drawn gun. His hands were at his sides, fingers slightly spread.

"Mr. Jones is a friend of mine, gentlemen," Gabe said. "And he's new in town. I wouldn't want to see him get into any kind of trouble."

The man with the Peacemaker still tucked in his belt said, "Your friend thinks he's too good to have a drink with Big Jim here."

"I told you to stay out of it, Hatch," Driscoll said, turning around to face Gabe.

"And I told you that Morgan's a friend of mine." He had no visible weapon, but he flexed his fingers and had the look of a man ready to take action.

He and Driscoll locked gazes for a tense moment. Finally the saloon owner shrugged and said, "Tell your friend he'd better be more sociable the next time he comes around here." He gave a curt nod to the man holding the gun, who immediately uncocked it and slipped it back into its holster. Then he pushed past Gabe and walked away.

Gabe gripped Morgan's shoulder. The big man was shaken by the encounter, and Gabe didn't blame him.

Deuce Connors had gotten his nickname from those two sidearms of his, and he handled them as slickly as anyone in Deadwood. "Let's get out of here," he said. "Parker's not around. He must be over at Mattie's."

Connors and the other gunman kept their eyes on them as they walked toward the door. "Friendly town," Morgan said dryly when they were out on the street.

"Yeah, well, most of the people are all right. Driscoll's just gotten too swelled for his britches. He's got the biggest saloon in town and owns most of those rentals up there." He pointed up the canyon wall to a section of tin-roofed shacks built practically on top of each other. "Charges sky-high rents for miserable huts that a pig would think twice about sleeping in. But there are so many danged fools arriving every day determined to strike it rich that he can set any price he wants."

Morgan spat into the dust as if trying to rid himself of the taste of Big Jim Driscoll. "He won't have my patronage again, that's for darn sure."

Gabe started down the street. "I'll walk with you to Mattie's," he said. "I wouldn't choose the Lucky Horseshoe myself except that it has the richest games in town. If you want to talk real money, you've got to be a customer of Big Jim."

They walked in silence for a few minutes. Then Gabe asked, "Why are you looking for Parker?"

"His sister wants him. It seems she's determined to make a happy home for him up there at the mine. She's over at the store right now buying soap and brooms and what all. Says she's going to clean things up."

Gabe chuckled. "Well, now, *that* should be interesting."

* * *

By the time an evasive Parker and an even more evasive Morgan had joined Amelia at the general store, she had finished making her purchases. She stood impatiently, surrounded by bundles and feeling a little self-conscious. The storekeeper didn't seem to mind having a strange woman planted in the middle of his store, tapping her foot and looking around restlessly.

Parker had refused to offer much in the way of an explanation for the delay, though he claimed to be pleased that she had found a project with which to occupy herself and agreed to return to the cabin with them. All in all, the trip to town had brought back Amelia's headache, and she decided to postpone her cleaning venture until the next day.

It proved to be a wise decision, since she awoke the next morning with a clear head and a renewed determination to make the best of her stay in the West. Even the weather seemed resolved to put on its best face. It was a brilliant, cloudless day. The stream sparkled like liquid diamonds and the valley beyond looked green and inviting. Amelia thought for a moment of taking a short ride across the meadow before she started her work, but firmly pushed the idea away. Her first task was to do laundry, and since she had never in her life washed so much as a handkerchief, she figured she'd better get an early start.

Parker was on his best behavior, evidently as determined as she that their six weeks would be pleasant. He agreed without fuss that Morgan should stop working on the mine long enough to help her fill the washtub they had cut from a barrel and haul water up to the new copper boiler she'd purchased in town.

Once she had her system set up, Amelia told Morgan that he could go back to helping Parker. She would handle things from here on. What could be that difficult about boiling and rinsing clothes?

Feeling a touch of that independence Parker had boasted about, she prepared the first batch. She remembered that Meggie, the Irishwoman who came in once a week to supervise the laundry at the Prescott household, always put the light-colored things together, particularly the more delicate...unmentionables. As she started to choose items from the pile that Parker had gathered for her the previous evening, it dampened her enthusiasm a bit to discover that it wasn't only Parker's *house* that hadn't been cleaned in weeks. But she persisted and added some things of Morgan's and her own until the boiler was chock-full. She ladled out a spoonful of soap. She had no idea how much to use nor how long the things should boil, but it didn't seem that such considerations should matter. After all, she had been the star pupil at Miss Longworth's Female Academy four years running. How hard could it be to do a little laundry?

Gabe gave his horse free rein across the last flat stretch of meadow. Yesterday he had resisted the urge to walk with Parker and Morgan to see Amelia. Her refusal to dine with him had made it fairly clear that she was not interested in cultivating their acquaintance. But this morning he'd found himself mounting up to ride out to the mine with absolutely no excuse whatsoever except the beauty of one of the last hot days of summer. Amelia Prescott might not want to see him, but she'd left him with a bur under his saddle that had to get combed out . . . or at least scratched a bit.

Parker and Morgan were upstream at the far end of the digs, so Gabe hitched his horse, untied a paper-wrapped package from the back of his saddle and headed for the little cabin. The paper contained a slab of salt pork. Not the most romantic of offerings, but he knew the state of Parker's larder and figured that by now the lad's Eastern visitors could be getting pretty hungry. They weren't used to living on scrawny rabbits and scavenged wild vegetables like the more veteran miners up and down the Black Hills.

He couldn't hear any noise from inside the cabin. Perhaps Amelia was upriver with her brother. Tentatively he pushed open the door and looked inside. He couldn't decide whether the scene that met his eyes was comical or tragic. Amelia sat next to a large tub with her legs stuck straight out in front of her. The dirt floor underneath her had turned into a giant mud puddle that had splattered her light blue dress with polka dots of mud. She was surrounded by soaked, muddy articles of clothing. The water in the tub was black. A copper boiler lay on its side by the fire, more clothes tumbling out of it onto the ground. Amelia held one item in her hands and was viewing it with an expression of mourning.

She turned when the door opened. "Oh, fine," she said. "Now my day is complete."

"You're glad to see me, I take it," Gabe answered. The comical was winning out over the tragic, but he kept his expression neutral.

"What do you want, Mr. Hatch?"

Gabe looked around the room. "I...ah...heard you were determined to clean this place up."

"Mr. Hatch," she said in a slow, deliberate tone, "I'm sure your business is with my brother. He's up the hill somewhere with Morgan. Please go find them and leave me alone. I am, as you can see, very busy.''

Her voice was a strong contrast to the forlorn picture she presented. No one would say that little Amelia Prescott lacked pluck. ''Can I help?'' he asked mildly.

Her chin came up another degree. ''I'm doing just fine, thank you.'' When he continued watching her with a sympathetic look in his eyes, she added, ''Except...except...''

Finally there was the slightest tremor in her voice. He moved closer, just to the edge of the ring of mud, and crouched down. ''Except what?'' he asked gently.

She pulled her bottom lip through her teeth. Her mouth was full and red, Gabe noted idly. Ripened.

She lifted the soggy piece of clothing from her lap, then let it drop with a sodden splash. With an intake of breath that could have been close to a sob, she said, ''This was my only nightgown.''

Gabe glanced at the garment. It appeared to be made plainly of a serviceable white cotton. What *had* been white cotton. ''Are you having trouble getting it clean?''

She shook her head. ''It's *ruined*. Look.''

He leaned close as she picked it up once again. The entire piece was covered with sticky black globs.

''What water did you use?''

She looked confused. ''Well, just...water. From the stream.''

''Ah.'' He stood and walked through the mud to pick up the fallen boiler. Then he began dumping the dirty clothes back into it. ''The streams around here are full of minerals. See how the clothes have turned yellow?''

He spoke calmly, as if to a child, and gave Amelia time to compose herself. She picked at one of the little black balls. ''Will these ever come off?'' she asked.

"Perhaps. With patience. But the way to start would be to wash everything again. Doesn't your brother have a rain barrel?"

She gave a forlorn shrug.

"You need fresh water and lots of soap. How much did you use?"

She cupped her hand to indicate the size of the spoonful. The skin of her palm was bright red.

"You've burned yourself!"

She quickly turned her hand over, but he reached for it and gently spread her fingers out. "It's nothing," she said.

"Didn't you pour cold water over the clothes before you took them out of the boiler?" She didn't answer. He dropped her hand with a shake of his head, then collected the soiled nightgown from her lap. It appeared to have fared worse than most of the other garments. "Whenever you have to use river water, you need to use a lot of soap."

"I didn't think it would make any difference."

He smiled at her. "It's not quite the same as turning on a faucet over a washtub back home, is it?"

"Mr. Hatch, I have never in my life turned on a faucet over a washtub."

Her expression had regained some of the defensive haughtiness he had found so intriguing the other day. He liked it better than the sadness he had seen in her eyes when he came in, which had put an uncomfortable soft spot in the middle of his gut.

"Well, then, you can learn from the beginning." He reached out his hand. After a slight hesitation, she took it and let him pull her up out of the dirt. "We'll start by moving this operation out of Mudville, here. There's a nice grassy bank behind the cabin that will do just fine."

By late afternoon it was done. Gabe's brisk manner and gentle jokes had helped Amelia overcome her initial embarrassment at seeing him, his white ruffled shirt rolled up to his elbows, scrubbing away at her most personal items of clothing. She'd never in her life seen a man do laundry, but Gabe seemed to think it nothing extraordinary. A few of the garments had been beyond remedy, including her nightgown. Sadly she'd crumpled it into a ball with the other ruined things and tucked them away in the corner of the cupboard to use as rags.

She sat back against the little hill bank and surveyed the results of their efforts. Freshly cleaned clothes, now only slightly yellowed, flapped in the breeze from the clotheslines Gabe had strung between three small trees in the back of the cabin. The boiler had been dried and put away in the cabin and the barrel washtub was emptied and lying on the ground bottom up.

She was glad that Parker and Morgan had taken their lunches with them this morning and had not returned to the house at midday. She didn't think she could bear having them see the mess she had made. They would be home soon, though, and hungry as usual. She didn't have an ounce of energy left to prepare a meal, and she had no idea what they were going to eat. The squirrel stew was gone, and neither Parker nor Morgan had been out to catch anything else. Remember stores? she thought to herself. Stores where you bought food in boxes and cans? Restaurants? Restaurants where you sat at tables covered with snowy linen and fine china and were served course after elegant course by a discreetly hovering waiter?

"Now what's the problem?" Gabe interrupted her thoughts.

"I beg your pardon?"

"You look gloomy again. The laundry's done. The floor inside has almost dried. The only thing left to do is get you cleaned up," he added, gesturing to her now completely filthy dress.

She felt her cheeks color. She couldn't believe she was sitting on the bank, her dress wet and clinging to her in what must be a most indecent way, her skirt pulled up inches above her ankles and her feet bare, since she had abandoned her soggy shoes halfway through the afternoon. She must look like the worst kind of hoyden. "I am a sight," she said ruefully.

"Yes, you are," he agreed easily, his eyes bright as they roamed the length of her.

"We've used all the rainwater."

Gabe grinned. "I don't think your skin will turn yellow if you use the stream. It's not even too cold this time of year. You'll find it refreshing."

Amelia's eyes widened. "You mean... *bathe*... in the stream?"

He nodded. "Unless you want to ride into town to Mattie Smith's. She's got a bathtub upstairs the size of a dance floor."

Amelia scrambled to her feet. "No...ah...no. I have no intention of ever setting foot inside that woman's establishment. And I'd appreciate if you wouldn't mention it when you come around here."

Gabe's grin died. "You could do worse than make friends with Mattie, Miss Prescott. She knows this territory, understands how to live out here. Whereas you—" he gave a suggestive glance at the laundered clothes "—are what we would call a tenderfoot."

"I know... I'm as green as spring grass. But I'm going to learn, Mr. Hatch. And I don't intend to learn from the likes of Mrs. Smith."

"You didn't object to learning from me," Gabe observed.

"I didn't really have much choice in the matter. But, anyway, at least you don't own a bawdy house. You're only a... a..."

"A dissolute gambler and unrepentant drunkard?" he supplied with a serious face.

Amelia's flush deepened. "You have told me that you don't make a habit of imbibing, and I shall take you at your word. However, you *do* make your living gambling, and I can't say that it's a profession I admire."

Gabe got to his feet, smiling once again. "At least you've forgiven me for my uncharacteristic appearance the day we met. It's a start."

"Please don't count on it being a start to anything, Mr. Hatch," she said primly. "I've promised Parker that I won't object to your presence here, since you seem to have *won* the right to be here. But that doesn't mean I have to entertain you or treat you as anything but a business associate of my brother."

He stood just down the bank from her, so that their eyes were nearly level. "Oh, but I was *greatly* entertained this afternoon, Miss Prescott, and you weren't even trying. I can't imagine what it would be like if you truly made an effort."

"Nor will you find out," she said, then spun on her heel and started down toward the stream. Gabe watched her go. Her wet dress clung to her back and hips and molded itself around her tantalizing little bottom. He gave himself a shake. It had been a long time since he'd resorted to paying for something that usually fell into his hands with very little effort. But perhaps he should give Mattie's girls another look. He sure was feeling the itch these days.

Amelia marched up to the edge of the stream, paused, then continued walking right into it, clothes and all. Gabe called to her in surprise, "You're supposed to go in *without* your clothes."

She didn't turn around. "Not likely with you standing there, mister. Anyway, the dress needs bathing, too."

She was up to midthigh when her heavy, wet clothes started dragging her along with the current. Gabe ran to the stream and plunged in after her, grabbing her hand and pulling her back toward shore.

"Lord almighty, woman. You don't need a teacher, you need a keeper."

Amelia pulled her hand out of his grasp, wincing. "You didn't have to grab me like that. I was fine."

"It was either grab you or go collect you in a heap five hundred yards downstream," he said angrily.

Amelia was rubbing her reddened palm.

"Your hand *is* burned, isn't it?"

"It hurts a little," she admitted.

They were standing in about a foot of water at the edge of the stream. Gabe gave an exasperated sigh, then grasped her shoulders and turned her to face him. Before Amelia could stop him, he unbuttoned her lace collar, took it off and flung it up on the bank. "Now the dress," he said, reaching for the top button.

Amelia took a step back into the stream. "Don't you dare!"

"I will if you don't do it yourself. Dress and petticoats, too. I'm sure you're wearing some kind of duded-up Eastern underclothes that will serve just fine to protect your modesty. Then you can go in, but stay on this side—don't go into the middle where the current's too swift."

Amelia looked around helplessly. "I can't... I have to..." Finally she concluded weakly, "Parker and Morgan will be coming home wanting their supper."

Gabe lifted his finger in the air. "I forgot. In all the fuss, I didn't mention that I brought supper—a ten-pound slab of salt pork."

"Salt pork," she said, looking uncomfortable. "Ah... thank you."

Gabe cocked his head and tried to get her to meet his eyes. "What's your favorite way to cook it?" he asked.

"Cook what?"

"Salt pork."

She looked up at him. "Fried?" she ventured.

He grinned. "Excellent. That's my favorite, too."

She looked relieved.

"But you've had quite a day," he said. "And your hands are burned. So how about if I go ahead and fix it while you're taking your bath?"

"You'd fix the supper?" Her chin dropped.

"It wouldn't be the first time. I rather like cooking, to tell you the truth."

Amelia felt a little dazed, and her feet were beginning to get numb from the cold water. The day had certainly not gone as she had planned. But she hadn't eaten since breakfast and if Gabe was willing to put some food on her table, she'd let him do it. She didn't care if it was rattlesnake. "I'd be very grateful, Mr. Hatch," she said after a moment.

He tipped up her chin to force her to look at him once again. "There's a price for my services," he said softly.

Something had changed in his voice, and it made the rest of her go as numb as her feet. "What do you mean?" she asked, her throat sticking on the words.

"You have to start calling me Gabe."

Amelia cleared her throat. "Back East it wouldn't be proper for—"

"You're not back East anymore, tenderfoot," he said with the same husky tone. Then he touched his finger to the tip of her nose and turned to leave. As he slogged out of the water in his wet boots he turned back to her and said. "Supper's on in half an hour."

Chapter Five

Parker and Morgan didn't seem the least surprised to find Gabe hunched over a big iron spider on the fire grate when they came in from their day's work. Amelia had been sitting in the rocker watching him, but she jumped up guiltily when her brother came through the door.

"I see you finished the washing, sis," he said. "Good job."

Amelia glanced down at Gabe, who gave her a conspiratorial wink. "Some of the things are a little yellowed," she said.

Parker laughed. "Yellow passes for white out here. Those kinds of things aren't as important as they were back home. Can you imagine what Mother would say to a batch of yellow clothes?"

Amelia giggled. "She practically has a case of the vapors when the laundrymaid puts a little scorch mark on one of Father's collars."

They all laughed together, then Morgan said, "Something smells mighty good."

Amelia's smile died. "Mr. Hatch...*Gabe*...brought us some salt pork and insisted on cooking it himself." She looked over at her brother, expecting to be reproved or at least teased for putting a guest to work, but Parker looked unaffected.

"Morgan's right. It smells wonderful. I could eat a polecat," he said.

Amelia let out a long breath. Gabe stood up holding the handle of the frying pan with a towel. "She's ready and waiting," he said.

Amelia had already set the table. She held out Parker's tin plates as Gabe served up the food. She had found it fascinating to watch him as he had efficiently and expertly prepared the food. He'd cut the pork into slabs, which he'd first parboiled, then rolled in flour and fried. In the grease that was left he'd fried onions, which he then poured over the cold potatoes Amelia had left from breakfast. To Amelia it looked and smelled more delicious than anything she'd ever tried in the elegant tearooms of New York City. They all sat down at the table and, with little conversation, dug in. She ate until she thought her sides would burst, and then, to the amusement of the three men, she ate a few bites more.

When they had finished, she insisted that *she* would do the washing up, and she literally pushed Gabe down into the rocker as Parker took out his bag of tobacco and passed it around. It was a new habit of his that Amelia found repulsive, but she refrained from commenting and went to wash the dishes. When she had finished, she stood silently for a few minutes, watching the men enjoying each other's company. Though she was utterly exhausted, she was reluctant to interrupt their camaraderie by insisting on having her bedroom to herself.

At the first lull in the conversation, Gabe looked over and saw her standing idly by the fire. "It's time for bed, gentlemen," he said, getting up. "Thank you for the fine evening."

"Thank *you* for the supper," Parker replied, also getting to his feet. He waited for their visitor to head for the door, but Gabe hesitated.

"I have a last little item of business with Miss Prescott," he said.

Parker lifted a questioning eyebrow.

"It will just take a minute," Gabe said. He made no move to leave.

Finally Parker shrugged and turned to go out. "C'mon, Morgan. That gold dust will be waiting for us bright and early tomorrow."

The two men left, leaving Amelia looking uneasily at Gabe. "I thank you for the supper, too," she said softly. "And for everything else today. Especially for not telling my brother what a coil I'd gotten myself into."

Gabe smiled gently. "It wasn't so very much of a coil. As you say, you're learning."

He still stood without moving, his eyes intense and gleaming in the firelight.

Amelia smiled nervously. "Was there something you wanted to talk to me about?"

Gabe shook his head, then advanced slowly toward her. She could see the stubble of his beard, the flinch of a muscle along his straight jaw. When he was close enough to see tiny reflections of the flames in the blue of his eyes, he stopped. She swallowed.

"You said you had some business with me." Her voice came out as a near whisper.

"Yes."

He was not smiling now, and something in his expression made the breath stop dead in Amelia's chest.

He leaned closer. She closed her eyes and had a swift, unbidden memory of the moment in the stagecoach when his hard thighs had rubbed against her.

Her entire body swayed as she felt him brush against her. Then she opened her eyes in surprise as he bent to reach past her toward a crock on the floor next to the fire. He scooped up a handful of the contents and straightened up, facing her.

"Give me your hands," he said.

Amelia was still trying to locate her last breath.

"Your hands," he said again, seizing one of them. His fingers were covered with pork grease, which he started to gently smooth over her still-red palms. He spread it slowly in small circles. "It might not smell as pretty as that lemon soap you like to use, but it should help that burn heal."

Amelia felt the light pressure of his fingertips all the way up her arms. She took a deep gulp of air, which seemed to steady her. "It was kind of you to think about it," she said.

Now he smiled at her, which lightened the tension that had grown between them. But Amelia's heart was still beating far too fast.

He finished with one hand and repeated his ministrations with the other. Then he stepped back and leaned over to grab a towel to wipe his fingers. "That should do it," he said. "Now I will bid you good evening."

He walked to the door, retrieved his hat and opened the door. "Thank you for a most enjoyable day, Miss Prescott," he said with a little bow.

As he started to leave, Amelia called, "Gabe." He turned back to her. "You may call me Amelia."

He looked taken aback for a moment. Then he grinned, nodded and went out the door.

"So what's put the bee in your bonnet, Gabe Hatch?" Mattie Smith and Gabe were in her office where Gabe was finishing up her monthly accounts. When she had given up the dance hall circuit and gone into business for herself, Mattie had insisted on two things. Her girls must keep themselves clean and healthy, and in return she promised to be scrupulously accurate in seeing that they got their fair share of the earnings. The latter had become easier when Gabe Hatch had come to town. Mattie had never much liked numbers herself.

"I don't know what you're talking about, Mattie," Gabe answered absently.

"Well, you snapped at Delia when she offered to take you upstairs for half the regular fee. Then you started entering the figures in last month's account. And in the past five minutes you've added the same column of numbers six times by my count. So I figure there's got to be something on your mind."

Gabe frowned and threw his pen on the desk. Mattie sat across the desk from him, curled up in an over-stuffed armchair that dwarfed her tiny frame. Except for her gray hair, she looked like a plump little child. "I guess I'm tired," he said finally, pushing back his chair. "Maybe I should finish up on these later."

"Maybe you should have taken Delia up on her offer," Mattie suggested. "Best cure for 'tiredness' I know."

Gabe smiled. "No, thanks." He winked at her and added, "Your girls are lovely, Mattie, but I'm still waiting for you to break down and make me an offer yourself. Why should I settle for second best?''

Dimples appeared in Mattie's soft cheeks, but she kept her voice stern. "Go on with you, Gabe. An old gal like me deserves some rest in her sunset years. I don't need any more hassling by young bucks like you."

"Sunset years," Gabe scoffed. "Why, you're barely reaching the noon hour, Mattie, love."

The dimples deepened. "You're full of malarkey, Gabriel Hatch. And what's more, you're trying to distract me by changing the subject. You still haven't told me what's wrong."

"Yes, I did. I'm tired. It was late when I came back into town last night."

Mattie leaned forward and demanded, "Came back from where?"

Gabe closed the book and stood. "From my partner's place."

Mattie's gray eyes gleamed wickedly. "Sure, now. Would that be the partner whose sister just arrived in town? A sister with the face of an angel and hair like the mane of a prize bay mare? Is that the partner you mean?"

Gabe rolled his eyes. "Parker's the only partner I have, Mattie, as you well know. As for his sister, well, yes...she's quite lovely."

Something in the tone of his voice made Mattie's expression grow serious. "You aren't getting yourself stuck on that fancy Eastern lady, are you, Gabe?" she asked, a line of worry creasing the skin between her eyes.

"Don't be ridiculous." He started toward the door. "I'll come back and finish these books tomorrow."

Mattie jumped out of the chair and went to put a hand on his arm. "You'd be better off with Delia," she said kindly. "Or any of my girls. Belle's mighty sweet."

Gabe patted her hand, then gently removed it from his arm. "I'm not interested, Mattie. At least, not today."

Mattie shook her head. "You oughtn't go messing with a lady like Miss Prescott. Why, they say her pappy's a genuine New York City banker. He's likely to send some of those Pinkerton boys to blow your head off."

Gabe leaned down and gave her a kiss on the cheek. "I don't think the Pinkerton agents are for blowing people's heads off, Mattie. But, at any rate, I have no intention of 'messing' with Miss Prescott. Or anyone else, for that matter. The only engagement I have planned is with a deck of cards."

Amelia sat in the rocker doing her best to mend her brother's tattered long underwear. She had decided to spend the day on a less strenuous activity after yesterday's marathon laundry session. And she found herself enjoying the task. Her mother would undoubtedly have been horrified to see her stitching away on a man's undergarment, even though it was her brother's. Back home she had never stitched anything coarser than fine linen with silk embroidery thread.

Suddenly Parker burst through the cabin door with a whoop of triumph. He took two leaps to reach her side, then lifted her out of the chair and spun her around. "We're getting closer, sis! Morgan's a wonder. He followed a vein straight back into a crevice that I'd never even noticed before. And it looks like it's rich with ore."

Amelia couldn't help being caught up in her brother's enthusiasm. She laughed and reached to straighten her tumbled chignon. "It's a fine millionaire you'll be making, Parker Prescott," she teased.

He set her down. "I came running to tell you," he said, trying to catch his breath.

"Do you think it could be the main strike you've been looking for?"

"I don't know, but it's shining brighter than the noonday sun, sis. Come on with me and see."

He half dragged her out of the cabin and up the hill to the spot where Morgan was waiting, an ear-to-ear grin on his face.

"We're going to make your brother a rich man yet, Missy," he said.

Parker slapped him on the back. "We'll all be rich—you too, Morgan. Part of everything you help me find should rightly go to you."

"You don't need to do that...."

"No, I mean it. And I'm sure Gabe will feel that way, too. Anyway, I have a feeling there's going to be plenty for everyone!"

Amelia tried to mirror her brother's excitement as he pointed out the thin line of gold that they'd traced back into the cliff. But she'd lost some of her enthusiasm at the mention of Gabe's name. As she had sat sewing all afternoon, her thoughts had turned too often to the attractive gambler. It had been a mistake to be nice to him yesterday, she decided, in spite of all the help he had given her. In one of the few moments her mother had taken the time to talk with Amelia about the relationship between the sexes, she had made it very plain that men who gambled and drank should be given no encouragement. And even without encouragement, her mother had warned, they were likely to practice their wiles on unsuspecting females. Amelia had been a bit vague about exactly what kind of wiles they would be practicing, but she had promised to remember her mother's words.

"So, what do you think? Isn't it something?" Her brother's voice had risen with his excitement, making him sound like the young Parker who had always made her tag along on his adventures as a child.

Actually, the vein looked very small to her, like a dribble of gold paint. But she smiled and returned the hug he gave her. "How long will it be before you can tell how extensive this is?"

Parker looked at Morgan. "We'll start in digging first thing in the morning," the Welshman said. "We should know something in a day or two."

Parker danced from one foot to the other as if he couldn't contain himself. "I've got to tell Claire," he said.

Amelia was silent. She had been meaning to talk to her brother about this folly of his in pursuing one of Mattie Smith's girls, but she hadn't found the right moment.

"C'mon, sis. Let's go into town and celebrate. You, too, Morgan."

He looked from Morgan to his sister. There was doubt on both faces. "We have salt pork left from last night for supper," Amelia said.

Parker took both her hands. "Millionaires don't eat salt pork. I'll take you to the Willard Hotel for a nice steak dinner."

Amelia hesitated at the hopeful look in her brother's eyes. She didn't like to dampen his enthusiasm, but she didn't want to encourage his trips to town and his visits to . . . that house. Nor was she anxious to run into Gabe Hatch. "I think we should stay home, Parker," she said finally.

The glow faded from her brother's face. "You can stay home if you like," he said stiffly. "I'm going into town to celebrate."

He turned down the hill, then craned his head to call back, "Are you coming, Morgan?"

The big man shook his head. "I'll stay here with Missy," he said soberly.

"Fine," Parker said. He gave his sister a frosty glance. "Don't wait up for me."

The next morning Parker was subdued and appeared to regret that he and Amelia had once again quarreled. Without saying much, he helped her build the fire to heat up the breakfast coffee. Both he and Morgan were anxious to get back to their discovery. They gulped down a cold breakfast of bread and dried fruit, then started up the hill.

Amelia had decided to tackle the task of cleaning the cabin. With a dirt floor, there was little she could accomplish by sweeping, but she wiped the dust off the furniture and window ledges and hung the blankets out to air on the clotheslines that Gabe had put up. The more she thought about that day of the laundry, the more mortified she became. When Gabe had been here, it had not seemed so outrageous. But thinking back on it—how he had found her sitting in the mud of her cabin, how he had actually unbuttoned and removed her collar, how she had nearly melted into a little puddle when he had been rubbing her hands—it all seemed utterly scandalous. She would take pains in the future to have as little to do with him as possible, she decided.

Morgan and Parker returned at midmorning, a little less ebullient about their find. They had followed the vein back until it disappeared deep into the rock. Morgan said that the only way to see if it led to a major strike was by blasting. Amelia was not at all in favor of such a dangerous approach, but after Morgan assured her that he had used giant powder back in Wales, she withdrew her objections. The two men went into town to purchase the materials, leaving her to her household tasks.

When they were gone, she took a minute to study the little room. There didn't seem to be much more she could do in the way of cleaning. Glass windows that let in the sunlight would help, but she supposed it was silly to think about such an extravagance when they were only going to be living here for another six weeks.

She stood the broom in the corner and decided to move on to another project. She had purchased some cotton ticking at the general store and was determined to make a mattress for herself. The soft grass of the meadow would do for filler, and it was a beautiful day for gathering it. Carrying a bushel basket that Parker had used to store his clothes, she started across the bridge to the meadow. She had gone only a few yards when a rider emerged from the woods on the other side of the clearing. Her heart skipped and she craned her neck to see if it might be Gabe, but as the rider came nearer she could tell that it was a stranger, a slightly overweight man with a bright plaid waistcoat and a fancy-looking derby hat. He looked harmless enough. Still, she wished Parker and Morgan were home.

"Good day, ma'am," he called to her. He was smiling and his greeting was hearty, but something about him made Amelia uneasy.

"Good morning," she answered cautiously.

He pulled his horse up and held tightly to the pommel as he dismounted. Then he walked toward her, removing his hat to reveal balding hair slicked to one side. "You must be Miss Prescott," he said. The words were polite enough, but the way his eyes narrowed as they ran the length of her body made her clutch the basket protectively in front of her.

"You have the advantage, sir," she said. "I don't believe we've been introduced."

He clasped his hat to his chest and gave a little bow. "James W. Driscoll. Proprietor of the Lucky Horseshoe. Your brother may have mentioned it."

"I'm afraid my brother is not home at the moment, Mr. Driscoll. You'll have to return at another time."

Driscoll took a step closer, his steely eyes squinting. He smelled sour, as if he had overeaten on onions and garlic. "Perhaps I can do my business with you instead of Parker. You're much prettier than he is."

His laugh made the jest sound vulgar. Amelia took a step back. "I'm sorry, sir. I never get involved in my brother's affairs."

"Perhaps you should," Driscoll said, his smile disappearing. "He needs someone to tell him that he shouldn't be gambling when he doesn't have the money to settle up his debts."

A chill settled over her. Was he telling the truth? Though she knew that Parker had lost half his mine in a poker game, she hadn't realized that he had continued such reckless playing. Surely he hadn't been foolish enough to put himself in the power of a man as unsavory as Driscoll.

"How much did he lose?" she asked. The chill had frozen into a knot in the middle of her stomach.

Driscoll cocked his head. "I thought you said you didn't get involved in your brother's business." His eyes were raking her again, lingering on the swell of her breasts over the edge of her makeshift apron.

Amelia took a deep breath, dropped the basket on the ground and folded her arms in front of her. "I don't," she said, keeping her voice firm. "But I do want to know if he's in some kind of trouble."

"He could be. Folks out here don't take kindly to welchers. I rode out today to offer to take over his debts for a share of the mine." He lifted his eyes to look over the array of equipment stretched along the stream. "Word about town is that he and that ox of a servant of yours might be on to something big."

The knot in her stomach was gone, replaced by a quickly rising temper. She held it in check. "I wouldn't know about that, Mr. Driscoll. But I can assure you, my brother is not a welcher. If he has debts, we will pay them. And I don't believe he'll need help from you. So if you don't mind—" she pointed to the bushel basket "—I have work to do."

Driscoll smiled broadly. A gold tooth gleamed from the right side of his mouth. "That's what I like," he said. "A woman with spirit. Perhaps you and I can work out something to bail Parker out of his troubles. I'd be willing to talk it over."

He moved closer and grabbed her chin. His heavy ring pressed painfully into the side of her cheek. From some well of feminine indignation that she hadn't even known she possessed, Amelia lifted her hand and slapped him. He let go of her and stepped back, his face mottling with fury and the mark of the blow.

"Bitch!" he hissed. He took the upper part of her arm in a painful grip and pulled her toward him.

In the intensity of their exchange, neither had noticed a rider coming across the meadow, but suddenly they both turned at the sound of approaching hoofbeats. With a wave of relief that left her weak-kneed, Amelia saw that the newcomer was Gabe Hatch.

"Take your hand off her, Driscoll," he said as he pulled his mount up to within two feet of where they were standing.

Driscoll released her arm and stepped back, looking up at Gabe without concern. "Miss Prescott and I were just having a little talk about her brother's gambling debts, Hatch. It's no business of yours."

Gabe swung off his horse. "Parker is my partner. If he has debts, I reckon they're mine, too."

Driscoll's gold tooth flashed. "Is that so?"

Gabe didn't hesitate. "Yeah, that's so."

The two men glared at each other for a long moment. Then Driscoll said, "Well, then, you and your partner owe me eighty-five dollars."

Amelia gasped at the amount, but Gabe calmly pulled a money clip from his vest pocket and peeled off some bills. "Here," he said, handing over the money. "I didn't know the Lucky Horseshoe was so desperate for cash that you have to make your money on a wet-behind-the-ears boy who can't tell a full house from his own behind."

Driscoll shrugged. "I'm not a nursemaid. If Prescott wants to play cards in my place, who am I to stop him?"

Gabe's face was set in angry lines, but he didn't argue the point. "At any rate," he said, "if you bother Miss Prescott again, you'll answer to me."

"Is your partner sharing *her* with you, too?" Driscoll sneered.

Gabe's hands flexed at his sides, but he made no move. "Get out of here, Driscoll, before I forget that there's a lady present."

Driscoll gave a crude laugh, then turned toward his horse. Gabe didn't take his eyes off him until he had mounted up and ridden halfway across the meadow. Finally he turned to look at Amelia. "You're a bloody little fool," he said. "You know that, don't you?"

Chapter Six

Amelia gave a start of surprise. She'd expected sympathy, a kind word and perhaps some angry comments against Driscoll. But she couldn't see any reason for his harsh words to her. "What are you talking about?" she shouted.

"You shouldn't be out here by yourself in the first place. But when you knew you were alone, what did you think you were accomplishing by slapping Driscoll? He's more than twice your size."

Amelia calmed down a little as she saw that Gabe's anger was disguising a real concern over the incident. "What was I supposed to do—let him insult me and put his hands on me?"

"He didn't hurt you, did he? Because if he did—"

"No," she interrupted. "He didn't hurt me, except..." She lifted a hand to the spot where Driscoll's ring had made a red mark on her cheek.

Gabe leaned close and looked at her face. His eyes were furious. "I should have laid the bastard out," he said in a low voice.

Amelia shook her head. "No, I'm fine, really. I don't want to cause any more trouble. Let's just forget about the disagreeable Mr. Driscoll."

He touched the bruised spot with two gentle fingers. "Do you know how to fire a gun?" he asked abruptly.

"A gun!"

Gabe nodded. "If Driscoll ever shows his face around here again, I want you to have a weapon ready."

"I've never even touched a gun, much less fired one. And I haven't the slightest desire to do so."

His fingers slid down her cheek to trace the fine line of her jaw. "You're in the wild West now, Amelia. Things out here aren't resolved at tea parties."

There was a little flutter of happiness inside her chest from hearing him say her name. She drew in a breath and waited for his fingers to leave her skin so that she could swallow the liquid that had pooled in her mouth.

He dropped his hand. The sun glinted highlights in his hair and mustache. Amelia tried to concentrate on what she was saying. "I ... don't think I could fire a gun."

"I'll teach you," he said. His deep voice had taken on that husky tone again. Something was definitely happening between them, and Amelia had absolutely no idea what to do about it. She'd read the classics. She knew that when men and women reached a certain age they formed attachments. She knew that there could be some kind of mysterious attraction. But she had always pictured it as civilized and stately, courtships such as those painted by Jane Austen, carried out in elegant drawing rooms. He picks up her lace fan. She hands him the tray of tea cakes. She hadn't ever imagined this kind of feeling that robs one of sense and of one's very breath.

"I—I don't think that will be necessary, Mr. Hatch," she stammered. "I'm rarely alone here, and you'll cer-

tainly never find me going into the Lucky Horseshoe.
I'll probably never see that man again.''

"It's Gabe, remember?'' he chided gently.

"Yes, Gabe. I've been in Deadwood a week, and
you've come to my rescue so many times already I've
lost count. I guess the least I can do is call you by your
Christian name.'' She smiled and began to relax as his
blue eyes stopped regarding her so intensely.

He returned her smile. "And you'll let me teach you
how to shoot a gun?''

She straightened her shoulders and took another deep
breath. "I suppose it couldn't be much worse than
learning to do laundry,'' she said with a rueful chuckle.

Gabe shook his head. He'd known girls from fine
families back in St. Louis, and he'd never met one who
could hold a candle to Amelia Prescott. It wasn't just
her looks, it was the way she tackled things that were
completely foreign to her with such determination. He
remembered the society girls back home crying buckets
at the least little contretemps. He'd never seen banker's daughter Amelia shed a single tear. Even now, after being abused by a scoundrel like Driscoll, she could
still muster a smile. "So,'' he said briskly, trying to ignore the sudden urge to take her into his arms, "when
do we start the lessons?''

Amelia reached down to pick up her basket. "Well,
not right now. I'm bound and determined to sleep on a
mattress tonight. My back's had enough of that wooden
cot.''

Gabe lifted an eyebrow. "What are you going to put
in your mattress, may I ask?''

Amelia smiled proudly. "Grass—from the meadow.
It'll be soft as a feather.''

"And will have the cabin smelling like a still inside of two days."

Amelia looked up with a frown. "What do you mean?"

"It's too moist. You close it up like that and it will start to ferment on you."

Amelia threw down the basket in frustration. "Can't I get even one thing right?"

Gabe picked up the basket with one hand and put his other arm around her shoulders. "I'm sure you get most things right, sweetheart. You're just a bit out of your element here."

He had let the endearment slip out without thinking, though now that it was said, he had no desire to take it back. Her thick sable eyelashes fluttered as she looked up at him in surprise, but she did not move out of the circle of his arm. Her mouth was slightly open as if she was about to say something. No words came out. Instead, she moistened her bottom lip with her tongue. Blood rushed to Gabe's head. He tightened his hold and bent to kiss her.

It was something neither had anticipated. Something he had not intended. But once their lips met he could not have stopped if a steam engine had been barreling down on him. He had to taste her. The basket fell once again to the ground and he wrapped his other arm around her, bringing their bodies flat against each other. The entire length of him hardened at the pressure of her softness. He deepened the kiss, just barely. Just enough to satisfy the flash flood of desire that had surged through him. When she made a little whimper at the back of her throat, he let her go instantly.

"I'm sorry," he rasped.

Amelia's eyes were glazed. "I…I guess you're right," she said, slightly breathless. "I definitely *am* out of my element."

Gabe shook his head, berating himself for moving so fast, for moving at all. "It's my fault," he said with a frown of worry. "A great rescuer I'm turning out to be. I'm no better than Driscoll."

She laid the tips of her fingers against the soft hairs of his blond mustache. "Don't say that. You're nothing like him." Suddenly she looked past him over his shoulder. "Oh, no."

"What's wrong?" He turned around.

Parker and Morgan were coming toward them at a gallop. Gabe silently called himself every kind of a fool he could think of. He moved to stand well away from Amelia.

It was apparent even from a distance that Parker had seen them in each other's arms and that he was spitting nails about it. He jumped off his horse and strode over to Gabe. "Just what did you think you were doing a minute ago with my sister?"

Gabe kept his voice even. "I'll thank you to lower your voice, Prescott. Your sister—whom you left alone to fend for herself—has had a tough morning."

Parker looked suspiciously over at Amelia. "What does that mean?"

Amelia's guilty flush had almost faded. She picked up on Gabe's cue to attack rather than defend. "It means that I had a visit this morning from a Mr. James Driscoll. He came to collect on *your* gambling debts. And while he was here he suggested that I personally could pay them off by accommodating him in certain unspecified ways."

The expression of shame on Parker's face at her mention of his debts turned to one of alarm. He looked at Gabe. "Did he hurt her?" he asked fiercely.

"No, he didn't hurt me," Amelia snapped. "Thanks to Gabe."

Parker looked down at the ground. "I'm sorry, Gabe. I . . . I didn't know what I was seeing here. I guess I owe you an apology and a heap of thanks."

"You owe me neither, Parker. But you *do* owe me eighty-five dollars, which is what it took to clear you with Driscoll. I'll wait to collect until you can take it out of your share of the mine. Maybe that will teach you to stay out of the games at the Horseshoe. They're too advanced for your skill and too rich for your purse."

"I hope you'll listen to him, Parker," Amelia said.

"Eighty-five dollars!" Morgan echoed, adding his look of reproach.

Parker held up a hand as if to ward off more scolding. "All right. I'm done with gambling. From now on I'm going to concentrate on the mine. It's a good thing you're here, Gabe. We can use your help with the dynamiting."

Neither Amelia nor Gabe acknowledged how they had turned the tables of guilt from themselves to her brother, but as the three men started up the hill he called back to her. "You might want to try hay for that mattress of yours, Miss Prescott. And we'll start those lessons we discussed tomorrow." Then he winked and sent her a smile that warmed her insides for the rest of the day.

"Hatch has crossed my path once too often." Big Jim was lying in his oversize bed. The place by his side had recently been occupied by one of the bar girls, a mousy little thing named Letty Sue who came at the saloon owner's call and never overstayed her welcome.

Deuce Connors was now perched on the end of the bed. It was not unusual for Big Jim to conduct business from his boudoir. "You want him killed?" the gunman asked nonchalantly.

"No. People are starting to set up a stink about all the killings in town. Some of the fine city fathers are already talking about how we need to get ourselves a real sheriff. I don't want to push the pantywaists into action. And Hatch is popular, even if he is a gambler."

"We could just rough him up a bit," Deuce suggested.

Driscoll reached to his nightstand for one of his Carolina cigars. "No. Not yet. I have a feeling Gabriel Hatch could be useful if a person just knew the right way to approach him."

"What do you mean?" Deuce reached into his pocket for a match to light Driscoll's cigar.

The saloon owner took a deep pull, then let the smoke curl lazily out of his mouth. "There's someone I want you to find for me. A former...acquaintance of mine from the gold camps."

"Does this still involve Hatch?"

Driscoll smiled and nodded. "We're going to prepare a little surprise for the meddlesome Mr. Hatch."

After the initial excitement about the discovery of the vein, the mood around Parker's mine had become subdued. There was gold, all right, more than he had found so far. But the pocket appeared to end at the place where it disappeared into the rock. Gabe left at mid-afternoon, saying that he had an engagement in town. At sundown Morgan and Parker abandoned their efforts and walked wearily down to the cabin. They were discouraged, sweaty and covered with dust from the blasting. Amelia put supper on the table with few words. She knew the disappointed look on Parker's face. And she knew that it would be pointless to try to cheer him. Her brother would regain his good humor in his own way and his own time, as he always did. Most likely by tomorrow he would be his old self, joking and dreaming of the next big find.

In deference to the men's disheartening day, she didn't mention how victorious she herself was feeling. Mentally she checked off the day's accomplishments. She had faced down the lecherous saloon owner. She had stuffed the ticking she had prepared with straw, making a nice plump mattress that was waiting on the cot to give her the first good night's sleep since she'd left New York. She had built up the fire by herself and had managed a passable stew and corn cakes that were only slightly scorched. And she had kissed Gabe Hatch.

She caught herself humming more than once as she washed the dishes. Then she would look over at Parker's gloomy face and feel a little guilty. She had only added to his dejection by scolding him this morning about his gambling debts. But, mercy, eighty-five dollars was a lot of money.

"So, will you go in with us, sis?"

Amelia snapped back her head and realized that she had been drying the same plate for several minutes. "Go where?"

"Haven't you been listening? We need some chisels to work out that vein. Morgan says we'll blast it to bits if we use any more dynamite."

"Chisels?" Amelia tried to concentrate on what her brother was saying.

Parker stood and gave a great sigh. "We have to go into town in the morning. And you're coming with us. I'm not about to leave you out here alone again for another visit from Driscoll."

Town . . . they would see Gabe. She gave herself a little shake. "Of course I'll go with you." She smiled brightly. "Perhaps we can all have dinner at the Willard Hotel."

"There," Gabe said, closing the black leather book with a flourish. "You're settled up for another month, Mattie."

Mattie was curled in the chair across from him as usual. "So, how much do I owe for your services, Mr. Hatch?" she asked.

Gabe gave a snort of indignation. "Since when have I charged you, Mrs. Smith?"

Mattie stretched out her legs. They didn't quite reach the floor. "Never. But I figured since it took you three times as long this month with your mind on other matters, so to speak, and since I hear you've taken to settling gambling debts for a certain partner of yours when the debts suddenly involve the sister of this certain partner . . ."

Gabe stood. He couldn't flatly deny his involvement with Amelia as he had with Mattie the other day. For the truth was, he had thought of little else since their kiss yesterday in the meadow. As Mattie had said, it was a foolish notion. He wasn't worried that Pinkerton men were going to show up at his door to blow his head off, but he did recognize that there was very little future for a well-bred daughter of an Eastern banker and an adventurer who made his living at the gaming tables. Still, there had been something about that kiss . . .

"I told you the other day that I don't intend on getting involved with Amelia," he said curtly.

Spry as a woman half her age, Mattie jumped from the chair. "So now it's Amelia, is it?"

Gabe shook his head tiredly. "Don't start on me, Mattie. I'm here to do your books, not to be dressed down."

Mattie gave him a sympathetic smile and took his arm as they walked out of the office. "I'm not about to dress down my favorite gambler. You're a good man, Gabe." She accompanied him out the front door. When they reached the front porch, she put an arm around his neck and pulled his head down so that she could reach to give him a kiss. "I know you'll do the right thing."

The late-summer sky was brilliant as they headed down the path to town. Amelia was in high spirits, teasing her brother into forgetting his disappointment and regaining some of his usual playfulness. At one point he plucked a pinecone off a tree as they passed and chucked it at her head, then tried to look innocent when she spun around looking for her assailant. In retaliation, she held on to an overhanging branch and let it go just in time to flop back at him, knocking his hat to the ground. Morgan regarded their antics with the same tolerant patience he had employed when they were children.

They settled down as they rode into Deadwood Gulch. Amelia was trying to look proper and dignified, but at the same time was avidly searching the streets for the sight of a tall, blond, mustached man. She didn't want to be obvious. Parker hadn't mentioned again the scene he had witnessed between her and Gabe, and she supposed they had convinced him that it was not what it appeared to be. But she wouldn't want to give him ideas by seeming overly anxious to encounter the gambler.

"That's Driscoll's place there," Parker said, pointing down the street to the right. Amelia followed the direction of his hand to the end of the street where a prominent sign said Lucky Horseshoe, then she quickly averted her eyes. She had no desire to see Big Jim's place, nor Big Jim. Deliberately she turned her head to the left toward Mattie Smith's innocent-looking little "house."

As if out of a nightmare, suddenly there was Gabe, his lean body bent over Mattie Smith. He had his arms around her... and he was kissing her! Like the sudden wind before a storm, all Amelia's good feelings of the past twenty-four hours blew away in a violent rush. She swayed in the saddle and had to hold on for a moment to steady herself. Parker continued on down the street, unaware that her life had turned upside down. Without conscious effort, she let her horse follow him.

By the time they reached the general store, the anger had begun to set in. And the self-reproach. How could she have been so stupid? She had lain awake last night picturing him—the way his sun-bleached hair and snowy white shirt collar contrasted with his tanned face. She'd remembered the way his mocking laugh turned tender when he was helping her out of one of her predicaments. She'd stared into the dark and tossed back and forth on her new straw mattress thinking about how soft his mouth had been, how hard his body had felt against hers. What a ninny she was! It was as if someone had knocked the air out of her. And it served her right. How she could ever have imagined falling for an unscrupulous gambler, a drinking man, a sidewinder who consorted with loose women...

"Sis!" Parker yelled. "Are you getting down or not?" He stood next to her horse waiting to give her a hand. "What's the matter with you?"

Amelia gave herself a shake and slid from her horse, ignoring Parker's offer of help. "Nothing's the matter," she snapped.

Parker shrugged and mounted the stairs to the general store. "Suit yourself," he muttered.

"Amelia!" The voice came from across the street. She cringed as she recognized its owner. She deliberately turned her back and marched up the stairs behind her brother.

The interior of the general store was dim after the bright sunlight out on the street. Amelia blinked and looked around. Normally she would be curious to examine the varied items crammed onto the crowded floor-to-ceiling shelves, but today she hardly noticed them.

"Amelia, didn't you hear me calling you?" Gabe came in the door half-running. Then, as if he realized that his eagerness to speak to her might sound strange, he added, "I wanted to see if you'd recovered from your ordeal yesterday." He glanced sideways at Parker, who was standing at the counter watching them intently.

Amelia tossed her head so hard that the ribbons of her bonnet came loose and it flopped back on her head. "I'm quite recovered, thank you, Mr. Hatch," she said in a tone that could frost a lake.

Gabe looked perplexed. "Is something the matter?"

"No." She looked over at her brother. "I'm heading back to the camp."

Parker scratched his cheek and looked puzzled. "We haven't bought the chisels yet."

"Morgan can help you. I ride slow—you two will probably catch up to me on the way home."

"Can I talk to you for a minute first?" Gabe asked. His expression had clouded.

Amelia ignored him. "I'll see you back on the road," she said again to Parker. Then she spun around and walked out the door, leaving all three men looking after her in confusion.

Gabe spoke first. "What's got into her?"

Parker spoke slowly. "I have no idea. But I learned back when I was still in knee breeches that when Amelia gets that ice in her voice and fire in her eyes, you're best off staying clear away."

"You don't think I should ride after her?" Gabe asked, troubled.

Parker shook his head. "Not unless you're a far braver man than I."

By the next morning Amelia's anger had subsided somewhat. After all, she had known what kind of man Gabe was from the day she had met him on the stagecoach. It was no one's fault but her own if she had abandoned every notion of good sense that her mother had ever taught her and become foolishly infatuated with him. Still, it hurt to think that he had cared so little about the kiss they had shared that less than twenty-four hours later he was kissing another woman. The two of them had been coming out of Mattie Smith's house. Heaven knew what had preceded the kiss. And in the middle of the morning!

Parker had asked her again the previous evening if something was bothering her. She had brushed off his questions, but when he had persisted, she had flat out lied to him for the first time in her life. She told him that she had left town abruptly because she had suddenly become afraid that she would encounter Driscoll. He had taken her in his arms and promised her that she wouldn't be alone again to be at the saloon owner's mercy.

He and Morgan had started out early this morning to tackle the gold vein with their new tools. After they left, Amelia halfheartedly straightened up the cabin, then sat down at the table and started to shell some peas. The men had taken along biscuits for a cold breakfast on the job, so they would be hungry at midday. The tedious task allowed her to put her turbulent thoughts in the background for the moment, but when she heard a horse approaching across the wooden bridge, she knew immediately who it would be.

She continued with her work and did not look up when a shadow darkened the doorway.

"Good morning." Gabe's deep voice was reserved.

"Morning." Amelia kept her eyes on the mound of pea pods.

Gabe walked into the room. "We're alone now. Tell me what's bothering you."

His directness surprised her and she finally lifted her head. He was wearing close-cut black trousers, a snowy white shirt and a blue vest that was exactly the color of his eyes. A single holstered gunbelt hugged his narrow hips. He had no jacket. His flat-brimmed hat was set back on his curly hair. It knocked the breath right out of her to look at him.

She decided to be just as direct. "Mr. Hatch, I made a mistake in the meadow the other day. It was a mistake I wouldn't want to repeat."

There was that flinch of his jaw that told her he was angry, but his voice was even. "Now, just exactly what kind of mistake are you talking about?"

She glared. "I let you . . . take liberties."

Gabe rolled his eyes in disbelief. "I assume you are referring to the fact that I kissed you. Pardon me if I'm wrong, but I don't remember hearing you express any objection at the time."

"I didn't. And that's why I'm not holding it against you. But as I said, I don't like making the same mistake twice. So I would appreciate it if you would keep your distance in the future." She gave a decisive nod as she finished her speech and went back to the peas.

Gabe walked toward her and leaned over the table, putting his hands on each side of the mound of pea pods. "Would you like to tell me what has caused your change of heart?"

She could hear the restrained anger in his voice, but she told herself it did not affect her. Why should he be angry because one woman had told him to stay away? He undoubtedly had dozens of others who would welcome him into their lives and their beds. Experienced women like Mattie Smith. "Let's just say that we are from two different worlds, Mr. Hatch, and it would be foolish to try to merge them."

"You're a woman and I'm a man, if that's what you mean. And, take my word for it, merging those two worlds can be a lot of fun."

She finally abandoned the pretext of the peas and straightened up. "I'm sorry," she said, looking directly at him.

There was leashed fury in his eyes, enough to make her push her chair back from the table to put distance between them. Her eyes widened as he reached for the gun at his side and pulled it out of its holster. She had started to stand in alarm when he laid the gun down on the table. "This is yours," he said.

"I beg your pardon?" She sat down again, hard.

"I promised to teach you to shoot, remember?"

Amelia eyed the gun as if it were a rattlesnake. "I...I don't think I want to learn anymore."

Gabe took a step back. "Suit yourself." He turned to leave.

"Gabe," she said to his back. When he paused she continued, "Don't forget your gun."

"I told you. It's yours. I bought it for you."

"Oh, but I can't...I can't take a present like that. Back East it would never be considered proper...."

He turned around to face her. The angry expression had been replaced by a smile that looked even more deadly. "We've already been through this. You're not back East anymore, Miss Prescott."

By the time she could think of a reply, he was out the door and riding away across the bridge.

Chapter Seven

"Where'd this come from?" Parker asked, picking up the revolver Gabe had left on the table. It was a small gun with mother-of-pearl stocks carved with the figure of a rose. Amelia hadn't touched it.

"Gabe left it here."

Parker looked puzzled. "He left his gun?"

Amelia knelt on the hearth and busied herself stirring the beans. "He, ah, he gave it to me. He says I should learn to shoot in case Driscoll ever shows his face here again."

Morgan was sitting on the floor across from her cleaning some mining tools. "Nothing good ever came from using a gun," he said firmly.

Parker opened the gun and spun the barrel. "Nice," he said with a low whistle. "I can't say I agree with you, Morgan. Out here, guns are a way of life."

"Well, I have no intention of learning how to shoot from Gabe Hatch," Amelia said firmly.

"Why not? He taught *me*," Parker said.

"He did?"

Parker nodded, then added with a laugh, "He won't shoot with me anymore, though, because now I beat him at the target every time."

Amelia was silent. She felt the slightest twinge of jealousy. Her brother had always succeeded at everything he tried. She would labor for hours to learn some new skill, and he would come along and in no time at all would be showing up the experts. It had been that way since they were babies. Some people would say that it was just the natural course of events since he was a boy and she was a girl. But she had never seen any good reason that someone should have an advantage just because he happened to have been born male.

"Well, I'm not interested," she said with a little sniff. Then she stood and lifted the pot of beans. "If you want some supper, put that thing away and set the table."

They had not yet finished breakfast the next morning when there was a knock on the door. Parker got up to open it and gave an exclamation of surprise when he saw that the early-bird visitor was none other than Gabe, and that he was dressed uncharacteristically in blue denim work pants and a rough linen shirt.

"Good morning," Gabe said calmly. He was without jacket or hat.

"What are you up to at this hour of the day?" Parker asked, offering his hand.

Gabe gave a deliberate glance over at Amelia and answered, "I seem to have found myself in the middle of a losing streak. When that happens, I like to change around my tactics."

Parker looked uncertain. "You mean, you've had some bad luck at the tables?"

"Where else?" His tone was cheerful. If Amelia had been back home she would have stalked out of the room and made a grand exit up the elegant Prescott stairway. But in their tiny cabin there was no place to hide.

"I've decided to work with you boys up here at the mine for a few days. Maybe with a little hard labor we can change both my luck *and* yours."

Parker grinned. "I'm all for that."

Morgan looked a little doubtful. He stood up from the table and pointed at Gabe's hands. "Have you ever swung a pickax with those, my friend?"

Gabe gave him a light cuff on the shoulder. "I can outswing you, you big oaf."

Morgan laughed low in his chest. "I'd just like to see you try that, cardplayer."

With a few more traded jests and insults, the three men jostled their way out the door and started up the hill, leaving Amelia staring after them with an expression of disbelief. The nerve of the man! He was going to work with them "for a few days." She supposed that meant he expected to eat with them, as well—dinners, suppers. . . . She could hear her brother now. Why not stay the evening, partner, and share a mug of mulled cider? Would she never be quit of him? She slammed the breakfast dishes into the basin, then paced back across the room and dropped heavily into the rocker.

His pants had had faded spots where his thighs had rubbed for countless miles in the saddle. . . . She rocked back and forth, rubbing her hands along the front of her apron as if trying to force away the strange warmth that had begun to build deep in her middle when Gabe had appeared in the doorway. It was against all reason, she told herself furiously. But she had a feeling that all the hard logic in the world was not going to make it go away.

* * *

Claire Devereaux had learned at an early age that survival meant keeping her mouth shut and her ears open. She'd never known her parents. They'd died in a shipwreck while crossing the Great Lakes. In the confusion following the disaster, Claire had been placed in a Catholic orphanage in Chicago. If she'd had other relatives on the ship or back in France who might have been able to claim her, no one had ever bothered to track them down.

When she was young she used to dream that a handsome French nobleman would arrive one day at the orphanage door and proclaim that she was a lost *comtesse* with an elegant château awaiting her back in the beautiful, sunny French countryside. Then she would wake up to the orphanage's required two hours of daily prayers before breakfast followed by a forced walk in the bare school yard, buffeted by the raw winds off Lake Michigan, and she would retreat into the silence that had made her one of the most docile of Sister Margaret's pupils, if not the most excelled.

Everyone at St. Stephen's had assumed that Claire would enter the novitiate when she reached the proper age. But Sister Margaret had nodded in understanding and gone to the chapel to pray when they had told her that Claire had run off to the West with a man she had met only once while doing the Saturday marketing.

Claire had never confided in Mattie how she had ended up ill and without money on the streets of Deadwood where Mattie had found her. But the older woman had taken pity on the fragile girl. She had nursed her back to health and had offered to lend her money until she could find a job for herself. Claire, however, had said she preferred earning her keep at once as one of

Mattie's girls. As soon as she was feeling strong enough, she'd begun appearing each evening in Mattie's pink-accented parlor, quietly taking the customers who were attracted by her slender beauty and the otherworld look she had about her.

It had been Parker Prescott who had put the first hint of animation on her face. It started when she discovered that he could speak fluent French. Though Claire had never learned the language herself, she could listen to him for hours, perhaps remembering some faint trace or nuance of tone from the land of her birth.

Parker had come every night for a week before he had asked Claire to take him upstairs. Under normal circumstances, Mattie would have encouraged the lad to make a decision or let another customer have a chance, but there was something so tender and innocent about the young couple, the breath of youthful idealism, that she let them talk together late into the night without interfering.

She could have predicted the result. Parker was coming almost daily and, of course, didn't have the money to pay. And Claire was growing increasingly reluctant to see other customers. Something would have to happen soon. But for the moment, it did Mattie's soul good to see the two youngsters so happy. Had she ever been that way? She couldn't remember.

She could tell when Parker was stretched. He came in the door, as he had tonight, with a hangdog look and a plea in his pretty brown eyes that it would take a harder woman than Mattie to resist.

"She's up in her room, Parker," she'd said. "You can go on up."

He'd flashed her a smile that more than covered the three dollars she was losing.

Claire was waiting for him, watching the door with an anxious face. When he entered after a brief knock, she ran to him and threw her arms around his neck.

"I was afraid I'd have to go downstairs tonight," she said in a shamed whisper.

He pulled her against him and thoroughly kissed her rosebud mouth, drinking from her, drawing kisses like a man suffering from a terrible thirst. "I can't stand to think of you down there," he said after their initial frenzy had passed. He lifted her easily in his arms and crossed over to the bed. "I want you to belong just to me forever and always."

She pulled him down beside her. "I do, Parker, *mon che-wee*. I will. Forever and always."

"Mon chéri," he corrected tenderly. "It's with an *r*. They just make it sound different."

"Someday I will learn French," she said fiercely. "When we go to France together, you'll teach me, won't you?"

Parker rolled over to sit back against the wall. "I'll teach you, my love. And I will take you to France."

"I wish we could leave today."

Parker stared into space. His hand idly caressed her long black hair.

"What's wrong?" she asked.

He looked down at her and smiled. "Just another disappointment. The vein we found has played out— another fool's mission."

"There will be another strike, a true one this time. I can feel it."

He leaned down and gave her a brief kiss. His expression grew grim. "And in the meantime, you go down each night to choose someone else to bring to your bed."

"They are nothing," she said. She pushed herself up to sit beside him and pulled his head against her breast. "I will give my heart but once in this life. It belongs to you and no one else."

He closed his eyes and held her tightly. "My darling Claire, somehow I'm going to get the money to get you out of here. I may be able to ask Gabe . . . or wire to my parents. I can't let you stay here any longer."

She shook her head. "Don't take on so. I don't care about this," she said, gesturing around the room with her arm. "My life now is you, and nothing else matters."

"It matters to me," he muttered. Then he pulled her under him on the bed. "Let's not talk anymore."

Gabe sucked in a deep drag from his cheroot. The bitter smoke suited his mood tonight. He intended on supplementing it with a bottle of Driscoll's best whiskey. And a game. He flexed his fingers and headed across the street toward the Lucky Horseshoe. It had been too long since he'd tended to business. He'd spent the week playing miner, and all he had for his efforts were a handful of calluses and an aching back.

Amelia had not addressed him with a complete sentence the entire week. He'd hung around until he thought Parker and Morgan would send him packing. But she hadn't suggested that he leave. She hadn't gotten riled. She'd just cooked and tended to all three men with brisk efficiency and a bland smile. And she'd made darn sure that he never had the opportunity to talk with her alone.

She'd begun to haunt him at night. He'd close his eyes and see her reaching across him to put a plate of flapjacks on the table, her gingham dress pulled tight across her trim breasts. Then he'd open his eyes and see her own luminescent brown eyes staring back at him, thickly lashed, liquid and wanting.

He couldn't explain even to himself how he had become so damned obsessed with her. She had made it quite plain that she didn't even want him around. And God knows, the last thing he needed in his life was a feisty Eastern beauty with the temper of a two-year-old. He'd be much better off returning to his sane, ordered life. It felt good to be back in clean, fine clothes, heading for a good night at the tables. Someplace where he knew he was welcome.

The Lucky Horseshoe was crowded. It seemed that every week more and more of the young men who had come to Dakota Territory to strike it rich were deciding that the only place they were going to find gold was on the gambling tables. It was good for Gabe's business, but he hated to see the desperation in the faces of the newcomers when their amateurish playing left them without anything at all. Parker Prescott was a good example. Gabe didn't know what fate had made him decide to come to the New Yorker's rescue the night they met. If he hadn't become Parker's partner, he would never have become involved with his sister. And he'd be sleeping a lot better at night.

The degree of his frustration was evident when he walked in the door of the Horseshoe and saw Parker gambling at a table across the room. Gabe's first impulse was to turn around and go back to his hotel. He'd had enough of bailing out the bloody young fool. But after a moment of hesitation he threw his cheroot on the floor and headed over to Parker's table. The boy had his coat off and his shirt sleeves rolled up, even though a chill evening air blew in through the saloon's open door.

"May I join you?" Gabe asked the group coolly.

A ponytailed cowboy named Snap Winters pushed back his chair. "Take my place, Gabe. Deuce is too lucky for me tonight."

Gabe glanced at the man across the table. Driscoll's henchman. If Deuce Connors was controlling this game, he would bet it was on Big Jim's orders. And Big Jim had a score to settle with the Prescotts.

"You ready to call it a night, Parker?" Gabe asked.

Parker looked bleak. "I can't. I'm in too deep."

"That's the time to quit, if you ask me."

"I'll be all right. I'm gonna win some of this back. C'mon. It's Jake's deal."

His fine New York speech was slurred. Gabe clenched his teeth. The damn fool was drunk. Had been *gotten* drunk, most likely. As if confirming his suspicion, the bar girl, Stella, came over to the table with a fresh round for everyone.

"Drinks are on Big Jim tonight," Connors explained.

"I'll bet they are," Gabe said under his breath. He reached out to take Parker's drink from the girl. "You've had enough, partner."

Parker nodded. "I think you're right."

Gabe sat back and concentrated on the other players as the next several hands unfolded. Deuce was not cheating, at least not at the moment. Which didn't mean that he hadn't been doing something underhanded before Gabe got to the table.

Parker was into the house for almost fifty dollars. Twice more Gabe suggested that he go home and try to recoup another day, and twice more Parker refused. He was growing more morose with every hand.

Except for Connors, who was a fair player, the rest of the table were easy marks for Gabe. They hedged their bets, telegraphed their hands, took foolish chances. Easy pickings.

Charlie Wilson, the stagecoach driver, threw his cards down in disgust after four losing hands in a row. "I can't play against you, Hatch," he said, getting up from the table.

Normally Gabe might not have been so ruthless with obvious amateurs, but tonight he had a mission. One by one he forced them out. Finally only Connors, Parker and Gabe were left.

Parker dealt the next hand, and Gabe felt a surge of satisfaction as he picked up the cards to see three pretty little sevens. He drew a five and a ten, but he didn't need them. Parker had drawn only one card. Gabe kept his face impassive and silently moved an entire pile of chips into the center of the table. Deuce looked at his cards, then at the stack of chips. "I'm out," he said, tossing down his hand.

Parker licked his lips, his eyes on the pot. The hand holding his cards shook. "I need this one, Gabe," he said. "But I can't match you. Will you take my marker?"

Gabe folded his hand and set it on the table. Slowly he shook his head. "No, but I'll take payment in kind."

"For what? There's not much I can put up—just the mine. I don't have anything else."

"You have a sister."

Parker's chair fell over backward as he leapt to his feet, his bloodshot eyes furious. "You bastard!" he said.

Play stopped at surrounding tables as men turned to find out what the fight was about.

Gabe held up his hand. "Don't get so het up. I wasn't insulting Amelia. I just wanted to propose a supper with her as payment of your debt."

"Supper?" Parker asked in a calmer voice. He reached back, picked up his chair and sat down.

Gabe nodded. "Alone." When Parker started to bristle again, he added, "You and Morgan can be within shouting distance. I just want a little time by myself with her."

"Why?" Parker asked suspiciously.

Gabe shrugged. "There are some things I'd like to discuss with her."

"You can discuss things with her any time you want. You've been out there with us all week."

Gabe tapped a single finger on his cards. "Supper with Amelia—alone. Take it or leave it."

Parker looked again at his hand and at the stack of chips on the table. He hesitated. Finally he took a deep breath and called, "Stella, bring me a piece of paper."

The bar girl said something to Roscoe, who reached behind the bar and came up with a sheet of paper and the stub of a pencil. She brought it over to the table and looked over Parker's shoulder as he scribbled something down. Then he threw the paper over to Gabe.

"What's this?" Gabe asked impatiently.

"My half of the mine."

"That wasn't the deal—"

Parker interrupted. "I'm not wagering my sister, Hatch. You've got half a mine against that stack of chips. Take it or leave it."

Gabe pushed back his chair. "Maybe you just weren't cut out for this town, kid. Why don't you pack up that

sister of yours and head back to New York?'' He spread
his hand on the table.

Parker's hand stopped shaking. He set down his
cards—two aces, two jacks and a queen. They made a
pretty quintet, but didn't mean a thing against Gabe's
three sevens. ''What are you going to do with the
mine?'' Parker asked dully. ''You won't work it yourself, will you?''

''I don't know,'' Gabe said. He folded the sheet of
paper Parker had written and tucked it inside his coat,
then reached to collect his chips. ''That will do it for
me,'' he said, glancing around at the onlookers. ''Good
evening, gentlemen.''

Without looking at Parker, he got up and started out
of the room. Just as he reached the door, Big Jim, who
had been watching the proceedings from behind the bar,
called out to him. ''I might take that claim off your
hands, Hatch. Give you a good price.''

Gabe looked back once at Parker, who still sat
slumped in his chair, then answered Driscoll, ''I'll think
it over.''

Charlie Wilson brought word of the disastrous game
out to the Prescott cabin the next morning. He'd shyly
taken a fancy to Amelia the night the stagecoach had
broken down, and he liked Parker, as did most folks
around town. Everyone was saying that it was a shame
for Prescott to lose everything he'd worked so hard for,
but that he wasn't the first young fool to lose it all to
liquor and cards.

After hearing the news, Amelia and Morgan waited
anxiously most of the day for Parker to come home.
When he wasn't back by midafternoon, Amelia told the
Welshman that she was going to town to find him.

"You know where he's going to be, Missy," Morgan had said with a sober shake of his head. "That Mattie Smith's place."

"I don't care if I have to go fetch him in Satan's living room," she'd retorted. "He's my brother, and I'm not going to let him destroy himself over a Western adventure that he obviously wasn't cut out for in the first place. It's time we gave up on this place and went back home where we belonged."

"Let's go get him, then," he said resignedly. But as they mounted up and started across the bridge, he surveyed the array of equipment Parker had assembled. "He's done a mighty fine job of it for someone not cut out," he observed dryly. "There's not a finer setup along this river."

"A lot of good it did him—he's worked for months now, only to lose it all on the turn of a card. It doesn't make any sense to me."

Morgan had not argued, and neither spoke on the trip into town. They went directly to Mattie's place, Amelia agreeing that it was the most likely place to find her brother. She hung back on the porch while Morgan lifted the brass knocker.

Mattie herself opened the door, sympathy in her gray eyes. "Come in," she said. "Your brother's here, Miss Prescott."

Amelia felt a rush of relief. At least he was safe and she would be able to talk with him. "Thank you," she murmured, following Mattie into the parlor where she had been reunited with Parker that first day.

"I don't know if he'll see you," Mattie said. "He's pretty low."

Amelia swallowed down a lump in her throat. "He's got to see me, Mrs. Smith. We've always taken care of each other...."

The little woman took Amelia's hand and patted it gently. "It's going to be all right, honey. Parker's a smart lad. Talented, too. Just not for poker playing, apparently," she added dryly. "Why don't you give him some time? He's had a bad night, but he's resting now."

Amelia looked through the parlor doors to the salon opposite, as if expecting to see her brother lying on one of the rosy-hued sofas.

"He's upstairs in Claire's room," Mattie said matter-of-factly.

"If I could just see him for a minute, see that he's all right... If he's sleeping, I won't wake him."

Mattie hesitated for a minute, then gestured to the chair by the fireplace and addressed Morgan. "Will you please excuse us for a minute, Mr. Jones? You can make yourself comfortable."

Amelia followed Mattie up the narrow, carpeted stairs toward the red-lighted room she had glimpsed on her first visit. Unable to resist the curiosity, she looked inside and was a little disappointed to see that it was nothing more than a nicely appointed parlor much like the one they had just left.

Mattie led her down the hall to a door at the end, then knocked on it softly. It was opened by a lovely, thin young woman in a neat cotton dress that looked very much like one Amelia might have chosen for herself. Her features were beautiful, but her skin was almost too white, especially in contrast to her starkly black hair.

"This is Parker's sister," Mattie said in a low voice.

The girl gave Amelia a quick, almost furtive glance, then stepped back to let her see into the room. Parker was seated on the bed. His clothes were rumpled and his hair was a mess. He wore no boots. His eyes were red, and if Amelia hadn't known better, she would have said that he had been crying.

"Are you all right?" she asked.

He gave a harsh laugh. "Never been better. I've lost the mine and every cent I own. I expect Driscoll's gunmen to show up any minute to shoot me for the fifty dollars I owe him. At least then I'll be out of my misery."

Amelia had the urge to go put her arms around him, but before she could move, Claire went to sit quietly next to him on the bed. He took her slender hand in his and held on to it as if it were a lifeline.

"I'll wire Father for the money."

"Over my dead body," Parker said furiously.

"But..."

He let go of Claire's hand and stood. "I came out West looking for independence, sis. And I got into this mess all on my own. Now it's up to me to get myself out of it."

"But they told me you lost the mine."

"There are other places no one has staked out yet—farther west. I should at least be able to pan out enough to pay off Driscoll. I just won't have money for anything else for a while." He locked gazes with Claire, and the anguish in both their expressions put a lump in Amelia's throat.

"Is the cabin still yours?" she asked.

Parker shrugged. "I guess so. The deed I signed over wasn't exactly explicit."

Amelia bit her lip. "When are you coming home?"

He shook his head. "Tonight... I don't know. You go on back and don't worry about me."

"But what if Driscoll's men come?"

"If Driscoll's men come you grab that pistol Gabe left you and aim it as if you knew what you were doing. Then tell them they can find me here."

He walked back over to the bed and flopped down on it behind Claire. "I've got to get some damn sleep before I can do anything," he said.

Amelia backed out the door. She met Claire's sad eyes. "Pleased to meet you, Miss…ah…" She stopped, swallowed hard and glanced at her brother. He lay with an arm covering his face. "Take care of him," she said softly.

Mattie was waiting out in the hall. She didn't say anything as Amelia followed her down the stairs. When they reached the front hall, Amelia stopped. "Mrs. Smith," she said, "I need to ask you something."

Mattie turned around. "Of course, my dear."

"Where does Gabe Hatch live?"

Mattie's face was unreadable. "He lives at the Willard Hotel, but he's not there now. He followed Parker here last night, said he wanted to be sure he was all right."

"You mean he's still here?"

She nodded toward the rear of the house. "In the card room. He and a couple of the girls are playing whist."

Chapter Eight

Amelia had not expected her confrontation with Gabe to be immediate. She had yet to sort out her muddled thoughts. But she followed Mattie to the back of the house and stood stiffly while she opened the door to a tiny room with dark green flocked wallpaper. Gabe was seated at a table in the center with two women. Neither one lived up to the description Amelia had in her mind of a "fallen dove." They both wore fairly modest day dresses, and neither seemed to have used a trace of face paint. But it was Gabe himself who drew her attention. After she had seen him—tried *not* to see him—in work clothes all week around the cabin, he looked quite different. Once again he was impeccably dressed in a finely tailored dark suit. His golden hair was brushed and gleaming. He looked fit and rested, quite a contrast to the pathetic picture presented by her brother. The thought made Amelia seethe, but she held on to her temper.

"Miss Prescott would like a word with you, Gabe," Mattie said as he looked up at them. He showed no surprise at seeing Amelia in the middle of a bawdy house with the woman she had sworn never to speak to again. Casually he laid down his cards and smiled at his companions. "If you don't mind, ladies . . . I shouldn't be long."

Mattie led them into the front parlor, which was un-occupied. The evening customers had yet to arrive. All three stood awkwardly for a moment, then Amelia said, "I'd like to speak with Gabe alone, Mrs. Smith, if you would be so kind."

Mattie bobbed her head and left the room, closing the glass parlor doors behind her. Gabe waited without a word.

Finally Amelia gestured at the sofa. "Should we sit down?"

He nodded and waited for her to take a seat, then pulled a small chair to sit across from her. He still had not spoken to her.

Amelia cleared her throat. "I once accused you of taking advantage of my brother," she said. He watched her dispassionately. His eyes were a darker shade of blue, somehow. Perhaps it was the dim parlor light. She continued, her voice catching. "How could you take his mine, Gabe? It was all he had."

Gabe stretched his long legs out in front of him. "If I hadn't, he would have lost it to Big Jim, which I sus-pect was the reason Driscoll got him drunk in the first place."

Amelia nodded, as if confirming something to her-self. "I imagined it was something like that. Though I don't approve of your profession, I don't think you're quite as unscrupulous as you may wish people to be-lieve."

A glint of humor lit his eyes. "I'm only *somewhat* unscrupulous," he clarified.

Amelia nodded. "I haven't quite decided how much."

Gabe sat up straight. "Well, thank you for that analysis of my character, Miss Prescott, but if you're through, I have a card game to finish."

Amelia leaned forward and spoke in a rush. "I understand you made Parker an offer before he lost the mine."

Gabe lifted his eyebrows in surprise. "Where did you hear that?"

"Charlie Wilson. He was out at our place this morning and gave us an account of the whole evening."

"Parker turned me down."

"Yes, he did. I want to know if the offer is still good."

He leaned back in his chair and folded his arms. "Just exactly what do you mean, Miss Prescott?"

Amelia's chin lifted. "If I agree to spend an evening with you, will you give Parker back his half of the mine?"

Gabe gave a low whistle. "That would be an expensive evening."

Her face was grim. "You're the one who made the initial offer. I'll meet your conditions in exchange for his half of the mine and the loan of fifty dollars to pay off Driscoll."

"Your brother already owes me eighty-five dollars from the last time."

"The only way he can pay you is by getting his mine back."

Gabe unfolded his arms. "You drive a hard bargain, lady."

Amelia's hands held each other in a death grip in her lap. She felt humiliated, but she was not going to back down at this point. There was too much at stake. "I'd like an answer," she said.

Gabe narrowed his eyes. "Why are you doing this? Without his mine, Parker will have to go on back to New York with you. Isn't that why you came out here in the first place?"

"Yes, but I didn't come out here to see him come home with his tail between his legs feeling like an utter failure. Anyway, he's talking about trying to find an unstaked claim farther west and starting over again."

Gabe shook his head. "He won't find anything west of here but prairie and Indians."

"He'll try, though. My brother is stubborn."

"It must run in the family."

Amelia felt trembly inside. Nerves were starting to set in. "You haven't given me an answer."

"Let me be sure I understand this. I'm supposed to give you half a mine *plus* fifty dollars for the privilege of one evening alone with you?"

She clamped her lower lip with her teeth and nodded.

Gabe cocked his head. "Would you do the cooking?"

A quick rush to her head made her sway against the arm of the sofa. He was going to do it. He'd been going to do it all along. He'd just wanted to make her squirm a little. She didn't care. Her brother's future was worth it. "Thank you," she whispered.

Gabe stood and walked toward the door. "Tomorrow night?" he asked.

She closed her eyes and nodded. "Tomorrow night."

In a terse conference with Morgan and Mattie Smith, Amelia had arranged a conspiracy to keep Parker in town until she had fulfilled her bargain with Gabe. She knew that her brother would be too proud to allow her to "earn" back the mine by such an arrangement. But she was sure that once the evening was over and Parker saw that she was none the worse for it, he would have to accept back the deed. As for the fifty dollars, she figured she would ask Gabe to pay it to Driscoll directly. Parker would just think that Driscoll had decided to give him more time to pay his debt.

Morgan had his doubts about the whole plan, but as usual he was willing to go along for Amelia's sake. Mattie Smith made no comment either for or against. She simply agreed to make sure that Claire would keep Parker occupied for the next day and a half.

Once that was out of the way, Amelia and Morgan left to go back to the cabin, stopping at the general store for some supplies. Gabe might be unscrupulous and infuriating, but he was, after all, giving up a lot just for an evening alone with her. She wondered why he was doing it. If he wanted to buy himself a woman, he had plenty to choose from at Mattie's for a tiny fraction of what the evening with her would cost. And, though women were scarce in Deadwood, she suspected he could find a few rancher's daughters in the surrounding territory who would be plenty happy to give him their company for nothing. At any rate, she had decided that the least she could do was give the man a decent meal. She would cook the rabbit that Morgan had shot and hung up out back of the cabin. And she would make a cobbler with the blackberries that grew down by the stream.

By the time they purchased their supplies and got back to the cabin, it was dark. They ate a cold dinner and headed for bed. It had been a long, upsetting day, and Amelia couldn't reach her straw mattress soon enough. But once the lamps were off she lay awake in

the firelight, staring up at the black ceiling. She'd seen
Gabe daily since her arrival in Deadwood, she told herself. Tomorrow night would be nothing different.
They'd eat dinner, have some civilized conversation by
the fire, then he'd bid her good-night and that would be
the end of it. Parker could have his mine again, and
things would go back to normal. But the churning in her
stomach wouldn't stop. She felt a tingling new aware-
ness of her own body as she lay in the darkness, while
pieces of memory from the day he had kissed her
flashed across her mind. It was just a supper. Morgan
would be right outside. So why did she feel this half ex-
cited, half guilty anticipation?

The gold watch Amelia wore just above her right
breast said exactly seven o'clock when she heard him
ride up. She'd pinned the watch on at the last minute as
kind of a talisman, something to remind her of home,
of the finer things in life. Her father had given it to her
on her fifteenth birthday.

She'd dressed with special care, discarding two frocks
before she settled on the peach-colored taffeta. She was
in a crude cabin in an uncivilized place keeping an assignation that she would never in her wildest dreams
have made in New York, but she could at least dress as
befitted the daughter of prominent banker Samuel
Prescott. She told herself that she was not wearing the
dress to impress Gabe Hatch. She chose it as a matter
of pride and good breeding, not because its rosy color
brought out the reddish highlights in her hair and the
blush of her cheeks. Nor because the lightly bustled
skirt made her waist look even smaller than Cynthia
Wellington's.

The dress, of course, had not fared well on the journey, but Amelia had hung it up in the steam of a boiling pot of water and it had more or less resumed its normal shape. Preparing for the evening had, in fact, occupied her entire day. Even after her restless night, she had awakened early and had gone out to pick the berries for the cobbler she had planned. It wasn't as easy as she had anticipated. After what seemed like a long time of picking, her basket still held only a paltry amount of berries. When Morgan awoke she enlisted his help, and the two of them finally were able to assemble a respectable quantity of fruit.

Morgan made no comment about the effort she was putting into the supper. When he came in from the mine at midday to find her covered in flour from making the cobbler, he simply scrounged in the larder for some jerky and biscuits to make his own lunch. "I owe the man a good meal," Amelia had said defensively. "He's bailing Parker out of a heap of trouble. And it's not the first time."

Morgan had regarded her with his wise, steady eyes and had merely said, "Let me know if you need help with anything, Missy."

But she'd been determined to do this herself, so she'd boiled the potatoes and cleaned the rabbit and steamed her dress and set out the cobbler in a Dutch oven that was by some miracle a part of Parker's sparse kitchen equipment. She'd even put candles and a jar of wildflowers on the table, though she had nothing to use for a tablecloth.

By seven she was exhausted, but pleased that she had worked hard to keep her part of the bargain. It wouldn't exactly be an evening at Delmonico's, but Gabe Hatch would get a decent meal for his money.

Gabe seemed to have taken some pains with his appearance, as well. He was wearing a navy blue suit that she had not seen before. He carried a bunch of flowers in one hand and a paper of sweets in the other. Amelia looked at them in surprise.

"I didn't know you had such customs out West," she said, opening the door wide to admit him.

He grinned. "I'm trying to impress you."

"You're succeeding," she said, returning his smile.

She took the flowers and added them to the jar on the table. "I don't have a vase," she said wistfully.

"They're just as pretty without one," he said. He laid the candy on the table, then took her hand and held it up so he could look at her dress. "Almost as pretty as you."

"Why, thank you, sir," Amelia said with a little blush. This wouldn't be hard at all, she decided with a giddy feeling of relief. It was just like back home with all the beaux who used to crowd around at the afternoon socials. They'd say pretty things and she'd bat her eyelashes and blush and the older folks would whisper behind their hands about what a charming young lady that Miss Prescott was. Of course, there weren't any old folks here tonight, nor any other beaux, for that matter.

"All through this long day I expected to receive a messenger telling me you had changed your mind," he said. His eyes roved over her as if she were one of the sweetmeats he had brought. She couldn't remember any of the beaux back home looking at her quite like that. Her smile wavered.

"I rarely change my mind, Mr. Hatch."

Gabe shook his head and finally dropped her hand. "Mr. Hatch? Well, now, that's a bad start to our evening. Up to a week ago you had agreed to call me Gabe. For the past week you haven't called me much of anything at all, a fact for which I'm still awaiting an explanation."

Amelia changed the subject. She didn't want to think about the scene on Mattie Smith's porch that had caused the abrupt change in her attitude. "Have you heard anything about my brother? Driscoll's men haven't been after him, have they?"

Gabe moved past her into the room. "They don't have any reason to be. I paid his debt last night after I talked with you."

Amelia stared at him. "But you said you expected me to back out of the arrangement."

He shrugged. "A skilled gambler knows when to cover his bets."

"I...thank you." She studied him a moment. "You're a good man, Gabe," she said softly.

"You won't tell anyone, will you?" he teased. "I wouldn't want to ruin my reputation."

She felt the beginning of a glow inside. He tried to put her at ease even when *she* was the one who owed *him*. With a half smile that seemed to emanate from somewhere in her chest, she showed him to a seat in the rocker while she worked at the fire to get the meal ready. Her cheeks grew red from the heat. On one side of her it came from the fire, on the other it was from his eyes as he watched her every move.

Gabe pushed himself back and forth in the old rocker. When he had impulsively proposed the bet at the tables with Parker the other night, he did not, for the life of him, know what had made him do it. Now he was here, alone with Amelia, an entire evening stretched out before them, and he still didn't know what he intended to do about it.

He had wanted to make her smile at him again, as she had the day he had kissed her, before she had mysteriously turned on him and frozen him out. Well, he'd accomplished that much. Of course, she had smiled at him because he was her only hope of getting her brother out of trouble. But if he had thought that was all there was to it, he could have given her the deed and the fifty dollars at Mattie's yesterday and washed his hands of the whole Prescott family. But instead, some perverse devil inside him had made him insist on the bargain. And tonight he fancied that there had been more than gratitude in Amelia's smile. Satisfaction curled into him like the smoke of a fine cigar.

"Do you like rabbit?" she asked, pulling a charred roasting pan out of the coals.

"My favorite food," he said promptly.

She looked up skeptically, then laughed at the gleam in his eye. "Well, then, you're in luck." Proudly she put the pan on the table. "I even know how to cook it now. The first one I did for Parker and Morgan was as raw as a pugilist's shiner."

Gabe threw back his head and laughed. "How many pugilists have you seen in your lifetime, Miss Prescott?"

She giggled. "Parker smuggled me into a match once. It was horrible. I spent the entire time with my face buried in his coat." She pulled the cover off the roaster. The meat smelled wild and savory and looked tender enough to eat with a spoon.

Gabe got up from his chair. "You've made me hungry."

She had, and not entirely for food. When he had promised Parker that there would be nothing untoward about an evening alone with her, he had thought he'd been telling the truth. He had had no intention of anything beyond, perhaps, kissing her good-night, seeing if his reaction to her was as strong as it had been the other day in the meadow. But the evening had barely begun and he found himself spinning dangerously into a loss of control. Just watching her move as she knelt by the fire, listening to the rustle of her dress, smelling the lemony scent of her, tantalizingly faint through the odor of freshly cooked food, was making him crazy. He sat down at the table and tried to keep his eyes from the tight swell of fabric over her breasts as she bent over him serving the supper. Her dress was the color of a blush.

Amelia was immensely pleased with her meal. She had fried up onions and turnips in pork grease as Gabe had shown her that first laundry day, which seemed like a lifetime ago. The rabbit was delicious, and she was able to accept Gabe's hearty compliments knowing that they were deserved. She herself had little appetite. She didn't know whether it was due to the exhaustion from tossing all night and working all day or to the way Gabe kept watching her with his dancing blue eyes. There were moments when she felt her heart thump out of place inside her chest. Jumpin' Jehoshaphat, but the man was handsome!

He was smart, too. After some initial tension when they first sat down, they both relaxed and began to talk avidly of subjects ranging from the classics to the presidential election to the New South. She told him of her young ladies' academy in New York City and he told her tales of the Colorado mining camps. She argued for the cause of women's suffrage and he told her how to hold back a kicker with a pair in five-card draw.

A sudden settling of the fire made them both start with surprise and a recognition of the passing of time. Amelia clapped her hand against her mouth with an exclamation of dismay. "The cobbler!" she wailed. She jumped up and went over to the fire, opening up the Dutch oven with a sinking heart. The berries that she and Morgan had been at such pains to collect had cooked down to a thick mush. The dough underneath was hard and stuck to the bottom of the dish. "It's ruined," she said sadly.

She looked like a little girl whose ice cream had fallen to the ground. Gabe couldn't resist getting up and going to her side. He put his arms around her. "It's no matter. The rest of the supper was so good that I don't think I could eat another bite, anyway."

She looked up into his face, tears brimming in her big eyes. "But all those berries . . ."

"Hush," Gabe said tenderly. "There are plenty more berries. Tomorrow I'll come and help you pick another batch."

She leaned her head against his chest. "I wanted everything to be just right."

He laughed softly and lifted her chin so that she would look at him. "I don't understand you, Amelia Jenks Prescott. You travel halfway across the country to track down your errant brother, you face down the biggest scoundrel in town, you bargain like a fishmonger to save your brother's hide—all without flinching. Yet here you are soaking my new suit over a spoiled pastry."

Amelia looked up at him. The tears shimmered in her eyes. "I guess I'm not all that tough," she said, trying to smile.

"You're pretty damn tough, if you ask me, lady," he said. Then he pulled her up to his mouth and kissed her, impatiently, as if he'd been waiting a long time to do so. It lasted only a few seconds before he set her down again with a jolt.

"What was that for?" she asked, bringing her fingers up to her mouth.

Gabe took a step backward and ran his hands back through the waves of his hair. "I just couldn't look at you anymore without doing it."

He seemed almost angry with her, and Amelia didn't know how to react. Her lips tingled and her stomach felt queer. She stepped around him and went to clear more dishes from the table. Her heart was racing like a runaway train.

"I'm sorry if I offended you," he said.

She turned back to face him, willing her body to composure, and was surprised to see that he looked shaken. For once he seemed to have lost that cool self-control. The knowledge gave Amelia a curious satisfaction. It made her want to move closer to him and see what would happen. But just as she started to do so, she remembered their first kiss in the meadow . . . and she remembered that he had been kissing Mattie Smith less than a day later.

She stopped and drew in a deep breath. "You didn't offend me, Gabe. I realize that kissing women is simply a matter of custom for you. You do it all the time."

Gabe looked puzzled. "What are you talking about?"

"You...and kissing. It appears to be a habit of yours."

Gabe took the plates from her and put them into the basin. "You're talking crazy," he said. "I haven't kissed another woman in...well, so long I'd be laughed out of the Lucky Horseshoe if I admitted it to the boys there."

So he was a liar as well as a libertine. What *was* she doing here with this man? The flutter of pleasure she'd felt from his kiss was completely gone, replaced by a smoldering burn. She put her hands on her hips. "You're a liar, Gabriel Hatch," she said.

His eyes opened wide. "I beg your pardon?"

"You're a liar. I myself saw you kissing Mattie Smith on her front porch in front of God and all mankind not a week ago!"

Gabe looked as though he'd been hit across the face by a board. He blinked twice, then stared, then began walking slowly toward her. "Do you mean to tell me...you blasted little idiot...that you've been treating me like a leper all week long because you happened to see me on Mattie's front porch?"

There was such amazement and such anger in his voice that Amelia took a step backward as he approached. "I saw you *kissing* Mattie on her front porch," she corrected.

He came closer and she started to cringe as his hands took a firm grip on her upper arms. "You were kissing her," she said again in a weak voice that faded into a whisper.

Suddenly his face changed. The anger drained away and he began to laugh, a great head-tossing laugh. "You're jealous!" he said finally.

"I...ah..." She didn't know why, but suddenly she felt a little foolish.

"Don't deny it," he said, his voice soft again. "Your face gives you away. You're plain and simple jealous. And of dear old Mattie, of all people!" He chuckled deep in his throat. His smile was tender as he took her face in both hands and forced her to look up at him. "Sweetheart, I work on Mattie's accounts for her every month. She's my friend." When he saw that Amelia was still regarding him with a doubtful expression, he added soberly, "Mattie tries to give me a little of the mothering I haven't had since my own mother died when I was six."

"But...you were kissing..." She seemed to have lost her voice.

Gabe grinned and cocked his head. "I can see you don't have all that much experience in kissing, Miss Prescott. If you did, you would know that what I was doing on the porch that day with Mattie was saying goodbye to a friend. Now this," he added, his voice gone velvet, "is *kissing*...."

He released her face, slid his arms around her and bent his mouth to hers, softly at first, but gathering confidence as she molded to him without protest. He touched her with just his lips—on the mouth, then her chin, her still-damp cheeks, her closed eyes, then back to her lips. If it hadn't been for the solid pressure of his arms around her she felt that she might dissolve.

"This is kissing," he repeated, husky and wanting. He took her mouth once again, but now he demanded more, opening her with his tongue, seeking heat and union, a mating of mouths, lush and urgent. It went on and on, and Amelia lost track of where she was. When he lifted her in his arms and carried her to the bed, she clung to him, her eyes closed, her body alive in ways she had never before known. The taffeta of her dress slipped sensuously along his wool suit as she wrapped herself around him. He tightened his hold on her.

The few steps across the room proved to be a long journey for Gabe. She was a light burden in his arms, but a heavy one on his heart. His body had raced way ahead of the action and was sending strident signals for release, but he took a deep breath and made himself concentrate on her lovely, trusting face. She was trembling and willing in his arms. He had enough experience with women to know that he could have her here and now if he wished. She was his for the taking. But inside him a long-buried vestige of conscience was demanding a voice. When he had proposed this evening to Parker, he had promised his partner that his sister would come to no harm.

She opened her eyes, questioning his hesitation. He smiled reassuringly and set her down on the cot, then sat down and bent to kiss her again, this time lightly. Her face was flushed to the color of her dress. Her rich brown hair framed her beautiful features. Her breasts rose and fell quickly in the first stages of arousal. She was incredibly, utterly beautiful, and she was safe from him . . . at least tonight.

"I want you, sweetheart," he said.

Through the glaze of desire in her eyes he could see the first touch of fear. But she nodded and said, "I want . . . something, too."

He smiled and put a light hand on her dress where the hard nub of a nipple showed. "I can see that." He made slow, warm circles with his palm against the silky taffeta.

Amelia looked a little uneasy. "Do we kiss some more first?" she asked.

"No," he said. "We don't. I've had about all the kissing I can take, tenderfoot." At her confused expression he added, "We're not going to make love. I promised your brother that nothing would happen to you if he lost this bet."

She tried to sit up, but he pushed her gently down on the mattress and ran his fingers through her disheveled hair. "He didn't make the bet," Amelia said with a frown. "I did."

Gabe nodded. "I know. But my intentions were the same when I made the bargain with you." He gave a rueful grimace. "Unfortunately, if I keep kissing you, my intentions might get overruled."

The clamor inside her body from their kissing had begun to subside, and Amelia wasn't at all sure she wanted it to. She felt cheated somehow, frustrated. She understood what Gabe was saying, and appreciated that he was going against the basic needs of his own body to take a nobler road, but she found herself wishing that he had just kept going on the road he had started out on. She closed her eyes and savored the light pressure of his fingers against her temples.

If she were back in New York, she would never in a million years have found herself lying wantonly on a bed next to a man she had known only a short time, letting him put his hands on her at will. But she wasn't in New York anymore. And in New York she had never encountered a man like Gabe Hatch.

She opened her eyes, sat up abruptly and threw her arms around his neck. "Intentions be damned, Mr. Hatch," she said.

Chapter Nine

They sat with their faces less than a foot apart, their lips separated by a breath. For a moment Gabe considered forgetting his scruples and giving in to what they both obviously wanted. He felt as if he were standing at the edge of a cliff and would fall off no matter which direction he stepped. Backing off now would likely cause Amelia hurt and embarrassment. But taking his seduction to its logical conclusion would be breaking his promise to Parker without any guarantee that Amelia wouldn't regret their actions in the harsh light of day. He made his decision. Steeling himself to keep his voice light and teasing he said, "You're a hussy, Miss Prescott."

"I don't care," she retorted.

He kissed her once more, tenderly, then pushed her away and stood. "You might care tomorrow."

She shook her head and regarded him seriously. "Maybe. If tomorrow I was waking up in my parents' home in New York City. But nothing seems the same out here. Maybe it's the freedom Parker keeps talking about."

Gabe removed his hat from a chair and put it on. "We may be free from our families or free from a certain place, but we're never free from ourselves. That's what you have to consider, Amelia—what's best for you."

Amelia got up from the bed. She felt cold suddenly, and shivered. "I didn't realize that people . . . I don't know . . . talked about this kind of thing. I thought it just happened."

"Often it does. But I didn't want to risk letting it just happen with us and then having you hate me tomorrow."

Amelia leaned the backs of her legs against the bed trying to keep them from shaking. She remembered her first impression of Gabe as a drunk and a gambler who had somehow cheated her brother out of his property. None of it was true. He might be a gambler, but at heart he was a thoroughly decent man. Certainly more chivalrous and considerate than any of the randy suitors back home who, according to her brother, discussed their sexual liaisons as if they were victories on a battlefield. "I don't think I would hate you," she said thoughtfully.

He took a step toward her and reached for her hand. "We have time, sweetheart. Time for you to consider if this magic we both feel so strongly between us is enough for you to give up the chastity that a prospective husband might expect when you go back to New York."

Even the touch of his hand began the warmth flowing through her again. "Do you always discuss your . . . love affairs so thoroughly?" she asked, at once stimulated and curious about the encounter.

"I've never before felt the need to discuss one," he answered soberly. "Don't think that I let you go lightly, Amelia. I'll likely not sleep this night with my body scolding me for my decision. But you are not like any woman I've ever met, and when we come together, it will be only after you tell me that you have made the decision to give me that gift.''

She went up on tiptoes and kissed him on the cheek. "I'll sleep on it," she said.

"Sleep on this," he whispered, then took her mouth in exquisite, gentle nibbles.

She closed her eyes, swayed, and then he was gone.

Gabe closed the door softly behind him with a smile of satisfaction. His body might have been cheated of fulfillment, but his heart was soaring. He'd told the truth when he'd said he'd never met anyone quite like her. He'd already seen her spirit and her quick mind, and now he'd sampled something of the passion that lay quick to arousal just underneath her prim Eastern facade. Though he'd put her off tonight, somehow he knew that it was inevitable they would experience that passion together—soon.

"Evenin', Gabe."

Gabe jumped as the voice out of the dark startled him. Then he turned to see the hulking shape of Morgan sitting right up against the wall of the cabin not two feet from the door. After a moment's irritation he asked in an amused voice, "Did you think you'd have to come dashing to her rescue, my friend?"

He could just see the gleam of Morgan's teeth through the moonlight as he grinned. Then there was a scraping sound and the moonlight flashed on the blade of a twelve-inch hunting knife that Morgan held in the air. "I wouldn't want to see anything happen to Missy," the Welshman drawled.

Gabe shook his head. "Save your weapons for hunting, big man. Your charge and I finished off the rabbit you caught." He tipped his hat and added, "It was delectable." Then he turned and went whistling down the path to his horse.

Parker was in a rare fury. He'd galloped up to the cabin just as Amelia was fetching water to make the morning coffee, and before his mount had stopped moving he'd jumped to the ground and stalked over to her.

"What happened between you and Hatch last night?" he demanded.

Amelia was taken aback by his vehemence, but kept her voice mild. "Whatever do you mean, darling brother?"

"Don't play stupid. I wrung the whole story out of Mattie when I figured out that she and Claire had let me sleep through the entire day."

"I honored your bet, that's all. The deed for the mine you tossed away like a used match is on the table. In exchange for an evening of my company."

"The bastard. I'm going to call him out."

Amelia laughed. "They don't fight duels anymore, Parker, and if they did, Gabe would never be ridiculous enough to let you challenge him to one."

They were standing right next to the stream. Parker knelt and splashed some water on his face. "How could you do it, sis?" There was anger and insult in his voice, which produced something of the same in hers.

"How could I do what? Entertain a gentleman here at the cabin while you slept in the arms of your mistress in town? Pray tell me exactly where the transgression lies in this scenario?"

Parker was silent for a moment. "It's not the same thing."

"You're right, it's not. Because I did *not* spend the night in Gabe's arms. But you might as well know, brother dear, that the only reason I didn't was that Gabe was too much of a gentleman to break his promise to you."

Amelia wanted to laugh at her brother's horrified expression, but she thought better of it. Until he had left for the West, her brother had been her protector for her entire life. She supposed it would take him a while to adjust to the fact that the freedom he had come out West to seek could be equally tantalizing for a woman.

She scooped up a bucket of water and turned back toward the house, leaving her brother sputtering as he tried to decide what to say.

By the time Gabe rode in that afternoon, Amelia and Parker had once again patched up their differences. When Amelia had told her brother to expect the gambler later that day, Parker had threatened to run him off the place. Then he had threatened to throw the deed back in Gabe's face. But he did neither. Instead he gave his partner a grudging thank-you for bailing him out one more time. Then, at Amelia's urging, he made a solemn vow that it would be the last time Gabe would ever need to do so.

"Your brother's not too happy that you paid off his debt," Gabe observed as they watched Parker trudge sulkily up the hill to work.

"He'll come around. I think he's glad to have the mine back."

Gabe waited until Parker had disappeared from sight, then put his arm around her shoulders. "He's protective of you."

She nodded and smiled up at him. "Yes. Back home I never really was interested in any of my suitors, so Parker didn't pay much attention. But I think he senses that you could be dangerous."

Gabe grinned. "He's right. I'm feeling very dangerous at the moment. And I'd like to kiss you. But with your brother just up the hill and that big Welshman waiting for me in the shadows with a butcher knife, I don't dare."

"A butcher knife!"

"When I came out of the cabin last night, he was practically lying across the stoop like a guard dog."

Amelia gave a little huff. "How silly. I'll have to talk with him."

Gabe pulled her against him. "Don't worry about it. He's just trying to see that you're not hurt. So we both want the same thing."

She skipped out of the circle of his arms and stood to face him. "Gabe Hatch, you try to look like an unscrupulous gambling man, but in reality you are one of the nicest men I have ever known."

Gabe's eyes darkened a shade. "I'm not always nice, Amelia. Don't start seeing me as something I'm not."

She refused to listen. "All right. Men can never accept compliments. But you won't change my mind."

He started to protest once again, but she stopped him by putting her fingers on his mouth. "If I remember correctly, you owe me some berries, mister."

Gabe shrugged off his misgivings and let her joyous mood overtake him. She looked as fresh as a berry herself today in a blue cotton dress and crisp white apron that cinched at her tiny waist. With the late-summer sun beating down in a last show of strength, they wandered leisurely along the stream, downriver from the mine so as not to encounter Parker or Gabe. Twice they stopped in the shelter of the bushes to cling together and explore the delights of deep, languid kisses that left them both breathing hard and wanting more.

When they returned, they worked together preparing the supper. This time Gabe made the cobbler. Parker and Morgan came in from working to find them laughing together like schoolchildren, and even Parker's sour looks through the meal could not dim their obvious delight in being together. Afterward, she walked with him out to his horse, but they were acutely aware of Morgan and Parker waiting like maiden aunts for her to return to the cabin.

"What would they do if I scooped you up on my horse and carried you away?" Gabe asked dryly.

Amelia giggled. "I don't know, but I wouldn't try it. You're the one who turned Parker into a crack shot."

"Which reminds me, we were supposed to have had a shooting lesson."

"But didn't because I was being foolish," she said, ducking her head.

"Correct," he agreed. "Now that you are being sensible once again, we'll reschedule it for tomorrow."

She looked up at him, beaming. "You'll come again tomorrow?"

"Didn't I just say so?"

"Don't you have to tend to your work for a while?"

"I'm tending to something more important than work at the moment, thank you, Miss Prescott."

Amelia felt as if her heart were melting. She didn't want to let him go. She wished it was tomorrow this minute so that he would be back. "If you're sure . . ." she said happily. She leaned very close to him.

"I'm very sure, tenderfoot." He glanced back to be sure the cabin door was still closed, then he took her in his arms and kissed her. "Of course," he added after a few more breathless moments, "we don't want to risk hurting anyone during our shooting lesson. So I think we'll have to go far off into the woods."

"How far?" Her voice was dazed.

He kissed her again and murmured, "Very, very far."

Amelia did not pay the slightest attention to her brother's objections the next morning. She just kept on humming and preparing the basket of lunch she intended to take on her excursion with Gabe.

"You can practice shooting out back of the cabin," Parker grumbled. "That's where he taught me."

"Perhaps he thinks I'll need a wider target space," she said lightly. Then she resumed humming.

Morgan added his reservations. "You get too far up into those mountains, you'll likely encounter bears."

"Gabe will have his rifle if we are disturbed by any ferocious creatures," she answered calmly.

She didn't resent their concern, but she was just as glad that they both had disappeared up the hill by the time Gabe rode up so that she could give in to her impulse to run to him and throw her arms around his shoulders as soon as he dismounted.

He kissed her hungrily. "Has it only been hours since we said good-night?" he asked. "Because it feels like days."

"Weeks," she agreed with a little sigh of happiness.

He looked around. "Did you tell your brother that we would need a little privacy today?"

"He's not too happy about it, but he's got to learn that I'm too old to need a nanny anymore."

"Yes, ma'am, you are," he said fervently, his eyes roaming down over her figure in a way that made her feel as if he had caressed her.

"I've packed us a picnic," she said.

He followed her into the house to collect the basket of food and the gun he had given her. Then they mounted and began to ride up into the mountains. The pungent pine scent of the Black Hills filled their nostrils as they climbed higher and higher. It was cooler today, and the crisp air seemed to make everything look greener, smell fresher. It was as if nature was determined to put on a final show before launching itself into the dying season of fall.

Amelia and Gabe talked about anything and nothing as they ambled along. They laughed over the strident demands of a mountain jay who seemed to be trying to collect some kind of toll for the use of his personal road. They stopped for a while to watch a pair of red squirrels with black-tipped tails, in the middle of a domestic quarrel.

"She's asking him why he stayed out so late last night," Gabe interpreted.

Amelia gave a bubbly laugh. "And he's telling her that a good wife is seen and not heard."

"And she says he'll hear a lot more if he doesn't stop squandering his money at the saloon."

"And he says that he works hard for his money and he can darn well spend it where he pleases."

The two squirrels stopped their scampering and faced each other, their little cheeks puffing as they continued chirping. Then one of them reared up on its hind legs and leapt onto a big rock, disappearing down the opposite side. Its companion hesitated for a minute, then followed it.

"Who do you think won?" Gabe asked.

"Probably neither. They were just airing their differences. Then they'll kiss and make up. Isn't that the way it usually goes with marriages?"

Gabe's smile dimmed. After a moment's hesitation he answered, "I suppose. Come on. There's a pretty little valley I want to show you just ahead. We can eat our lunch there."

Gabe's valley turned out to be a wildflower-covered meadow nestled between two craggy peaks that towered over them in majestic silence, looking very much like the stereopticon photographs she had seen of the great Rocky Mountains.

She sat with her back propped against a tree, Gabe's head in her lap. He chewed idly on a long stalk of grass. She had been making a chain of clover flowers, but had abandoned the effort in favor of letting her eyes delight in the view.

"I've never seen anything so beautiful," she said, looking up at the mountains while she idly sifted her fingers through his soft hair.

Gabe's eyes were closed. "Nor have I."

She tweaked his ear. "You're not even looking."

"Yes, I am. It's the most beautiful thing I've ever seen, and I can see it with my eyes closed." He reached up and ran his hand across her face.

"I'm talking about the mountains."

"I'm not."

She leaned contentedly back against the tree. She was relieved that Gabe had regained his good humor. For a while after they had stopped to watch the red squirrels he had seemed withdrawn. He had eaten his lunch absently, without complimenting her on the food as he usually did. But soon he had become his usual self, attentive and charming, and now he seemed relaxed and happy.

"We haven't done any shooting," she said.

Gabe opened his eyes and looked at her upside down. "We've been too busy, I reckon."

She laughed. "Parker will want to know what I learned in all this time up here."

"Tell him it's none of his business."

"I can't do that."

"Why not?"

"Because he's my brother, and we've always taken care of each other."

"Mmm." He seemed unconvinced, but too lethargic to argue the point. How could she explain the special bond she and Parker had always had? They'd been more than brother and sister. They'd been best friends and parents to each other, too. But then, Parker hadn't consulted her when he decided to fall in love with his Claire, had he?

"I wish . . ." she began uncertainly.

Gabe opened his eyes again. "You wish what?" he encouraged.

After a slight hesitation she continued, "I'm beginning to wish that I could take off to some wild new place where no one knew me, just as Parker did."

He threw away the grass he'd been chewing and twisted around to sit up facing her. "What would you do there in this wild new place, tenderfoot?"

She met his eyes and blushed.

"You don't need to go anywhere for that," he said tenderly. "If you're sure it's what you want."

"It's what I want," she said, her voice barely audible.

He leaned toward her, making her look at him. "You realize we're not talking marriage and a brownstone on Park Avenue... happily ever after?"

She nodded. "I don't care. Those things weren't important to me even when I was still back in New York. Out here they don't seem to make any difference at all."

Gabe moved closer to kiss her. "I've never met anyone quite like you."

"The only problem is..."

"What?"

"You know... my brother, Morgan and his hunting knife. I might as well be back at the Cotillion Ball with a chaperon hovering over each shoulder."

Gabe stood and reached out a hand to her. "Why don't you let me worry about that?" he said. "For now, we'll have that first shooting lesson so you can show your brother that you spent the entire day in respectable, educational activity."

She let him pull her up, and turned her face to accept his kiss. Then she stammered, "So how...? When...?"

He gave her a smile that sent a liquid rush of feeling through her middle. "Just leave it to me."

Gabe rarely had visitors come to his room at the Willard. Most people just looked for him at the tables at the Horseshoe. When he answered the knock on his door, he half expected to see Parker and Morgan glaring at him from behind, respectively, a drawn six-gun and a menacing hunting knife. Guilty conscience, he supposed.

But instead of his partner and the Welshman, his visitors were David Harrington, the town banker, Peter Stuber, owner of the dry goods, and Nels Nelson, who had recently purchased the Willard Hotel. He'd beaten each one of the men in friendly card games over the past few weeks, but he wouldn't exactly have considered any of them a friend.

"Come in," he said, hastening to button up his half-open shirt. Late nights playing meant that he usually slept far past what was considered normal by most of the respectable folk in town. His schedule had been further skewed lately because he'd spent so much time out at the Prescott place that he often didn't start his game until nearly midnight. And when he did get to his bed, swift, hot fantasies of Amelia kept him staring into the dark for hours. If she hadn't changed her mind, this evening the fantasy would become reality, and he hoped like hell that he would be able to have enough control to take it slow and lingering as she deserved.

"What can I do for you gentlemen?" he asked.

Tall and overly lean, David Harrington spoke for the group. "Some of the merchants around town have been getting together trying to come up with some solutions to all the problems here in Deadwood."

"You've got your work cut out for you," Gabe observed dryly.

"We know. But if we want to turn this town into a decent place to live, something has to be done."

"There were twelve gunfights out on the public street last week," Stuber put in. "I had a bullet come through my store window. It dinged the ostrich feather right off one of them fancy new hats just in from Boston."

Harrington continued, "The walls of the canyon are turning into shanty towns—a ramshackle collection of shacks built practically right on top of each other. One stray spark could start a fire that would burn half the town. There's no order to it, no rules, no law...."

Gabe frowned, looked over at the stout little dry goods owner and then back to Harrington. "Excuse me, gentlemen, but exactly what does all this have to do with me?"

The banker had muttonchop whiskers that looked too big for his lean face and twitched when he took a deep breath to say something important, as he did now. "We're forming a kind of committee—the Board of Health and Street Commissioners."

"Sounds impressive," Gabe observed.

Nels Nelson was a blond, quiet man with typically Scandinavian reserve, but he had a sharp intelligence and dry wit that had made Gabe like him at once when he had arrived in town a few weeks back. "Look, Gabe," he said. "We know that we're businessmen, not lawmen. But right now there is no law in Deadwood, and we figure we can't just sit back and let the town go to ruin."

"Well, I admire your intentions."

Nels shook his head and continued more insistently. "But we need help. We can't face up to men like Big Jim Driscoll all by ourselves."

Gabe's eyes widened in surprise. "You intend to go after the Lucky Horseshoe?"

"Not if it stays legal. We wouldn't be fools enough to try to shut down gambling in Deadwood. But we do intend to make some ordinances that would prevent Driscoll from building any more of those shacks and renting them out to the miners at five times their worth."

Gabe gave a low whistle. "He won't be happy about that."

"No, he won't," Harrington said. "Which is why we want you on our side."

"Why me?" Gabe asked with a look of confusion.

"Because you're not afraid of Driscoll. We've seen you stand up to him. And you're good with a gun. Which is one of the few things people like Driscoll respect."

"I don't even *own* a gun," Nels put in.

"I'm no gunfighter," Gabe said hastily.

"We know that," Stuber answered. "And we don't want a gunfighter. That would just put us in the same category with them. But we can use a leader who can talk with Driscoll on something of his own terms."

Gabe considered for a moment. It had been a long time since he'd considered himself part of the respectable elements of a town. Back in St. Louis he'd never dreamed he'd be anything else, but after the debacle of his marriage to Samantha, it hadn't seemed to make any difference anymore. He liked the three men standing in front of him. It would be nice to see people like them take control over this area so that when the gold played out and the adventurers grew tired of the game, a new breed of good, solid citizens could establish themselves in the Dakotas.

"What are your plans?" he asked.

"Our first plan was to get you on our side," Nels said with a laugh.

Gabe smiled. "And then?"

"Driscoll's shantytown. We want to make him clean it up or tear it down."

Gabe nodded. "All right. I'm with you."

"Wonderful!" Harrington's smile pushed his whiskers back to his ears. "We'll start today. We can meet at the bank right after closing."

Gabe walked over to his dresser and picked up his tie. "Not today," he said, keeping his voice steady, though his heart had started to race. "We can meet tomorrow. Today I, ah, have a prior engagement."

Chapter Ten

"**Y**ou're sure you feel all right about this, sis?" Parker asked, fastening on a pair of suspenders he'd bought that day at Stuber's Dry Goods.

"Now, don't you look elegant?" she teased, giving one of the braces a little snap. "I'll be fine with Gabe, Parker. You should know that by now."

"Morgan could stay with you. Claire asked me especially to be there to help out with the surprise, but Morgan wouldn't have to go."

"Poor Morgan. He hasn't done anything but work or play bodyguard with me since he got here. Mattie's birthday party will do him good. I'm still not saying that I approve of that woman...or her girls," she added.

Parker gave her a quick peck on the cheek. "But you have to admit Claire's a beauty, isn't she, sis? And she's sweet, too. I wish you could get to know her."

Amelia didn't want to talk about Claire. Not tonight. Her stomach had been jumping all day as she considered and reconsidered the decision she had made. Gabe had not put on any pressure. He'd left it all up to her. But now that she'd said yes, he wasn't the kind of man to vacillate and give her time to get cold feet. The "surprise birthday party" that had materialized overnight was proof of that. It would leave them alone—really alone this time.

"You can bring your Claire out to supper one of these days," she answered absently.

"Truly, sis? You'd be willing to talk with her, to sit down at table with her?"

Amelia gave her brother a hug. "If you're in love with her, she must be very special, regardless of what she does for a living. We both should have gotten at least that much from Mother and Father—that people shouldn't be judged by what they are forced to do by life's misadventures."

"You're a peach, sis," Parker said with a grin. "And you sounded just like Mother right then, which is not all bad."

Amelia's smile was halfhearted. No misadventure of life was forcing her to make love to Gabe Hatch. It was simply something she wanted with all her heart. And if what Parker wanted was Claire, who was she to stand in judgment?

"Bring her out tomorrow after the party, if you like."

Parker beamed, then they both turned and stared as the door opened and Morgan came in. He was wearing a new red wool shirt with a string tie. His black hair was slicked back from his face with some kind of grease. His face was scrubbed shiny and he was newly shaved. "Why, Morgan," Parker teased. "You're as shiny as a new nickel. Looks like you're going to a party or something."

The Welshman grinned sheepishly. "That's the idea, isn't it?"

"You look very nice, Morgan," Amelia said gently.

"Now, if Gabe would only get here, we could be on our way," Parker added impatiently.

"Why don't you two go on ahead?" She consulted her watch brooch. "Gabe said he'd be here at seven, and it's almost that now."

"I don't like to leave you alone...."

"Go on...you're going to miss the surprise if you don't get started." Amelia hoped she could convince them to leave before Gabe arrived. She was sure that her face would give her away the minute she saw him, and then Parker might never agree to leave.

She ushered them out the door just in time. As they started across the meadow Gabe's horse emerged from the woods on the other side. The three riders stopped and exchanged a few words, then continued on to their respective destinations. Gabe undoubtedly was cooler about this assignation than she was. He probably had no trouble facing her brother without giving a hint of why they so desperately wanted to be alone.

She went across the bridge to meet him, and reached up and held his hand as he walked his horse to the other side. Just the firm grip of his fingers was enough to quiet the nerves that had been plaguing her all day, and when he jumped down and kissed her, all doubts fled.

"So we're alone at last," he murmured wickedly. "You're at my mercy."

"I think I've been at your mercy, Mr. Hatch, practically since the day we met."

"Except for the week you pouted and treated me like something smelly you might scrape on the bootjack."

"Even then," she said with a sigh. "I was so miserable."

"Ah, sweetheart. If I had my way, you'd never be miserable again in your entire life."

"I don't think that's possible," she said practically.

"No. But tonight we'll make believe it's possible, all right?"

She nodded, her cheeks growing warm and her insides churning. "Shall I make us some supper?"

"Oh, no. You're not doing any work this evening. Just go on in and grab a wrap while I saddle your horse."

"Saddle my horse?"

"Or do you want to ride double with me?"

"Ride *where?*"

He turned her around by the shoulders and gave her a little pat on the bottom. "Just get your shawl. I'm in charge tonight, remember?"

She went into the cabin and took a last swipe at her hair. She'd left it down, which meant that it looked thick and disheveled no matter what she did to it. She hadn't anticipated a horseback ride.

When she came out her horse was saddled and Gabe helped her to mount. He still refused to tell her where they were going, but the view of the setting sun over the mountains was so spectacular that she stopped pestering him. The ride was fairly short. They left their little Pronghorn River and followed a stream that connected to it. After only a few minutes' ride up the mountain they emerged on a clearing rimmed with towering pines. A tiny cabin stood in the middle, smoke curling up from its stone chimney. The border of trees made it seem as if the little house was completely shut off from the rest of the world.

"Who lives here?" Amelia asked.

"We do—for tonight, at least."

At her questioning look he laughed and jumped off his horse. "The miner who built this place gave up last month and went back home to Tennessee. I had loaned him some money, so he left me the house to pay off his debt.''

She jumped down into his arms and followed him inside. The cabin was even smaller than Parker's, but it was clean and smelled fresh, and up against the far wall was a wide cot with what looked for all the world like a real feather bed.

She looked at Gabe in amazement. ''All the comforts of home,'' he said. He gestured to the food spread out on the planked table. ''I brought it out from the Willard. That's why I was a few minutes late.''

Amelia turned around in a circle to survey the room. The fire burned merrily. There were flowers on the table and oil lamps already lit in the two windowsills. The bed looked plumped and freshly aired. Gabe had gone to some trouble to prepare this place. ''But why did we have to come here? Parker and Morgan are gone for the evening....''

''They'll be gone for the whole night if Mattie's girls manage things right. But you never know. I didn't want to risk interruptions.''

He walked up behind her and put his arms around her. ''Anyway,'' he said softly in her ear, ''I wanted us to have our own little world tonight. I want to take you away from everything you have ever known.''

Amelia felt a knot inside her throat. She turned in his arms. ''For the whole night?'' she whispered.

He nodded. ''Don't worry. Parker and Morgan are going to be having a good time, too.''

She blushed. ''Morgan will be surprised.''

Gabe led her to a chair by the little table. ''Not as surprised as Mattie will be to learn it's her birthday.''

''You mean it's not?''

"Nope."

Amelia looked distressed. "But..."

He sat down opposite her and winked. "Don't worry. Her birthday's next week. She'll just think the girls got the date wrong. Mattie's too nice a person to spoil her girls' efforts with details."

"Too nice?"

"Yes." He gave her a look of reproach. "Mattie's one of the most caring women I've ever met, in spite of her profession. I've seen her turn down some of the richest bankrolls in town when she thought the men were too drunk to treat her girls properly."

"But a surprise party when it's not even her birthday," Amelia chided. "You could just have waited until her birthday came to plan all this."

"No," Gabe said firmly, a flare of blue fire in his eyes. "I couldn't. I don't think I could have waited another day."

Heat radiated from Amelia's cheeks. She looked around nervously. "Whew, it's warm in here. We don't really need the fire, do you think?"

Gabe gave her a knowing smile. "The sun's almost down. It will start to cool off quickly. Autumn nights can be chilly this far up in the mountains."

Amelia loosened the top button of her dress. "So...I suppose we should eat," she suggested a little too brightly, opening up the cloth that covered a basket of chicken.

Gabe reached across the table and grabbed both her hands. His eyes held hers. "Listen to me, tenderfoot. Nothing's going to happen tonight that you don't want to happen. You're in control. Understand?"

"I don't feel much in control," Amelia whispered shakily.

"Come on. Where's the brave girl who came by herself all the way out West to rescue her brother?"

"I wasn't by myself. I had Morgan with me."

Gabe's voice was low and intent. "You aren't by yourself tonight, either. You have me with you."

The strength of his hands seemed to flow through hers, bringing confidence and assurance . . . and something more—a vague wanting deep down inside her. She wanted this man. She wanted to feel his hands on her, his lips on her. . . .

She pulled her hands out of his with a laugh. "If you don't want your food to go to waste, you'd better let go of me, Gabe. I can't seem to think clearly when you're touching me."

There was a slight flare of his nostrils and a predatory look in his eyes that she had not seen before, but it was gone in an instant, replaced by his customary smile. "By all means, sweetheart. It's bad enough that I've kidnapped you and spirited you away to my lair in the mountains. I wouldn't want to be accused of starving you, as well."

His teasing broke the tension, and the rest of the meal passed in easy conversation. Amelia laughed so hard at his stories that once she choked on her food and had to stand up and pound on her chest to recover. She and Parker had shared a good deal of fun growing up together, but the overall tone of their household, set by their crusading parents, had been serious. "I haven't had enough laughter in my life," Amelia declared as she wiped her eyes for the third time.

"Carlyle says that humor is not found in laughter but in still smiles, which lie far deeper. He also says that the essence of humor is love. I've seen you and your brother share many of those still smiles, Amelia."

"Thomas Carlyle, the philosopher?" Her father was an admirer of some of Carlyle's theories on the integrity of the individual.

Gabe nodded with a gentle, still smile of his own. Amelia gazed at him in amazement. He was a gambler who told tall tales like a shantyman, but he also quoted Shakespeare and read modern intellectuals. He made her happy when she was feeling sad and gave her strength when she was feeling weak. In a moment of stark revelation she realized that she had fallen totally in love with him.

"I . . . I can't eat another bite," she said.

He pushed back his plate and stood up from the table. "Do you think it's cooled off enough now to sit by the fire?" he asked with a hint of teasing in his voice.

She nodded. There were two chairs pulled up in front of the fire. One was an oversize chair with leather padding, the other a Shaker-style stool with half a back. She was a little surprised when he motioned her to the stool and took the big, comfortable chair for himself.

"Would you like a glass of brandy?"

"Brandy?" Amelia's eyes widened. There had, of course, never been a drop of spirits in her home, though she had been offered a ladylike glass of sherry at various social functions in other places. "I don't think so," she said.

"Do you mind if I have one?" For the first time she noticed a dark, round bottle and two shot glasses sitting on a little table at the side of his chair. He reached to pour himself a glass without waiting for her answer. When he pulled the cork out of the bottle she could detect a pungent but not unpleasant smell. He lifted the small glass in a toast. "To new horizons," he said.

The fluttering in her stomach began again. She had not realized that her decision to make love with him would turn out to be such a prolonged process. Suddenly she wanted to hurry on with it. As if he sensed her impatience, he put the glass back down on the table and said in a low voice, "Come here."

She paused. Then she pointed to his chair. "Come there?"

He nodded. Standing, she glanced over at the puffy feather bed. Weren't these things supposed to take place in a bed? Uncertainly she took the two steps over to his chair. He pulled her down into his lap. "That's better," he said.

Now she understood why he had taken the comfortable chair. It fit the two of them nicely. She perched a little awkwardly on his legs and put an arm around his shoulders to steady herself. But he wasn't satisfied with the position. He spread his legs slightly, then grasped her hips and nestled her back against him. She felt the hardness of his thighs along her bottom as she had that first day so long ago in the stagecoach. He turned her shoulders so that one of her breasts pressed on his chest and leaned her back against his arm. "That's definitely better," he said, his voice now husky and stroking.

Then he began to kiss her, deep, drugging kisses with a bite of brandy and the urgency of a passion too long leashed. He concentrated all his attention on her mouth, expertly teasing, tonguing, sucking until her lips were so sensitive she felt as if a mere breath of air could start up the magic once again.

She was hardly aware that Gabe had begun to move his hands over her dress. But suddenly his fingers reached a breast and lingered, caressing, gently molding. And the other hand stroked her stomach where she had begun to feel a hard, odd building of pressure. She moaned involuntarily. He renewed his kisses and began slowly unbuttoning her dress. His fingers searched and found bare skin, then dug deeper to reach her hardening nipples. He aroused first one, then the other with gentle tugs of his fingertips. Then he bent his head to surround them with a soft, swirling tongue. Amelia gasped and pushed herself back against the arm of the chair as sharp pulses of feeling shot through her.

Her gasp was almost Gabe's undoing. In a few short minutes he had become more aroused than he could remember since he had first learned about sex in the hazy summer meadows back in St. Louis. Amelia might be an innocent, but her mouth was a naturally erotic instrument, and her breasts were perfection, full and pink tipped. Her reaction to his stimulation was quick and impassioned. He had thought to spend long moments of leisurely foreplay in the chair before taking her to his bed, but he could see now that neither would wait. In one easy movement he stood, carrying her with him. Her dress was half-off. He ran his tongue along one of her smooth ivory shoulders.

Willing his racing body to calm down, he continued to undress her. "You may do the same to me," he told her. "Do you want me to turn off the lamps?" He'd expected shyness, but as she answered his question with a shake of her head she looked intrigued and almost...lustful.

Their clothes were dispatched and he took a minute to run an appreciative glance down her long-limbed body. She made no effort to hide her high breasts nor the triangle of chestnut hair that covered her sex. Gabe had urgent, hot impulses to throw her down and bury himself inside her, but instead he took a deep breath and spoke. "I've never seen anything so beautiful, sweetheart." He ran his hands from her hips up to just under her breasts. "You're almost too perfect to touch."

She leaned up and kissed him wetly as their naked bodies came together for the first time, smooth against hard, curves against planes. "But I want you to touch me, Gabe," she murmured. "Everywhere. Teach me."

And he waited no further, taking them both down on the bed where they sank into its softness and into each other, rolling and stroking and rubbing together intimate parts until finally he guided her hand around him and showed her how they would become one.

Amelia moved her hands up to take a tight hold on his shoulders. There was discomfort as he moved inside her, but it was in the distance, like a light through a fog. Mostly there were the wrenching waves of feeling and a powerful, overwhelming sense of merging herself with another being. At the very end she lay still and let the sensations carry her into another world, one from which she didn't care if she ever emerged.

"Are you all right, sweetheart?" Gabe asked with sudden concern. Amelia's cheeks were wet with tears that she didn't remember shedding. She didn't know how long she had been unaware of her surroundings.

She pulled him against her, unwilling to let go.

"I didn't hurt you?" he asked, the anxiety sharper in his voice.

She tried to chuckle but it ended up as not much more than a smile. A still smile, she thought to herself. "I love you, Gabriel Hatch," she said. She hadn't meant the words to come out, but she was too depleted to feel regret. The declaration seemed the natural result of what they had just experienced together. She hadn't said it consciously or to oblige him to return the sentiment.

But when he stiffened and didn't say anything, her common sense began to return and she realized that she might have just said the very thing that would have him up on his horse and running the other direction. "I'm sorry," she said. "I know that's not what you wanted to hear. It just came out. I'm not trying to force you into some kind of commitment."

He rested on an elbow, looking down at her. His face was flushed from their exertions, his hair tousled. He looked pensive. "How could you think I wouldn't want to hear it?" he asked. "Who would not want to hear a declaration of love from a beautiful, intelligent—" he stopped and kissed her nose "—*passionate* woman?"

"But I mean—"

He put his hand on her mouth. "I know what you mean. I'm honored, sweetheart. Touched by your words and honored that you allowed me to be the first man to make love to you. If my life were different, I would..."

He stopped for such a long time that Amelia thought he had lost track of his thoughts. "Is it because you're a gambler?" she asked.

He came out of his reverie and regarded her with a bittersweet smile. "It's because I'm not the right man for Amelia Prescott, the banker's daughter from New York City. I'm not the right man for any woman."

Amelia gave a puzzled frown. "I think any woman would be lucky to have you, Gabe."

He gathered her in his arms. "There are things about me that you don't know, sweetheart. But we don't have to let any of those things spoil our night together."

Amelia's body was still limp. She let herself mold against him. She wanted to ask him what things he was talking about. She wanted to know everything about him. What he liked, what he thought about. He had, as he had said, brought her to a whole new world, one she hadn't even known existed, and she wanted to let him know what it meant to her. But there would be time to talk. For now she was content to revel in the unique, utterly unexpected pleasure of her silky, naked skin rubbing against his. The feelings began to build once again as he, too, decided that there had been enough talk.

This time he went more slowly. His hands caressed every inch of her body before he finally reached that secret, hidden place and lingered there, parting her and teasing with dampened fingers until tremors began inside her and he hastened to enter her and join in her release.

Then he held her tenderly and kissed her eyes and her mouth and, pulling a coverlet over them both, cradled her to sleep like a newborn babe.

Amelia's eyes flew open in horror. The sun was streaming in through the little cabin windows. She sat up, allowing the coverlet to fall and expose her nakedness. Gabe was naked, too, still asleep beside her. In spite of her anxiety, she took a moment to enjoy the sight of him. The hair on his body was much darker than his blond head and mustache. His upper body was tanned as if he spent time out of doors with no shirt, though she didn't know how this could be when he spent all of his time inside a smoky saloon. Perhaps it was just from the week he had worked out at the mine. But the muscles in his arms and chest had not developed over just a week. Nor had they come from dealing cards.

Scolding herself for her indulgence, she pulled the coverlet back up to her chest and smoothed it over him, then bent to give his shoulder a tentative push. She had barely touched him when his hand snaked up and grabbed her wrist, pulling her down on the bed and underneath him in one smooth move. She could swear that he had been sleeping only seconds before, but there was no doubt about the fact that he was already aroused. "Spying on me, were you?" he growled. "There's a penalty for that."

He turned her in his arms and gave her a playful slap on the bottom that turned into a caress as their bodies moved together once again in a quick frenzy of passion.

Gabe collapsed on top of her, his body damp and sticking. "Good morning," he said lazily.

Amelia lay underneath him with a silly grin on her face. She hadn't realized it would be like this...making love, being in love. So all consuming. So explosive. So *frequent*. He had awakened her in the middle of the night with apologies that proved completely unnecessary after just a few minutes of attention by his hands and lips. And they'd made long, leisurely love in the dead stillness of the night before once again sinking into sleep in each other's arms. And now this...morning thing.

"How are you feeling, tenderfoot?" he asked after several minutes.

"Tender," she replied ruefully.

He rolled off her, his eyes worried. "Damn. I...I ought to be shot for a randy bastard." He put his hand over her private place and made a gentle circle. The warmth of his palm felt good. Amazingly, she wasn't the least bit self-conscious at the intimacy. She'd given herself to Gabe, and there were no reservations to her gift.

She smiled up at him. "Don't say that. I'm all right."

"I should have been gentler. We shouldn't—"

She reached up and smoothed the hairs of his mustache, cutting off his words. "I wouldn't change last night for anything in the world," she said.

"There's one thing I would change," he said, unexpectedly.

"What?"

He gave her a quick kiss, then threw his long leg over her, climbed out of bed and went across the room to rummage in a saddlebag that lay on the floor by the door. After a moment he turned and held up an ivory silk nightgown.

"What's that?" she asked, mystified.

"It's a present. Yours was ruined, remember?"

"But, Gabe, I can't accept a gift like that."

"Why not? Who will ever know? It's not as if you're going to wear it out to tea when you get back to New York. I wanted you to wear it last night, but, ah, things went a little faster than I had anticipated."

She laughed and her eyes shone as he walked over and draped the soft silk over her. "Put it on now for breakfast," he said. "I want to see you in it."

She smoothed the fine fabric with her hands. The low neckline was edged in delicate lace. She'd never worn anything so fine just for sleeping. But then, she remembered with a sensual smile, she'd been doing a lot more than sleep last night. Suddenly she sat straight up. "Gabe, it's morning!"

"Yes, it is, sweetheart." He smiled at her as he pulled on his pants.

"I've got to get back to the cabin. What if Parker came home after all? Or Morgan. Morgan wouldn't ever leave me alone all night. He'll be sick with worry."

She sat with the coverlet and the nightgown pooled around her waist, her breasts bare to view. Gabe's eyes were on them as he said, "You underestimate the talents of Mattie's girls. I'd be surprised if those two show up back at your place before late afternoon."

"But we can't be sure...."

Gabe suddenly picked her up off the bed and set her down on the floor. "The only thing we can be sure of, tenderfoot, is that if you don't get covered up, I might *never* let you out of that bed."

He reached for the nightgown and lifted it over her head. It shimmered down her body like a caress and clung to her curves. The lace bodice showed through to her skin, revealing the top halves of her breasts. Gabe whistled. "I don't know that that's much better."

Amelia had never before known what it meant to feel seductive, to bask in the look of desire in a lover's eyes. Her lips curved into a new, uniquely feminine smile. "You want me to take it off?"

"Oh, no, you don't, you little minx. We're not starting in again. I've already pushed way too hard for your first experience with all this, and I'm not laying a hand on you until you've had some time to recover." He led her by the shoulders over to the table and pushed her down on a chair. "You sit down over here and behave yourself while I rustle us up a nice big breakfast. How about bacon and eggs?"

"That would be very nice," she said demurely. Then she added with a wicked gleam in her eye, "But, Gabe..."

"Yes, sweetheart?" he asked, scooping a spoonful of grease into a big frying pan.

"I should warn you that bacon and eggs always give me an incredible amount of energy."

He shook his head with a grin on his face that lasted all the way through breakfast.

Chapter Eleven

"What shall I tell Parker if he's arrived back before us?" Amelia asked anxiously as they rode down the mountain path toward the Prescott cabin.

"Don't tell him anything. Just turn the tables like we did the other day—scold him for staying out all night himself."

She nodded and lapsed into silence. Gabe waited a few moments, then said, "Or you could tell him the truth."

"The truth?"

"That you and I spent a long, wonderful night in each other's arms and neither one of us has a single regret."

Amelia's only reply was a noncommittal "Mmm."

Actually, Gabe admitted, he did find that a regret or two was trying to surface. Amelia was above the age of majority, and he had let her be the one to make the decision, but he now found himself feeling a little guilty. Since Samantha had betrayed him, he had had very few scruples as far as women were concerned. But all at once he was putting himself in Parker's shoes. If Amelia decided to tell her brother about their night together, Parker would have every right to nail Gabe's hide to the nearest door.

He'd been foolish to think he could treat a woman like Amelia as casually as he had his many other liaisons over the past few years. What if she got pregnant from their encounter? he thought with sudden horror. He'd been so enamored that he'd not even thought to be careful.

The cabin looked shut and empty, and there was no sign of Parker's and Morgan's horses. Both Amelia and Gabe breathed a secret sigh of relief. The question of what to tell her brother could be put off, at least for the moment.

Both were subdued as they reached the door. Amelia jumped from her horse without waiting for his help. He stayed mounted. "Aren't you coming in?" she asked, her voice a little stiff.

He shook his head. "There's something I have to do in town. I'll be back for supper, if that's all right."

She looked up at him towering over her on his horse. It seemed cold to part without even a kiss goodbye after so much warmth over the past twelve hours. "Of course," she said. "Until this evening, then."

As if he could read her mind, he jumped from his horse, took her in his arms and kissed her. "I'll be carrying you with me all day—" he tapped his finger over his heart "—in here. And I'll carry the memory of last night with me to the grave . . . and beyond."

He touched her cheek, then turned to get back up on his horse. She watched until he disappeared across the meadow, then walked slowly back into the cabin. Would her brother be able to tell the difference in her? she wondered. It seemed impossible that she would look the same after going through something so incredible.

But a quick glance in her mirror showed no outward sign of everything she had felt and done during the past long night.

She tucked the mirror away in her valise with a sad smile. She and Parker had never kept secrets from each other growing up, but she was afraid that for the time being her night with Gabe was one experience she would not be sharing with her brother.

Big Jim Driscoll was seated at the oversize desk that filled most of the small office at the back of the Lucky Horseshoe. The desk and the big leather armchair that went with it forced visitors to stand by the door or take an awkward seat in one of the three tiny straight-backed chairs that were jammed up against the opposite wall. Deuce Connors usually preferred to stand.

"We've heard from Cooper out in Denver, Big Jim, and I think you'll be pleased."

The saloon owner puffed on his cigar, filling the room with smoke. "He's taken his time about it. Has he found her?"

Deuce waved the stream of smoke out of his face. "Yes. Turns out she's dancing for her supper these days. Her latest protector skipped out and left her high and dry with nothing but debts to pay."

"Poor Samantha," Driscoll said with a satisfied sneer. "I always told her she'd regret not having been nicer to me. She had a great body and she knew how to use it, but she was too damn uppity for her own good. More trouble than any broad is worth."

"I think you'll find her a little more humble these days. She's made the rounds of the mining camps, I guess, which ain't the easiest life for a woman."

Driscoll shrugged. "Maybe I'll give her another chance after we've finished dealing with Hatch. He still thinks she's dead?"

"The bitch told Cooper that she hasn't had any contact with her husband since she left St. Louis."

"I want her here," Driscoll said tersely. "If those crybaby merchants really do try to put Hatch at the head of their precious committee, I want to be sure we have our pretty little ace in the hole."

Deuce took another swipe at the smoke then grinned at his boss. "I figured as much. She'll be arriving next week."

It was well after noon when Morgan and Parker showed up, sheepishly apologizing for not returning the previous evening. Amelia pretended to be put out by their transgression. It was easier than she would have thought to keep her new secret to herself, even when Gabe showed up for the evening meal with a huge bunch of flowers.

They laughed and talked through the supper as they had other nights, and Parker did not object when Gabe asked to walk with her in the moonlight afterward. They did not make it even as far as the bridge before they were in each other's arms in a long, needy kiss.

"I don't know what you've done to me, tenderfoot, but I can't seem to keep my hands off you," Gabe apologized.

"You didn't hear me asking you to keep them off, did you?"

"No. But I'm going to. Tonight you'll be back under the watchful eye of your brother, and I'll be up at our cabin in that big lonely feather bed, thinking of you all night long."

"You're not returning to town?"

He shook his head. "No. Because I intend to be back here first thing in the morning to take you off for a shooting lesson—a real one this time."

Something in his tone made her ask, "Is there some reason you want me to have another lesson?"

"Not really...." He hesitated, then said, "Well, let's go sit for a while on the bank and I'll tell you about it."

She followed him to a grassy spot, a little frown of worry on her face.

"We had a meeting in town today."

"Who is 'we'?"

"A group of citizens. They're forming an organization called the Board of Health and Street Commissioners."

Amelia laughed. "Street commissioners?"

"I know it sounds ridiculous in Deadwood, the most lawless town west of the Mississippi, but this group seems to be in earnest. They're tired of the crime and the poor sanitation. They intend to do something about it."

Amelia suspected she wasn't going to be pleased about the rest of Gabe's story. "What does this have to do with my shooting lessons?"

"The commission is setting itself up against Driscoll. He's madder than hell about the whole thing."

"But that doesn't mean—"

"And I'm going to be the chairman."

Amelia's mouth snapped open. "You?"

He nodded.

"But...you're a gambler. I would think that you represent one of the elements these 'solid citizens' would be against."

His tone became stiff. "Maybe they think it takes a thief to catch a thief."

Amelia bit her lip. "I didn't mean to imply that you were outside of the law, Gabe."

"Thank you for that much of a vote of confidence, anyway," he said dryly.

"I just don't understand why these men picked you."

"I think for the most part it's simply because no one else has the guts to go up against Driscoll."

"I don't blame them. I wish *you* didn't have the . . . nerve, either."

"So now you want me to be a coward?" Gabe's brief irritation gave way to amusement.

"There's nothing wrong with a little cowardice, if you ask me," she grumbled.

He reached over and lifted her to his lap. "Let's not talk about it anymore. I don't want to quarrel."

"I don't, either," she agreed, leaning against his chest with a contented sigh.

"But before I start kissing you and make us both wish we were anywhere but a hundred feet from your brother and your bodyguard, I need to talk to you about one more thing."

She nodded dreamily. "I'm listening."

He reached into his coat and drew out a brown paper package. "This is for you." He cleared his throat. "It's so you can take certain, ah, precautions."

She took the package from him. She could feel that there was a bottle inside. "Are you trying to turn me into a drinker of spirits, Mr. Hatch?" she teased.

But he stayed sober. "It's vinegar," he said. "And a sponge. It's, ah, you should bathe with it, ah, down there."

Amelia gave him a totally mystified look. "What in heaven's name are you talking about?"

He hugged her closer and tucked her head under his chin so that she wouldn't have to look at him. "Sweetheart, we weren't very careful last night. And when a man and a woman do what we did, sometimes there are...consequences."

Amelia gasped and a sick feeling washed through her. How could she have been so stupid? For years she had listened to her mother's dire tales of fallen women, poor unwed mothers who ended up begging shelter in one of the various homes her mother's friends supported. Amelia had even visited some of the "lost souls." But she had not once considered the possibility of becoming pregnant from what she and Gabe had shared.

"I...what do I have to do?" She felt slightly sick.

Gabe didn't look much better. "I don't know. There's something about vinegar if you can get it, you know, inside you.... It's what Mattie's girls use," he finished lamely.

Amelia closed her eyes. So now she was in the same category with Mattie's girls, trying to make sure that she would have no lasting "consequences" from her actions. The romance and warmth of the little cabin in the pines seemed farther and farther away.

"Don't, sweetheart," Gabe said, turning her face up to his. "Don't look that way. This doesn't change anything about last night. It was beautiful...you were beautiful...and what we had was something that many people never find in all their lives."

His words were reassuring and the kisses that accompanied them even more so. By the time they got up to walk back to the cabin and say good-night, Amelia had almost forgotten about the brown paper package.

It was only after Gabe had left with promises to be back early in the morning that she began to think about it again.

As comforting as his words had been, wouldn't it have been more comforting to hear him say that he loved her, that he wanted to be with her always, and that, if a child should result from their love, they would raise it together?

She lay awake long into the night, considering. She had known from the beginning that Gabe was a gambler, not a man to settle down with a family. "No happily ever afters," he had said. But she couldn't believe that he was unaffected by what they had found together. Perhaps she had given him the impression that she would never accept marriage to a gambling, drinking man. He might feel that with his style of life there was no way he could have a wife and family, that he didn't deserve the option. But if there was one thing she had learned from her parents, it was that people can shape their lives in any way they wish, if they will only take responsibility for them.

He was coming tomorrow for her shooting lesson. Perhaps she would just turn the tables on Gabriel Hatch and give him a few lessons of her own.

"It's not like you to talk about giving up, my love." Claire sat curled up on the bed stitching on a worn dress while Parker paced the tiny room like a caged tiger. On most nights he was so fascinated by her unusual beauty that he forgot about his mine and money problems and gave himself up to the wonder of their love for each other. But tonight not even her quiet, serene voice could calm him down. The vein that he and Morgan had tackled with such hope had played out for good that morning. And a thorough survey with Morgan's experienced eye had indicated no sign of any other promising area. They were back to seining the stream, and, even with the new equipment he had purchased, they weren't panning out more than three or four dollars' worth of dust a day. At that rate he'd never be able to rescue Claire from the profession she had been forced into.

"I don't see any other way, Claire. If I go back home with Amelia and start to work with my father, I'll be able to get together some money and send for you."

Claire looked skeptical. "And what would your parents say about you sending money out to a strange girl who makes a living as I do?"

"I'd be in for a lecture from my mother, that's for sure. But it wouldn't be the first time. I think they'll come around."

She put aside the dress she'd been mending and moved up to her knees to reach out to him. "But you've always said that you didn't want to go to work for your father, that you hated New York City."

Parker gave a deep sigh, then took her in his arms. "I know. It's not what I had hoped when I came West. I guess I'm just another fool chasing a mythological golden fleece." The newspapers had taken to calling the gold rush prospectors "argonauts" after the legendary Greek heroes.

"You're the least foolish man I've ever met, Parker Prescott," Claire said firmly. "And the nicest. And," she added, kissing him on the cheek, "I'm madly in love with you. So watch who you're calling crazy."

With his first smile of the evening, he collapsed with her on the bed, but when she began to kiss him he pulled away. "There's another reason why it might be a good idea for me to go back," he said.

She sat up and propped herself against the wall. Obviously his mind was still on his dilemma, and she was willing to listen as long as he needed to talk. "What other reason?"

"It's Amelia . . . I'm worried about her."

"Is she ill?"

Parker frowned and pulled himself up to sit next to her. "She's been acting strangely. Gabe Hatch has been coming around all the time lately and the two of them go off alone."

"I see," Claire said, raising her eyebrows.

"No, it's not like that. He's giving her shooting lessons."

"Shooting lessons," Claire repeated in a tone of disbelief.

"Hell, he gave me shooting lessons when I first came out here."

"Parker, darling," Claire said patiently as if speaking to a child, "in case you haven't noticed, your sister is a beautiful woman. There's no way a man like Gabriel Hatch is spending all that time with her just to teach her how to use a gun."

"Yeah, well, that's kind of what I'm afraid of," he said, slapping his raised knee.

"So maybe he's giving her lessons in more than shooting. Amelia must be willing if you haven't heard any complaints. What's wrong with it?"

"What's wrong with it! She's my *sister,* Claire."

Claire was silent for a long moment. "Let me see if I understand. It's all right for *you* to fall in love and come in here to make love to me every night, but it's not all right for your sister?"

"He's a *gambler.*"

"And I'm a prostitute."

"It's not the same."

"No, it's not. He makes a lot more money than I do."

Now she was glaring at him. Parker spread his legs out on the bed and reached for her. "Forget it," he said grumpily. "Let's make love."

She held him off another moment. "There's nothing I'd rather do, Parker, but making love to me won't solve your problems, and it won't keep your sister and Gabe Hatch apart if they're determined to be together."

"I just don't want to see her hurt," he said, pulling her underneath him.

She began to unbutton his shirt and whispered in his ear, "Don't worry, my love. If your partner Gabe is even half as good as you, she won't be hurting at all."

It was hopeless, Amelia decided. She simply could not seem to fire a gun in such a way that the bullet had a remote chance of reaching its target. Gabe had been patient and encouraging, but even he was starting to see the enterprise as futile. Of course, it didn't help matters that every time he tried to assist her by putting his arms around her and showing her how to aim, both were so distracted by the proximity of their bodies that the lessons ended up hurried and haphazard. Some days they didn't even make the attempt, heading directly to Gabe's little cabin to spend the afternoon in each other's arms.

The speech Amelia had so carefully prepared the night Gabe had brought her the detested bottle of vinegar had still not been given. Somehow it seemed easier just to live in the moment, enjoy the pleasure they were able to give each other, rather than talk about things such as commitment and family. But today Amelia had determined that they would have their talk no matter how much Gabe's skillful lovemaking distracted her. Parker had become increasingly suspicious of the amount of time they were spending alone. The six weeks he had asked for to prove himself at the mine were almost up, and, to Amelia's surprise, he had started to talk about going back to New York City. She had accomplished the mission she had set out upon, but she felt no satisfaction in the knowledge. Parker was defeated and surly, and she herself could hardly bear to think of the moment when she would have to say goodbye to Gabe. She wouldn't let that moment come without a fight.

Gabe was unloading her little pistol and checking out the action. "Maybe there's something wrong with the sight," he speculated.

Amelia gave a rueful laugh. "I'm afraid it's *my* sight, not the gun's, that's at fault."

"No matter. I never really expected you to have to fire the thing, anyway. If you can just learn how to point it and look halfway in earnest, that should be enough to scare off any miscreants."

"Well, why didn't you say so in the first place? We could have just skipped all these lessons."

He put the gun in his saddlebag and came over to give her a kiss. "We could have spent all our time on those other lessons . . . at which you've grown more than proficient, I might add."

Amelia smiled and returned the kiss.

"Shall we, ah, resume them now?" He had that look in his eyes again that never failed to make her feel feminine and wanted. But today she was determined to tend to business.

"How about if we just sit along the river for a while. I'd like to talk to you about something."

He agreed easily, slipping a blanket from behind his saddle for them to sit on. "What's on your mind?"

He spread the blanket for her. She sat down and took a long look around the clearing. The woods had turned into a patchwork quilt of autumn colors dominated by the rich gold of the beech and aspen trees. There was a fall briskness to the late-afternoon air, and the lazy summer hum of insects had given way to the sounds of great flocks of birds and fowl overhead on their journey south. Parker was right. The West was beautiful...and free. She'd learned a lot in the few short weeks she'd been here.

"Parker has as much as admitted that the mine is not going to pan out within the six weeks we had agreed on," she said as Gabe dropped down beside her.

There was a sudden coldness in his eyes. He looked away.

"It means that we will be heading back to New York," she explained, not certain that he understood what she was saying.

He nodded. "I know."

He certainly wasn't doing anything to make this easy. "I don't want to leave you," she blurted.

He still did not look at her. "I guess we knew this couldn't last forever," he said finally.

She smoothed her hand against the rough nap of the blanket. How could he be so nonchalant about a subject that had her heart swelled near to the breaking point? She took a deep breath and tried another tack. "Gabe, remember when we talked about...consequences of lovemaking?"

He jerked his head around and grabbed her shoulders. "What are you saying? Do you think you might be...?"

She gave a desperate little laugh. "No, that's not what I mean. I just wanted to know.... Well, would it be so terrible if something like that happened?"

Relief flooded his face, and he relaxed his grip on her. "Amelia, I told you from the beginning that this was not going to be happily ever after."

"Haven't you sometimes thought that you might like to have a child of your own?"

His expression was shuttered. "I'm sorry," was all he said.

He was *sorry?* What was that supposed to mean?

"So you haven't?" she persisted.

Gabe stood and walked down to the edge of the water. "I don't think I'm cut out for that kind of a life, Amelia. That's why I had reservations about us in the first place. You should have all of that—a home, little children running around." He turned to face her. "Hell, one of these days you will have it, I'm sure. And the man who shares it with you will be the luckiest man on earth."

She had the urge to shout that the only one she wanted to share that kind of life with was him, but his answer left no doubt that he was not interested, and she had already said as much as her pride would allow. She stood and picked up the blanket. "I guess there's nothing more to talk about," she said dully.

Gabe walked up the bank and took the blanket from her, winding it angrily into a tight roll. "I wish I had some different answers for you, sweetheart. I haven't ever meant to lead you to expect anything more from me."

She shrugged. "You haven't misled me. My heart has been, perhaps, but not because of anything you've said."

He put an arm around her and started toward the horses. "Shall we go to our cabin? We have a while yet before supper."

She shivered. The air was chilled with the first hint of winter. "I don't think so," she said. "Parker is starting to feel uncomfortable about the amount of time we're spending alone."

"Do you want me to talk to him?"

She looked up at him, her eyes bleak. "What would you say?"

He stared down at the ground. "I don't know."

She waited several minutes for him to say something more, but when he didn't speak she pulled out of the circle of his arm and mounted her horse. "Come on," she said. "I want to go home."

Chapter Twelve

Gabe threw his cards on the table in disgust. "I'm out," he said, pushing back his chair. He couldn't keep his mind on the game tonight, and for a gambler, that was the one cardinal sin.

He walked over to the bar. "Give me some of that stuff Driscoll keeps under the counter," he told Roscoe.

The bartender lifted an eyebrow, but reached down and pulled up a bottle with a fancy-looking label. Gabe usually stayed with beer or even coffee when he was playing, but he was finished playing for the night. He was in the mood for something that would burn all the way down and stay lit.

One of the bar girls sauntered in his direction. He discouraged her with a glance. The last thing he needed tonight was a woman. It was a woman who had his head muddled in the first place. His head and a good deal of the rest of him. He knew he had hurt Amelia yesterday when she'd talked about having a family. Had he ever thought about it? she'd asked, her great brown eyes looking as if they could see into his very soul. Hell, he'd thought about it for ten long months as he'd combed every mining camp, every saloon, every hellhole in the

West trying to track down his wife and what might be his son or daughter. Then he'd thought about it a lot more in the year that followed when he'd decided that drunk felt better than sober.

He wasn't interested in going through all that again. He had a good life—friends, an easy living, enough money to satisfy himself and help out a down-on-his-luck cowhand now and then. He had women—occasionally—though nothing even mildly approaching the sensual frenzy he'd found himself in with Amelia over these past few weeks. It was a good life. He didn't need the rest of it.

So why did he feel as if he'd just slammed head-on into a brick wall? He'd tried to do her a favor by not going out there today. Do them both a favor. But his insides ached for her. Every time he closed his eyes he saw her face—blushing, laughing, tender, now tense with desire, now impish with teasing. And he heard her voice in his head. *Haven't you sometimes thought that you might like to have a child of your own... a child of your own?* It bounced around in his brain like a rubber ball.

His child... and Amelia's. What a combination that would make! If only... That was the trouble. There had been too many "if onlys" in his life.

He drained his third glass of Driscoll's whiskey. Driscoll himself was nowhere around tonight, but Deuce Connors had been watching him all evening with a sly smile that made Gabe wonder what the hell he was up to. Driscoll had undoubtedly heard by now about his involvement with the Street Commissioners. He hoped Big Jim continued to let him play cards at the Lucky Horseshoe, but if they told him he wasn't welcome, he'd find other places to have a game. And he figured that even Deuce would think twice before challenging Gabe to a gunfight. He'd had no use for guns as a lad back in St. Louis, but once he got out West the skill had come naturally to him, and he'd had to prove it a time or two since he'd arrived in Deadwood. Whatever kind of reprisal Big Jim might try for his action on the commission, Gabe figured he'd be ready.

He flipped a silver dollar on the bar and turned to leave. He had every intention of seeking his bed at the hotel to sleep off the whiskey, but somehow his feet took him instead to the livery. He looked over at his horse, who whinnied gently in recognition. With a sigh of inevitability, he saddled him up and headed out into the night.

He was just going to be sure she was all right, he told himself—to be sure that she was not resenting him, not regretting after all her decision to make love with him. But his heart was telling him that it was finally time to tell Amelia the truth—that he had been such a miserable failure as a husband and prospective father that he wouldn't dare inflict himself on another woman, especially one he loved.

His heart grew heavier as he headed up the path to Parker's cabin. He hadn't consciously deceived her by not telling her the truth about his marriage. But he knew that he'd been wrong to keep it from her. Amelia had had the right to know about his past before he had ever touched her.

It was almost midnight, not a proper hour for a call. But after waiting this long he suddenly couldn't wait another day to tell Amelia about his past. He wondered how she would react. She'd been surprisingly tolerant of so many things that he would have thought a well-bred girl from back East would abhor. He supposed it was a tolerance bred into her by her socially conscious parents. But the story he was about to tell her might strain even Amelia's forbearance to the breaking point. He sighed and looked up at the full moon. It would be hard enough to send her away without thinking that she would spend the rest of her life hating him.

Amelia was not asleep. She had gone to bed early, telling Morgan and Parker that she was worn out from battling laundry all day long, which was the truth. The work had helped her stop thinking about the conversation yesterday with Gabe and had made the day go a little faster as the hours passed without a sign of him. But now as she lay alone in the cabin, she couldn't put off her thoughts any longer.

She'd finally brought up the subject. She'd as much as said that she wanted to marry him, wanted to have his baby. Her instructors back at the academy would be mortified. And he...he had grown stiff and withdrawn and reminded her of the warning he had given her before they'd ever made love.

In a way, he was right. He had told her exactly what to expect from him—and what not to expect. He had taught her so much over these past wonderful weeks— not just about sensuality, but about caring and about the kind of communion two people can have with one another when everything is turning out just right. She supposed she should be grateful for that much. He had indicated that she would now be more receptive to finding that kind of love with someone of her own kind back in New York. Perhaps he was right. He'd been right about so much. But somehow she couldn't imagine that she would ever find with anyone what she'd had with Gabe during these golden autumn days.

Her heart gave a little leap as the door scraped softly. Parker and Morgan never came into the cabin while she was sleeping. Could it be a bear? She'd heard that the furry black critters would tear an entire door off its hinges to look for food inside if they were hungry enough. But if it was a bear, it was being remarkably discreet.

The door creaked open and moonlight splashed across the cabin floor. Amelia's heart took a larger jump as she recognized Gabe's dark outline. He held on to the edge of the door and seemed to be trying to see into the darkened room.

"What are you doing here?" she whispered.

Now that he was here, Gabe was asking himself the same question. He'd told himself that he'd ridden out to have a civilized, rational talk with Amelia, to tell her about his marriage. To tell her how he had already failed one woman in his life, how he'd driven her away. He was ready to have Amelia regard him with horror as he told her how his too-beautiful, too-young, too-weak wife had been horrified to find herself pregnant with a child she never wanted to have. How she'd sworn never to be tied to the middle-class drudgery of their life in St. Louis. How she'd run off with the first unscrupulous bastard who had offered her flattery and the promise of wealth and luxury.

But the minute he saw Amelia sitting up in her bed, her body outlined in vivid detail by the silky nightgown he'd given her, every word that he'd planned to say fled plumb out of his head. He came stalking across the room, his eyes taking in every detail of her. And instead of a confession, the words that came out of his mouth were, "We've never made love in your bed, tenderfoot." In an instant she was in his embrace.

Amelia laughed from sheer joy, sheer *relief* at feeling his arms around her again when she had begun to think she had felt them for the last time. "My brother and Morgan are asleep in the lean-to right behind this wall," she whispered. "Remember the hunting knife?"

He'd never been hungrier for her. He'd never been hungrier for anything in his entire life. "We'll just have to be quiet, then," he murmured in her ear, taking them both down to the mattress.

"Shouldn't you close the door?" she protested.

His eyes were already narrowed with desire. "I want to see you," he muttered, pushing the shoulder of her nightgown down to reveal a moonlit breast.

Amelia's words, too, died in her mouth as she felt the soft touch of his tongue against her nipple. She wove her fingers through his hair as he lavished exquisite attention on first one side, then the other. Her nightgown had worked itself up around her waist, and she felt the rough brush of his serge pants against her soft skin. She moved underneath him, building the liquid heat inside. He sought her lips, urgently, drinking from her, murmuring soft words of need.

There seemed to be no time. She bunched the silk of her garment with tightened fists and he unbuttoned his pants. Their joining was frantic and release almost instantaneous for them both.

"Thunderation, sweetheart," he said breathlessly after taking a moment to recover. Their bodies were still joined amid a jumble of clothing. Slowly he pulled away. "If we could bottle this up we'd have one hell of a medicine show."

Amelia wiped tears from her eyes. "It was nice," she said inadequately.

"Nice?" He chuckled, pulled gently away from her and shifted his weight so that he could strip off his clothes. When she started to rearrange her nightgown, he interrupted his own efforts. "This comes off," he said, pulling it over her head. "I want you naked in my arms."

Amelia glanced at the open door. "What if someone comes in?"

"It's the middle of the night. They're sound asleep."

He finished removing his clothes, then pulled her against him. "Parker's a light sleeper," she said doubtfully. "And I think we...we did make some noise."

"We won't make any sounds this next time."

"Next time?" His hands and lips were on her again. Amelia's stomach lurched in anticipation.

"Hmm-mmm," he said. He had moved lower and was trailing kisses up the inside of her thigh.

She gripped the mattress ticking and took in a breath. "How—how can you be so sure I can stay quiet?" she asked. She felt like screaming this very minute. His fingers caressed her sensitive private area, then parted her to make room for a warm, moist swipe with his tongue. She gasped and he stopped, moving up to take her mouth in a deep kiss.

"Do you trust me, sweetheart?" he asked, his voice husky. At her nod he continued, "Then don't worry about making sounds. We're going to put that beautiful mouth of yours to another use."

Amelia lay awake, nestled against Gabe under her coverlet. The past hour had been filled with carnal delights that she had never even dreamed existed. Things she hadn't known that two people could do to and with each other. She could close her eyes and still feel the gentle, sucking pressure of his mouth, the skillful rhythm of his fingers. Her body quickened again at the mere thought. What was to become of them? Surely now, after the incredible intimacy they had shared, Gabe would not be willing to let her get on a stage-coach and leave him forever. And she didn't think she could bear to do it.

It was warm and snug under the covers with him. She wished that the world would freeze at this very mo-ment and stay just so forever. But of course, it was a fantasy. And Amelia Jenks Prescott had never in her life been one for fantasies.

"Are you sleeping?" she asked softly.

He turned his head to kiss her. "No, I'm just think-ing."

"About what?"

"Us. You and me. What we have together." He in-terrupted himself for a moment to grasp her chin and look into her face. Amelia held her breath as she waited for him to finally say that he loved her, but instead he said, "You're so beautiful."

She swallowed down her disappointment. "I was thinking about us, too. About the fact that it's almost time for me to go home."

Gabe ran a finger along her cheekbone, down the bridge of her nose. The delicious lethargy of their love-making had been replaced by a growing ache like a ball of unshed tears in the center of his chest. He couldn't imagine letting her go, and he was beginning to think that no matter what the odds against them—against *him*—he simply would not be able to give her up.

Perhaps, after all, there might be some hope for them. Was it fair that a man should be condemned to go through life alone because of one mistake made long ago? He would never be able to forgive himself for not being able to make his marriage work, for not seeing the desperation that had overtaken his young bride, but it appeared that he was being offered a second chance—a chance for redemption. And he would be a fool not to give it a try. He and Amelia had a lot working against them. They were from two different worlds. But he had once been a part of a world not so different from hers, and there was no reason he couldn't be so again. First, however, he would have to tell her about Samantha. "I need to talk to you about something," he began.

He could feel her tense slightly in his arms, as if sensing the gravity of what he was about to say. "What is it?" she asked.

"I've told you before that you don't know everything about me... about my life before I came to Deadwood, before I met you...."

"No one's past should be held against them, Gabe. I've already explained to you that—"

"You low-down bastard!" Parker's voice exploded from the doorway, making them both jump.

Gabe sat up, shielding Amelia behind him. "Take it easy, Parker," he said with authority.

"Get out of my sister's bed, you snake." Her brother's voice shook with rage. "And put on your gun."

Amelia sat up, holding the blanket to cover herself. "Parker! Don't be an idiot. No one's going to put on any guns."

Parker took his eyes from Gabe and looked at her for the first time. "What's this all about, sis?" he asked. His tone was pleading, as if he were begging her to tell him that things were somehow not as his eyes were seeing.

Gabe had slipped from the bed and was putting on his clothes. ''Amelia's a grown woman, Parker. She has the same right to explore life that you do.''

''Don't say my sister's name, Hatch. I can't stand to hear it on your lips. We've been your friends, invited you into our home, and this is how you've repaid us.''

''Why don't you ask your sister how she feels about it before you judge me, Parker?''

''I don't have to ask her. You're obviously as good at seducing girls as you are at . . . cheating at cards.''

The words were deliberately provocative. Not a gambler in Deadwood would let them pass without a challenge. But Gabe just tightened his jaw and glanced back at Amelia. ''I'm sorry,'' he said to her. ''I'd better get out of here before the bloody fool gets hurt trying to avenge your honor.''

She gave a quick nod. ''Yes, go. I'll deal with him. You go on back to town. We'll talk later.''

He picked up his hat from the floor and started walking toward Parker, who stood planted in the doorway.

''We're not finished, Gabe,'' he said.

Gabe stopped and took one look back at Amelia's wide, distressed eyes. Parker's abrupt arrival had neatly punctured the dreams he'd been spinning of changing back to a life of respectability. ''Yes,'' he said curtly. ''We're finished.'' Then he brushed past Parker and went out into the night.

Amelia dug under the covers for her discarded nightgown and slipped it on. Parker didn't speak. When she was fully covered she sat up on the edge of the bed, gripping her knees. ''I love him, Parker,'' she said simply.

He came into the room, slamming his open hand on the back of the door. "How could you love him, sis? He's a gambler...a drifter...he never stays in one place. He has been following the gold strike money from town to town."

"How could you love a woman like Claire?" she asked softly.

"That's different. Claire loves me, too. And she's sweet and caring—"

"And a prostitute," Amelia finished sharply.

Parker came over to the bed and dropped heavily next to her. "And a prostitute," he agreed with a sigh. As usual, his quick temper was also quick to subside. After a moment he gave a bitter chuckle. "A fine pair we make, eh, sis?"

Amelia smiled sadly. "What would Mother say if she knew we've fallen in love with just the kind of people she's spent her life crusading to save?"

"We could tell her we're continuing on with her good work." Now there was even a hint of humor in his voice.

"I don't think she'd approve of our methods," Amelia observed dryly.

"Does he want to marry you?"

Her chin came up. "He hasn't offered."

"He damn well *better* offer."

"Don't start again, Parker. This is between Gabe and me. I don't need my brother to fight for me anymore. I'm a big girl now."

He put an arm around her and hugged her lightly. "I'll never stop being your brother, no matter how big you get, sis. And, whether you like it or not, tomorrow I'm going into town to have a little talk with Mr. Gabriel Hatch."

* * *

Driscoll sat up in his bed, his eyes roaming idly down the tightly corseted figure of the strawberry blonde Deuce Connors had just ushered into his room. He clamped his cigar in his teeth and smiled. "I'd forgotten why it was I put up with you for so long, baby."

Samantha Hatch acknowledged the backhanded compliment with a bat of her thick lashes and a practiced smile with no warmth. Driscoll couldn't remember if the lashes were her own, but the green eyes were, and underneath the whalebone those curves were definitely real.

She didn't speak. Driscoll glanced over at his gunman. "You can go, Deuce."

When the door had softly closed, he motioned to her to come closer. "Don't you have a welcome for your old *friend,* Samantha?"

Reluctantly she moved toward the bed. "The way I remember it, we were never friends, Jim. Lovers, yes, but not friends."

"You were always better in bed than anywhere else," Driscoll sneered.

Samantha shrugged. "I guess we're all given our special talents. Yours was cheating at cards, if I recall."

Driscoll grinned, unoffended. "I don't have to cheat these days. I've got people to do it for me. I'm a big shot now, Samantha. You don't know how lucky you are that I decided to look you up."

"Right. I'm just about the luckiest woman in the West, I reckon." The green of her eyes turned dark as she sat on the edge of the bed.

Upon closer look Driscoll could see the powder that brightened the sallow complexion and covered the fine lines of her face. He surmised that Samantha had not found her years in the camps to be easy. But they hadn't defeated her. There was still a vestige of the spirit he remembered in her expression. And the beauty of her features could not be marred by a few years of wear.

"This time we're going to do things right, baby, and you'll find it will be worth your while."

She tilted her head, eyeing Driscoll's swollen paunch. "What do you have that I haven't already been offered by a dozen other lecherous fools out in the camps who've struck it rich?"

Driscoll took a hard grip on her arm. "If you've had so many great offers, how come you're here—on *my* train ticket, wearing a new dress that *I* paid for?"

She winced at his touch, but didn't pull away. "Times have been tough lately," she admitted. "The gold's playing out."

Driscoll gave a satisfied nod. He pulled her closer to him on the bed and spoke with his mouth just inches from her face. "You'd just better remember that, Samantha. Because we can do this one of two ways—hard or easy. Easy means you can have things real nice for a while, for as long as you keep on making me happy. Hard means you're going to do what I say anyway, but it won't be anywhere near so pleasant."

"I'm partial to pleasant."

"Good girl."

She reached down and uncurled his fingers from around her arm. "But I'm not for sale like some kind of hurdy-gurdy girl."

Driscoll put his hand behind her neck and dragged her roughly down to the bed. "You're costing me a damn sight more than a hurdy-gurdy girl, Mrs. Hatch. And I intend to get my money's worth." He let go of her neck. There were bright red marks where his fingers had pressed into her soft skin. She lay still, and he began to gently caress her long hair.

Samantha's eyes had taken on a dull sheen. "So what am I here for, Big Jim? You haven't brought me all this way for the pleasure of my company."

Big Jim wound a strand of her hair around his fist and tightened it. "You, my dear, are about to be reunited with your long-lost husband."

Since the year he had spent drowning the last vestiges of his marriage and former life in whiskey, Gabe had kept to a strict rule of never indulging in hard liquor two days in a row. Today he had considered breaking it for the first time, but had finally talked himself out of it. Instead he was on his fifth cup of the Willard's scalding black coffee. The stubby waiter, who had the unlikely name of Algernon, would keep filling up his cup as long as he liked. Gabe was a congenial guest, overly generous with his tips, and the hotel staff liked having him around.

He should be looking for a game. He'd neglected his playing lately in favor of more satisfying pursuits. But after last night it appeared that those would be at an end. He swallowed half a mug in one long gulp, hoping it would burn away the ache inside.

Even if Parker hadn't discovered them, it was time for it to end, he told himself. He didn't deserve a woman like Amelia, and she didn't deserve being made to fall in love with someone like him who had nothing to offer her. But how could he let her go? That was the one part of the equation he couldn't resolve.

He sat with his back to the wall, the position of choice in all the local establishments since Bill Hickok had bought a bullet in the back at Saloon No. 10 earlier that summer. They'd let the killer go free after a vigilante trial—just another example of the sorry state of justice in Deadwood. Maybe now that Amelia was leaving, he'd dedicate some real effort to the Street Commissioners and their cause. It might be one way to fill up the void she would leave in his life.

At first he hardly noticed the commotion going on in the lobby through the restaurant archway, but his head turned as the voices grew louder. It appeared that mild-mannered Nels Nelson had asked someone to check his guns at the desk before going into the dining room. Nels evidently lost the argument because a minute later Deuce Connors stalked through the doorway, his two six-guns still in place at his sides.

Gabe started to get up to see if Nels wanted his assistance, but suddenly he sat back down hard in the chair as he caught sight of Connors's two companions.

Big Jim Driscoll had his head turned back toward the hotel owner yelling, "We're trying to show our guest here some Deadwood hospitality, if you don't mind, Nelson." On his arm was a woman... or a ghost.

Gabe blinked his eyes and looked down into his coffee cup as if wondering if he'd somehow been drugged. But when he looked back up she was still there, smiling at him from across the room.

It felt like a punch in the stomach. She looked the same, but not the same—almost a nightmare version of the young woman he had known so long ago in St. Louis. She still had the same strawberry blond hair, the same fatally pretty face that had attracted the attention of one too many men. But her mouth was painted a garish red and her eyes were heavily rimmed with black. Her skin was an unhealthy yellow and had begun to sag

at the neck. Those sparkling green eyes that had so
tantalized him as a youth had grown old and hard.

"Hello, Gabe," she said as she and Driscoll moved
toward him across the room. Her voice was the same.
It slid into his middle like a shot of brandy.

"Samantha," was all he could say. He felt sick, and
he felt an insane desire to laugh. Shouldn't he have
learned by now how life has the habit of slamming you
down just when you think you're about to climb on out
of the muck? He'd had the audacity to consider the
possibility of starting over again—of starting a new life,
without recriminations, without a past. So now here she
was, in the flesh, come back like a spirit from beyond
the grave . . . to haunt him.

"It's been a long time." She let go of Driscoll's arm
and moved closer to Gabe's table. Driscoll took a step
back and watched them with a look of satisfaction.

"They told me you were dead. There were sheriff's
reports, a death certificate."

"I know," she said breezily. "I had certain . . .
complications at that point in my life which made it
easier to stay dead for a while."

Gabe belatedly got to his feet. "Was I one of those
complications?" he asked angrily.

"Not really. I thought I'd left you behind in St.
Louis."

"I searched for you for ten months."

She paused a moment. It seemed that something like
regret flickered behind her eyes, but Gabe couldn't be
sure. "I'm surprised . . . and flattered. Perhaps if you'd
paid that much attention to me back home, I'd never
have left."

"Dammit, Samantha. Why couldn't you have talked
to me—"

She interrupted him with an upraised hand. "I learned a long time ago not to try backtracking down a cold trail, Gabe. Let's just leave it alone."

He could hardly believe his ears. Leave it alone? After love, marriage, conceiving a... He took a long breath and asked the question that had tormented him for nine long years. "What happened to the child you were carrying? Did you have a miscarriage or..."

She opened her mouth slightly and licked her lips. Once the gesture might have interested him. "You needn't concern yourself," she said vaguely.

For nine years he had mourned the loss of his unborn child—had seen it in his mind the way it would have been, a fine son or daughter to care for and love. Now she had the nerve to tell him not to concern himself. To leave it alone.

Driscoll stepped forward and reclaimed Samantha's arm. "I'm sure you and your *wife* will have many happy occasions to renew your acquaintance, Hatch, but I've promised her supper, and, since the hospitality around here seems wanting, I believe we'll take our business elsewhere."

"I want to know what you're doing here, Sam," Gabe said, stretching a hand toward her as if to stop her from leaving. "And why you never contacted me...."

Samantha danced lightly away from him. "We'll talk later, Gabe, darling. It *is* good to see you again." Her voice lowered as she added under her breath, "Surprisingly good."

Algernon had stopped offering to fill up his coffee cup, but Gabe still sat at the table in the Willard, too stricken to go anywhere else. Samantha's appearance had generated dozens of questions, but he wasn't about to fight Driscoll for her company. In some ways he was just as happy to have some time to sort things out before he had to face her. For nine years he'd mourned her, hated her, missed her, cursed her. He'd thought a dead wife was a complicated burden on a man. However, he was quickly realizing that a live one was even more so.

Samantha's arrival had put thoughts of his confrontation with Parker temporarily out of his mind, but he wasn't surprised to see his partner entering the hotel lobby. At least he didn't appear to be carrying a gun. Saving Parker the trouble of asking for him at the desk, Gabe called out to him. Parker turned his head, glowered, then walked over to Gabe's table.

"Sit down," Gabe said, shoving a chair out with his foot.

Before it tipped over Parker caught it and sat.

"Want some coffee?" Gabe asked.

Parker nodded and waited while Gabe signaled to Algernon. The waiter bustled immediately over to the table with a toothy smile that died when he saw the expression on the partners' faces.

"Coffee for my friend," Gabe told him.

Neither said anything as they waited for him to bring a cup and fill it from a tin pot. When he had left, Gabe asked, "How is Amelia?"

Parker started to bristle, and Gabe raised his hand in a gesture of peace. "I swear I never meant to hurt her, Parker. It just happened. We fell in love." It was the first time he had declared it aloud. Amelia should have been the one to hear it, not her brother. But the way things were going, he might never have the chance to tell her. "People fall in love, Parker," he continued. "You should know that, dammit—you fell for Claire like a double-roped bull.''

''I know. My sister pointed out the same thing to me at length last night after you left.''

''I don't blame you for being upset. If she were my sister, I'd probably have torn my head off.''

''I might still do it.''

Though he could tell that Parker was still angry, his voice held none of the rage he had turned on him last night. Gabe looked him up and down and allowed himself a small smile. They were of similar builds, both lean but strong, well muscled. Parker had eight or nine years more youth, but Gabe had a lifetime more experience, and today he was feeling every mile of it. ''It would be a good match,'' he said.

''I'm not here to fight you.'' Parker didn't return his smile.

''What did you come for?''

''To ask you to marry her. She says she's in love with you, and that you're not exactly indifferent to her.''

Gabe drained his cold cup of coffee, set down the mug and rested his hands on the table. What they said was true—the universe had a twisted sense of humor. ''I'm already married, Parker,'' he said bluntly.

Blood rushed into Parker's face. ''I don't believe it.''

Gabe looked at his hands. ''I'm having a hard time believing it myself, but it happens to be the truth.''

''When . . . how . . . ?''

''I was a callow youth of eighteen, thought I was in love, picked the wrong woman and have regretted it almost since the day it happened. What else do you want to know?''

"So where do you keep your...wife?" Parker looked around the room in disbelief, as though expecting the phantom woman to appear at any minute.

"I don't keep her anywhere. Up until this morning, I hadn't seen her in nine years."

Parker's face was resuming its normal color but he was still breathing hard and his knuckles were white where they gripped the handle of his coffee mug. "What are you talking about?"

Gabe gave a deep sigh. "I thought she was dead, Parker. In spite of what you might think of me, I'm not such a cad that I would sleep with Amelia knowing that I already had a wife. But it turns out that all this time Samantha wasn't dead at all."

"I don't understand."

"She left me, ran off with another fellow who promised her a fortune in the West. I looked for her for months, but finally was told she'd been in a stagecoach that was buried by half a mountain out in Colorado."

"She never tried to get in touch with you all these years?"

"Nope. Not until Big Jim did me the favor of bringing her here to Deadwood."

"Driscoll?"

"Yes. I'm not quite sure what his motives are, but being Driscoll, I'm sure he has something in mind."

"Are you..." Parker's eyes were troubled. "Will you be living with her now? As husband and wife?"

Gabe met his partner's gaze head-on. "There's only one woman I love in this world, and that's your sister. Samantha and I lost out on our chance together long ago."

Parker shook his head and looked at the opposite wall. "I'm sorry for you, Gabe. But I can't condone your dragging my sister into your messed-up life."

"Nor should you. I don't condone it myself. Even before Samantha showed up, I knew I wasn't the right man for Amelia. I intend to step honorably aside and let her go back to New York with you, unharmed, I hope."

Parker looked back at Gabe, once again growing angry. "I guess that depends on your definition of 'harm.'"

"I didn't say she would be untouched by it all. Hell, I can't imagine that either of us will ever forget what we've had together. But it's impossible to go through life untouched. Who would want to?"

"I just hope she can get over you."

"She'll get over me—a beautiful, spirited woman like Amelia is going to have so many men after her she won't have time to think about a gambler from out West."

"I don't know . . ."

"I went out there last night with the intention of telling her the truth about my marriage so she would understand."

"She didn't know you'd been married?"

"No," Gabe answered with a guilty flush. "She still doesn't. I, ah, never got around to telling before you interrupted us."

"You *are* a bastard, Hatch," Parker said with disgust but without much energy.

"Yeah," Gabe agreed.

They stared into their empty cups for several minutes. Finally Parker said, "Don't tell her."

"Excuse me?"

"Don't tell Amelia that you're married. She's going to feel . . . sordid enough about this whole affair when we get back to New York."

"But that's just the point, there was nothing the least bit sordid about it. I don't want her to think—"

"Do you think telling her that you were committing adultery with her will make her feel better?" Parker said, raising his voice.

Gabe motioned him to quiet down. Fortunately the restaurant was empty. "Adultery's a harsh word, Parker."

"What do you call it, then?"

"I didn't know my wife was alive."

Parker shook his head. "Amelia and I were raised in a household where things were either good or bad. Women's suffrage was good, slavery was bad. Philanthropy was good, drinking was bad. Guess which category a married man sleeping with my sister would fall into."

"Maybe things out here in the West aren't quite so black and white as they are back East." Gabe tapped his fingers on the table in irritation. "We seem to have a lot more shades of gray. You've learned that yourself by falling in love with Claire."

"I know, but once we go home we'll be back to those same standards of Eastern society that we were brought up with. Which is one of the reasons I wouldn't go home if I had a choice in the matter. Amelia, on the other hand, is still part of all that. It comes more naturally to her."

"Nevertheless, I think I have the right to explain to her . . ."

Parker stood and leaned his hands on the table to bring his face close to Gabe's. "You don't have the right to anything, Gabe. You've done enough. Now just leave us alone so that we can get back on track with our lives. We're packing up and going home, and, as for the mine, *partner,* it's yours. You can have the whole bloody, worthless thing."

He turned and strode out of the room. Gabe looked after him sadly, his irritation dying as swiftly as it had arisen. The lad was right, of course. The most decent course would be to leave Amelia alone. He wished he'd left her alone last night, before her brother had gotten involved. But perhaps it was for the best. Parker could help her get her life back on track, as he had said. He took a ragged breath. The thought of not seeing her again was almost unbearable. But with Samantha back in his life he no longer had a choice. And he'd get through it somehow. He'd done it before.

He got up from the table, threw down some money and headed out toward the saloon. Perhaps he'd break that hard liquor rule after all, just this once.

Chapter Thirteen

Amelia didn't know if her brother had told Morgan about Gabe's presence at the cabin last night. The laconic Welshman had not made any mention of the incident. Everyone had slept later than usual, and Parker had left shortly after their late breakfast to ride into town. Morgan had helped Amelia clean up the dishes, and then had volunteered to begin packing up their things. They walked together out to the clotheslines to take down the remaining linens.

"After all the fuss coming out here to get Parker," Morgan said, "I'm feeling kind of bad that we're making him give up and come back home."

"I know what you mean," Amelia answered. "He seems like a different person from the one who first brought us out to this valley six weeks ago." She turned her head to look at the surrounding hills. "I've gotten kind of used to it here, too. After this, New York's going to seem mighty crowded and ugly."

"And lonely?" Morgan asked with a raised eyebrow.

So he did know. Leave it to Morgan to let her come around to talking about it in her own time instead of jumping on her with reproaches.

"Yes, lonely. I've fallen in love, Morgan. And no one ever told me that it could be so painful."

"It's a lesson we all have to learn sooner or later."

Amelia looked up sharply. Morgan's face was hidden by a blanket he was folding. "Did you have to learn it, Morgan?" she asked softly.

He lowered the blanket. His eyes suddenly looked as black as the coal he had mined back in his native land. "Yes, Missy, I guess I did."

"But all these years... you've never..."

He smiled. "Your family has given me all the love I've needed, Missy. The kind of love that's not—as you say—painful."

"But you had that kind of love once. Was it back in Wales?"

He nodded. "It was a long, long time ago. Sometimes it seems almost like a dream to me now."

Amelia dumped her handful of clothes on the grass and turned to him. "Let's go sit by the water. We can finish up here when Parker comes back."

Morgan followed her over to the bridge and they sat down, dangling their feet over the edge. Underneath them the stream rushed along, decorated by swirling leaves in bright autumn colors. Morgan leaned back on his hands and looked up. "It sure is beautiful under this wide Western sky," he said with a sigh.

Amelia reached over and put a hand on his arm. "Tell me about when you were in love, Morgan," she said gently.

He covered her hand with his own, dwarfing it. "Like I said. It was long ago. I fell in love, and she fell in love with me. Her name was Gwendolyn, and she was the prettiest girl in the shire."

"And what happened?"

"We had a problem. It turned out that Gwendolyn was in love with someone else at the same time."

"Is that possible?"

"It was for Gwendolyn."

Amelia had known all her life that Morgan had been rescued "from the depths," as her mother so delicately put it. But ever since Amelia could remember he had always been the stable one, never losing his temper, never showing too much emotion. She'd never heard him talk in this stricken tone before.

"So she married the other man?" she asked.

"Yes." He was silent for a long moment. Then he brought his big hands in front of him and stared at them. "And then I killed him."

Amelia gasped. "Oh, Morgan!"

Slowly he formed his hands into fists and lowered them to his side. "She made the wrong choice, as it turned out. I think the man loved her right enough, but he loved his liquor more and it made him crazed. One night after a bout he beat her savagely. She came to me the next morning, and before sundown that day he was dead. My brothers put me on a boat to America the same night." Morgan gave an odd shake of his big shoulders.

"Your mother and father have always known the truth, Missy. I don't want you to think that I lied to them."

"Of course not," she stammered. "I just . . ."

He reached over and patted her shoulder. "It's as you say, love can be a painful thing."

Amelia was trying to think of something to say when they saw Parker crossing the meadow. She jumped up. For the moment Morgan's confession faded into the background as her thoughts turned to what had passed between her brother and Gabe. At least Parker was unharmed, she saw with relief. She had hoped that Gabe would find a way to avoid fighting him.

As he approached she waved a hand and called, "Are you all right?"

His smile was not as bright as normal, but was reassuring just the same. Morgan stood and said, "I'll let you two talk." Then he walked with his long strides over to the cabin.

Amelia walked across the bridge to meet her brother. He dismounted and took her in his arms. "Did you see Gabe?" she asked, impatient to hear what had happened.

He turned and started across the bridge, leading his horse. "Yes, I saw him."

"Well?"

"Nothing. We talked. I didn't hurt him, if that's what you mean."

"What did you talk about?"

Parker turned to her with a look that was half sympathy, half exasperation. "We talked about the fact that you and he can never be together. It was a mistake from the beginning, but it happened, and now we have to just try to forget all about it."

"Just like that?" Amelia bit her lip and tears glazed the edges of her eyes.

Parker put his arm around her shoulders. "I'm not saying it will be easy, sis. But believe me, Gabe Hatch is not the man for you. And once I get you back home to New York, I hope you'll be able to put all this behind you."

Amelia pulled out of her brother's grasp. "So we're going home?" she asked, her voice brittle.

"Yes," Parker replied wearily. "We're all all going home."

Neither Parker nor Amelia had had the spirit to go into town, so Morgan had gone by himself to purchase the tickets. There was a stage leaving the following day that would take them all the way east to the railroad spur in Aberdeen. He had hired a wagon at the livery to bring their things back into town. Parker was leaving behind most of what he had accumulated during his stay, including the mining equipment. It was up to Gabe, he said, to decide if he could sell the place or if it would just all sit there and go to ruin.

Amelia couldn't help thinking of the other abandoned cabin farther up in the mountains where she and Gabe had spent so many stolen moments. Gabe had not come. Parker told her that he and Gabe had agreed that it would be best if they didn't see each other again. It seemed impossible that everything they had shared could end without so much as a goodbye, but she was too numb to argue the point.

The little cabin looked neat and fresh. The mattress she had labored over still lay on the cot, plump with fresh straw. Amelia knew that her store mattress back home would never quite feel the same to her again.

"I think that's about everything," Parker said, tying some twine around the last bundle. "We can head out first thing in the morning to be sure we get it all packed on the coach."

"Will it all fit?"

"I think so. If it doesn't, we'll just leave it behind. Nothing here is that important." He sounded as if nothing anywhere was important to him at the moment. Amelia felt much the same.

"Here comes Morgan with the wagon."

Parker stood. "After we load it, would you mind terribly if I . . . if I'm not here tonight?"

Amelia lowered her eyes. "You're going to be with Claire?" He, at least, would have a farewell.

"Yes. She's pretty upset that I'm leaving, even though I've promised her that I'm either going to come back or send her money to come."

Amelia looked up in surprise. "You're that serious?"

"She's the one I want, sis. I don't care about her past or anything else."

"Do you think you'll feel the same way when you get back home?"

He gave a firm nod. "I'm sure of it."

"I wish Gabe felt that way about me," she said wistfully.

Parker looked uneasy, but all he said was, "I'm sorry, sis."

The clattering sound of the wagon stopped and Morgan came in the door. His face was grim.

"What's the matter?" Amelia asked.

"There's trouble in town."

"What kind of trouble?"

"Smallpox."

"Dear Lord!" Amelia exclaimed. Her mother had helped out in smallpox epidemics that had swept through the poor emigrant neighborhoods of New York City. She'd described the plight of the victims in graphic detail and had insisted that her children be vaccinated against the dreadful scourge.

Morgan looked nervously over at Parker, who said loudly, "What is it?"

"Some of Mattie's girls have been infected."

Parker ran across the room to grab Morgan's arm. "Claire?" he asked.

Morgan's black eyes were mournful. "Miss Claire's one of them."

Amelia walked slowly out of the telegraph office. She had just sent another wire to her parents, letting them know the circumstances that had prevented her and Parker from starting for home. She knew her parents would be understanding. In fact, they would expect the children of Samuel and Caroline Prescott to do their humanitarian duty and help out in such a tragedy.

And she and Parker had done what they could. A doctor had been called in from Rapid City and had set up a makeshift clinic near the shantytown where the epidemic had hit hardest. Amelia had volunteered her services nursing there, while Parker and Morgan had gone immediately to Mattie's. So far four of her girls had been stricken. Amelia had tried to persuade Morgan to go back and stay at their cabin since he had never been vaccinated against the disease, but he had refused. "The good Lord already knows when it's my time, Missy," he'd told her. "I'll just leave him in charge of the matter."

Amelia had taken a room at the Willard, and that morning Parker had come to find her there to ask if she would come help out at Mattie's. A fifth girl had come down with the high fever that characterized the first stages of the illness. And Claire was gravely ill, he'd told her, his voice choking. He'd been sitting up with her for the past two nights, but the disease continued to ravage through her frail body until Parker despaired for her life.

Amelia promised to join him at Mattie's after she'd
checked in at the clinic. She was tired. Everyone had
been working nonstop during the three days since Morgan had ridden out with the news. When she had first
moved into the Willard she had been a little jumpy, expecting to see Gabe around every corner. But she soon
was too involved in her nursing and too exhausted to
worry about running into him. The past two nights she
had arrived late to her room and had fallen immediately into a dreamless sleep.

Still, she wondered where Gabe was. Surely he wasn't
off at the saloon playing cards while the rest of the town
fought off the epidemic. She walked across the street
toward Mattie's. The flowers on her front porch were
drooping. Evidently no one had thought to water them
in the past long week. Amelia remembered her first
pleased impression of the little clapboard house and
how she had then been horrified to learn what business
Mattie ran from it. It was surprising how her ideas had
changed over these few weeks. After Mattie had helped
her out when Parker had lost the mine, Amelia realized
that her outrage over Mattie and her girls had faded almost completely. Now she mounted the steps to the
place without a qualm. It didn't matter who the girls
were or what they did for a living. They were sick, perhaps dying, and she would give them all the help she
could.

She wasn't prepared, however, to have the door
opened by Gabe. He had a week's growth of beard and
looked tired. His shirt was open at the collar, revealing
just the top edge of the dark blond hair of his chest.
Amelia tightened her grip on her beaded reticule.

"Hello, tenderfoot," he said. There was that special smile in his blue eyes that he seemed to have invented just for her, but it was different somehow, guarded.

"Hello," she said. Telegrams, stagecoaches home, even the smallpox were temporarily forgotten.

"How have you been?" he asked, his voice subdued.

"Fine."

"I understand you've been working over at the clinic. Holding up the family tradition, eh?"

"I guess so." After the initial glow of happiness at seeing him, she began to feel awkward. The last time they had been together was the night they'd been discovered naked in bed by her brother. Since then he'd made no attempt to talk with her or even inquire as to her well-being. And he'd told her brother that he wanted no further part of her life. "What are you doing here?" she asked.

"Mattie needs help right now." He reached out and took her hand. "And, as I've told you before, she's my friend."

"Right." Amelia pulled her hand out of his and looked away. "Well, I'm looking for my brother. I assume he's with Claire. He says she's pretty sick."

Gabe hesitated for a minute, then stepped back and let her enter. "They're upstairs in Claire's room. She's been out of her head most of the day. I'm afraid her chances are not good."

"Oh, no!" She clutched at his arm, but at his grim nod she pushed past him and headed toward the stairs.

There had already been several deaths over in the shantytown. Just yesterday one of the patients Amelia had tended at the clinic had died—a young prospector from Philadelphia who had sounded much like Parker did when he first told her about his dreams for this place. The boy had even looked a little like her brother. With no family to claim him, his body had been sent to an unmarked grave in a special section out on Mount Moriah that had been set aside for the smallpox victims.

Amelia looked back once at Gabe standing at the foot of the banister, looking up at her with an inscrutable expression, then she pushed all thoughts of him out of her head. It was Claire she had to think of now. It was terrible to see any beautiful girl dying so young, but this girl was Parker's first love. He had been in despair anyway over the failure of his mine. What would happen to him if he lost Claire, too?

"Do you want me to come up with you?" Gabe asked softly from below.

She hesitated a moment, then said without looking down at him, "Thank you, but I think my brother and I can get along just fine without you."

They both knew there was a double meaning to the words, but Gabe said nothing to refute them. Out of the corner of her eye she saw him nod and head toward the back of the house. Amelia continued down the hall to Claire's. The tiny bedroom was stifling. Towels had been hung over the two small windows to keep any air from filtering in. They also blocked off most of the light, making the room look dingy and depressing. Parker was sitting on the bed holding Claire's hand.

"She's slipping away from me, sis," he said. His eyes were red and there was heartbreaking sadness in his voice.

Amelia crossed the room to his side. The girl's breathing was labored. Her skin, where it wasn't covered with dreadful blotches of red, was a translucent white. In her white gown with her black hair flowing around her shoulders, she looked like an angel already.

Amelia squeezed her brother's shoulders. "What have you been doing for her?"

He swiped his hand across the bottom of his nose. "Just cool rags to bathe her. And some willow bark tea for the fever."

"Dr. Wheelock has been using a kind of root—it comes from the pitcher plant."

A gleam of hope lit Parker's eyes. "And it's been working?"

Amelia gave a little shake of her head. "I don't know. Nothing seems to help much."

Parker stood up from the bed. "I'll go see him. We've at least got to give it a try."

She motioned him to resume his seat. "I brought some. I'll go mix it with liquid so we can get it down her throat."

Parker grasped the edge of her fingers, holding on hard. "I'm glad you're here, sis."

She nodded. "You should have come to get me before this."

"I knew you were working at the clinic and...I didn't know if you'd feel comfortable helping out in a place like this."

"If you need me, this is where I want to be," she said firmly. "I won't leave you again." She gave his hair an affectionate ruffle. "Now let me go get this medicine ready."

She left the room and closed the door softly behind, leaning back against it for a moment. From her three long days working with Dr. Wheelock she had started to be able to recognize the bad signs. And Claire looked bad. She thought about going to find the doctor to bring him to look at her. But she knew that he could really do nothing more than watch and try to keep the victims comfortable as the disease ran its deadly course.

She went downstairs and made her way to the back of the house to the kitchen. Gabe and Mattie were both there. Mattie was stirring two heavy pots full of boiling clothes while Gabe fed sticks of wood into the belly of her big wrought-iron stove. He straightened as Amelia entered. "Did you find your brother?"

She nodded. "And Claire. You're right. It doesn't look good."

Mattie waved the steam away from her face, then wiped a tear from the corner of her eye. "She's been so happy these past few weeks with Parker. She'd built up such high hopes of starting a new life with him."

"Maybe they still can. We can't lose hope," Amelia replied. "I'm going to prepare some medicine that Dr. Wheelock gave me. It hasn't seemed to do much good with the cases over at the clinic, but you never know. Would you like me to make some for the other sick girls?"

Mattie's soft face brightened. "Bless you, child. None are as bad as Claire, but their cases aren't as advanced as hers yet. Delia's just starting with the blisters."

Amelia knew all about the deadly progression. "What about you two?" she asked. "Aren't you afraid of the infection?"

Mattie shook her head. "They're my girls, dear. I'd not leave them to the care of anyone else."

Gabe's reply surprised her. "I guess I can't very well head up the Board of Health in this town if I turn tail at the first sign of disease."

She hadn't realized that he was taking the new commission so seriously. It was yet another side of this complex man, one that she would evidently never have the opportunity to explore.

"I'll just mix up a batch for everyone, then," she said.

Mattie's sharp eyes were on her as she avoided brushing against Gabe on her way to the cupboard to take down a dish. "Will you watch these things for a while, Gabe?" she asked briskly. "I'm going to go check on the girls." Before he could answer she bustled out of the room, leaving them alone.

Amelia found a pestle in a drawer and began to mash the root she had brought.

"Mattie's not one for subtlety," he said. "She's leaving us together so we can talk over our problems."

"Do we have problems?" Amelia tried to make her voice airy, but the words stuck in her throat.

Gabe crossed the room, took the bowl and pestle out of her hand and set them on the counter. "I've started out to find you a dozen times since that night. But each time I'd see your brother's face in front of me telling me not to bother you anymore. And I'd remember that I don't want to hurt him . . . or you. The last thing I ever wanted was to hurt you, Amelia."

"Parker's trying to protect me."

"I know. And I can't tell you how it galls me to realize that he's absolutely right in trying to keep you from seeing me."

"So we'll just leave it at that, then, Gabe. There are other people we need to be thinking about more than ourselves right now."

He nodded. "I know. But I wanted you to know that if I didn't seek you out it wasn't because I didn't care."

His words didn't change their situation, but they did make Amelia feel a little better. At least he was concerned about her. It made it easier to accept the fact that, even after his rejection of her, she still had felt her heart quicken when she had walked into the kitchen to find him there. She still had the urge to run a finger along the fine line of his jaw and feel the new whiskers growing there. She still felt the tingle in her lips when she thought about his mouth on hers.

"Thank you," she said in a low voice. Then she reached for the medicine and began to work again. He waited for her to add something more, but when she remained quiet he turned back to the stove. "These are done," he said. "I'm going to hang them out back to dry."

For the next twenty-four hours Amelia scarcely left Claire's bedroom. She saw nothing more of Gabe, and Parker never mentioned his partner's name. Mattie came regularly. In the middle of the night she spent several minutes on her knees praying next to the sick girl's bed. By then it didn't seem the least bit incongruous that a bawdy house madam should be offering up prayers to spare the life of a girl who worked for her as a prostitute. Amelia had come to see them simply as people. Mattie's grief was heartfelt and touching.

Parker refused to leave Claire's side and would not eat anything at all. He had drunk half the cup of tea Amelia had urged on him. His eyes looked sunken in his face and she couldn't rouse even the least animation in his voice. Claire was dying. And there was nothing any of them could do about it.

The end came a little after dawn. Claire had never regained consciousness. The last few hours her breathing had become more peaceful, and when it finally stopped altogether, it was several minutes before anyone moved to confirm the sad fact. Parker sat in a chair next to the bed, holding her hand against his cheek. Amelia got up and went to stand behind him, putting both hands on his shoulders. For the first time ever he shrugged away her touch.

Mattie had picked up a mirror from the little dresser and walked over to hold it over Claire's nose. It stayed clear.

"She's gone, Parker," Amelia said in a pained whisper.

He just shook his head and clutched at Claire's hand.

Mattie took Amelia's arm. "We'll just leave them alone for a few minutes, dear," she said. Tears were streaming down her cheeks.

Amelia took a last look at her brother, then let the older woman lead her from the room. Once outside the door, the two women came together in an embrace. "She was so young," Amelia said, her own tears starting to flow.

Mattie nodded and hugged her closer. They stayed that way for several minutes. Then Amelia pulled away and wiped her eyes. "Parker's devastated. I don't know what to do."

"The only thing that will help your brother is time, my dear. You'll just have to give him that."

Amelia nodded. It was oddly comforting to be with Mattie, a little like having her own mother there beside her, though she was sure that Caroline Prescott would be horrified to be compared to a brothel owner. "Shall I go back in to him?" she asked.

"Give him a few more minutes. Come downstairs and have a cup of coffee. It will brace you for what needs to be done."

Chapter Fourteen

Amelia had seen nothing of Gabe since Claire's death, and she began to wonder if her presence at Mattie's house had caused him to leave. But when she finally asked about him, Mattie explained that he'd been working with the other commissioners disinfecting the areas where the disease had been the worst and burning the contaminated property of the victims.

"They were at it all night," Mattie told her. "With great bonfires just west of town."

"Does he know about Claire?" Amelia asked.

She nodded. "I talked to him myself, but he said that it wouldn't help Parker any to have him around and that he'd best leave you two alone."

Perhaps he was right, but Amelia couldn't help wishing for the comfort of his presence. She didn't think it would affect Parker one way or another. Nothing seemed to. Since they'd finally led him away from his vigil at Claire's bedside, he'd sat in the parlor staring into the fire, not wanting to talk or eat or drink or even sleep. Amelia was at her wit's end. Give him time, Mattie had said. But how long could she let him go on like this, as if he had died right along with Claire?

Claire's body had already been taken away for a quick burial. Funerals were not being allowed for fear of contagion. Amelia busied herself helping Mattie. Fortunately none of the other girls seemed to be suffering as severe a case as Claire, but all of them were in misery as the welts on their skin began turning into nasty sores. As was typical, their faces and necks were the most affected, and Mattie spent a lot of her time reassuring them that there would always be a place for them at her house even if the disease left them with scars.

Gabe finally returned the afternoon following Claire's death. Amelia's expression clearly showed how glad she was to see him. He responded with a tired smile. "I'm sorry about Claire. How's your brother doing?"

"Not good. He won't even talk to me."

"He hasn't slept for days so I suspect he'll crash before too long. When he wakes up, he'll start to pull out of it. Mattie will help him come around."

"Do you think so? I've never seen him like this before."

They were in the kitchen again. Amelia had just finished washing up the noon dinner dishes. Gabe went to put his arms around her. "You've had a rough time of it yourself," he said. "How long's it been since you've slept?"

It felt inexpressibly comforting to lean up against him and feel his warmth around her. She closed her burning eyes. "A couple of days," she answered him.

Before she knew what he was doing, he had lifted her easily in his arms and headed through a back hall to a downstairs bedroom. "What are you doing?" she asked.

"Putting you to bed. I want you to sleep until supper." Holding her with one long arm, he bent to pull back the covers of the bed. It was a brass bed with a real mattress, linen sheets and a patchwork quilt.

"Whose room is this?"

"Mattie's. I'll let her know you're in here. No one will disturb you."

"But I should..."

He set her down and began to pull off her shoes. "You should nothing. Just lie back and go to sleep."

She struggled to sit up. "Honestly, Gabe. I don't even know if I can. I feel so wrought up...."

He pushed her down again and this time held her there, his hands on her shoulders. "Close your eyes," he said.

She finally stopped protesting and complied. He released her shoulders and ran his hands along her arms, straightening them out along her sides. "Just relax," he said in a soothing tone. He pulled the covers up around her and tucked them under her chin. "We'll just put you in a nice warm little cocoon and let you forget the rest of the world for a while." He ran a hand lightly over her forehead, then smoothed back the hair from her temples. "There's nothing you can do for anyone right now, sweetheart." His hand made light circles along her temples. "Nothing to do but sleep...."

Amelia was dreaming. She and Gabe had taken a walk in the hills around the little cabin they had shared. It was green and peaceful and the air smelled piney. Then gradually the trees changed and paths appeared and the green became Central Park back home. They were dressed up in fine clothes and greeted friends as they walked along hand in hand. She was so happy that she stopped him right in the middle of a busy thoroughfare and went up on her toes to kiss him. She had meant it to be a brief, light kiss, but once they started it was as if the trees, the park, all the people strolling by faded into the background and it was just the two of them, their lips and tongues intertwining to stoke that magic fire inside....

And then it wasn't a dream, and Gabe's lips were on hers, gentle but insistent, and he was murmuring in her ear, "I had to kiss you, sweetheart, you look so beautiful...."

She gave herself up to the sensations—the skillful demands of his lips and tongue, the soft brush of his mustache, the abrasion of his unshaven whiskers. He worked and worked her mouth until the kiss had traveled to every part of her body. She turned on the bed to give him access to her hardening breasts. He accepted her unspoken invitation and began to unbutton her gown.

But as the haze of sleep left her she became gradually aware of the clatter of dishes in the kitchen just down the hall. She remembered that she was in Mattie Smith's room, in her bed. Parker was here in this house—devastated and alone. Her ardor began to cool.

Gabe sensed her withdrawal at once. He pulled back. "I'm sorry," he said. "That was stupid of me, unforgivable. This isn't the right time nor the right place."

Amelia looked up at him sadly. "Is there a right time and place for us, Gabe?"

He took a ragged breath. His features still had the stamp of arousal that she had come to know. She could see him trying to pull himself back to rationality. "I don't know, tenderfoot," he said finally. "Maybe we'll find a way somehow."

It was the first time he'd allowed for any hope for a future for them, and Amelia seized on his words. "Truly?"

He stood without answering her question. He had been ready to give Amelia up the day Samantha had come back, but something had happened to him through the course of this past week of witnessing so much death. As he had worked side by side with the men of the commission, fighting for the health and integrity of their home, he had begun to realize that there are some good things in this life that are worth struggling for. And when something comes along as powerful as what he and Amelia had found together, it was a cruel waste to let it go. He knew that he was not a free man—he was legally tied to a woman who had betrayed him, deserted him. But he owed Samantha nothing. He'd searched for her, mourned her, punished himself by leaving behind everything he had started to build in St. Louis. He'd paid his debt for a bad marriage. He was, however, still married to her, and until he resolved that situation, he wasn't free to make Amelia any promises.

"I came to wake you because your brother was asking for you, and I thought you'd want to go to him," he said, knowing that mention of her brother would end any further discussion between them.

Amelia sat up immediately. "Of course I'll go to him. Has he eaten anything yet?"

"I don't think so, but Mattie spoke to him for a long time this afternoon and at least he's started talking."

He stood and let her slip out of the bed. Hastily she rearranged the covers, gave her hair a quick pat and said, "Maybe we can talk later—after supper." Then she was gone.

Gabe sat down again on the edge of Mattie's bed and stared after her. He was due at a meeting of the commission. At least there he knew what had to be done. It felt good to be embarked on a project that would lead to a better life for the settlers who would become the real citizens of Deadwood once the gold panned out. And if he could straighten out Deadwood, he ought to be able to straighten out his own life, too. He stood with sudden resolution. He still had connections with some lawyer friends back in St. Louis. It shouldn't be that complicated to end a marriage in which one spouse had deserted the other for nine years. If he sent some wires and worked fast enough, perhaps he would have something to tell Amelia before she and Parker were ready to start home.

Gabe's new determination stayed with him as he and Nels Nelson headed toward the Lucky Horseshoe for their meeting with Driscoll. It was too bad that his involvement with the commission might mean that he couldn't play at the Lucky Horseshoe. But if things worked out as he had begun to hope, he wouldn't be gambling much longer. The son-in-law of a New York banker needed a more respectable profession to support his new wife. The idea made him whistle as he walked alongside Nels. None of the other commissioners had been eager to accompany Gabe, but Nels had finally volunteered.

They were to present the saloon owner with an ultimatum about the shacks he owned up in the shantytown. If Driscoll was willing to clean them up, make repairs, establish a sanitary system and keep the tenants to no more than four per shack, they could stay.

Otherwise, the commission was going to condemn the lot and burn them down.

Gabe expected opposition. Big Jim hadn't amassed his fortune by being civic-minded. But for once there was an organized group standing up to him, and Gabe hoped he would decide that the wisest course would be to comply with the commission's demands.

It was almost dark by the time they reached the saloon. The evening action was just starting to get lively. Two bar girls, Stella and Big Jim's most recent mistress, Letty Sue, were sitting together at the bar sizing up the night's pickings. The black piano player, Four Fingers Gallagher, had started in on a minstrel song called "Camptown Races." The middle digit of his left hand had been shot off in a gunfight in Wichita, but it was not apparent from the way he played.

"Where's Big Jim?" Gabe asked Deuce Connors as they walked in the door.

Deuce looked disdainfully at Nels. "Who wants him?"

"Mr. Nelson and I have a matter we need to discuss."

Deuce tipped his head. "His office—in the back."

They made their way around to a walled-off area behind the bar. Deuce followed them and reached around them to knock on the door.

"Come in." Gabe recognized Driscoll's muffled voice.

There was barely space for them to enter the tiny office. Deuce stayed in the doorway, apparently waiting for a word from Driscoll, who looked up from his papers with a scowl. "Yes, gentlemen?" he asked impatiently.

Gabe pushed his way between the visitor's chair and the desk to allow Nels more room. "We need to talk to you about your rental properties, Big Jim."

"Who's we?"

"Nelson and I represent the new Board of Health and Street Commissioners."

"Well, now, don't that sound fancy."

Deuce chuckled from the doorway behind them.

Gabe decided to come right to the point. "The commission has voted to condemn your properties unless you agree to clean them up and install a sewage system."

Driscoll laughed and put his hands on his round belly. "Excuse me one minute gentlemen," he said, then looked over at Deuce. "Will you kindly tell Mrs. Hatch that her husband is paying a visit?"

Gabe's jaw tightened. "She's got nothing to do with this, Driscoll. Our business is with you."

Nels looked puzzled. But to Gabe's surprise, the hotel owner addressed Driscoll with an authoritative tone. "The smallpox started up in those shacks, Mr. Driscoll, and unless we as a city do something about the conditions here, we're going to end up a ghost town."

Driscoll stood up slowly. "That's a meritorious notion, Mr., ah . . ." He waited.

"Nelson. Nels Nelson," the hotel owner supplied.

"Mr. Nelson. A mighty meritorious notion. Trouble is, I've got all I can do to keep up those places the way I do with the pitiful rents those squatters up there pay. Half the time they light out to go back home before they even pay me."

"You'll just have to raise those rents, then, Mr. Driscoll," Nels continued in a businesslike tone. "It's a simple commercial proposition, just like running my hotel.''

Driscoll leaned across his desk. ''It would also be a simple commercial proposition for me to establish a policy forbidding Willard Hotel guests from patronizing the Lucky Horseshoe.''

Nels looked taken aback. ''Why would you do that?''

Driscoll smiled, then shifted his eyes to the door. ''Ah, here she is. Come in, Mrs. Hatch. Have you met Mr. Nelson?''

Samantha gave the gaping hotel owner a dazzling smile and extended her slender hand. ''Pleased to meet you.''

''Mrs. Hatch?'' Nels asked in confusion with a glance at Gabe.

''Samantha and I were married—many years ago,'' Gabe explained tersely.

Samantha moved close to put a hand on his arm and look up into his face. ''We're still married, husband dear, last I heard.''

Gabe looked around at Nels's gaping expression. ''Yeah, well, that's a situation we're going to have to discuss,'' he said to her in a low voice. ''But not here.''

Driscoll stood. ''Go ahead and discuss it if you like, Hatch. After all, I think the Board of Commissioners would be interested in knowing that your *wife* is currently living in a saloon because she has nowhere else to stay. In fact, I think the whole town will be interested in that information—beginning with the delectable Miss Prescott.''

''Perhaps I should leave,'' Nels stammered.

Gabe flashed an angry look at Samantha. ''Nothing can get settled between us until you agree to see me,

Sam. I'm not about to discuss the private details of our lives with Driscoll hanging on every word."

"I'm available, Gabe," she said.

"You haven't been. I've been here asking to see you every day. They keep telling me you won't see me."

Samantha turned to Driscoll. "Is that true, Jim?"

He shrugged. "You can see him any time you want."

"You're darn right I can," she said angrily, turning back to Gabe. "I'll meet you tomorrow morning."

"I'll be here at nine."

"No," she said with her little cat's smile. "I'll meet you at the hotel—in your room."

She should have taken more time to recover from the effects of Gabe's kisses, Amelia realized as she entered the kitchen. Mattie's look left no doubt that it was apparent what she and Gabe had been doing in Mattie's bedroom. But it was too late now. She put her cool fingers against her swollen mouth and held them there.

"I've fixed some soup for your brother," Mattie said briskly, turning back to the stove. "You can take it in and see if you can get him to eat some of it."

Amelia was grateful for the older woman's discretion, but she still felt much as she had when she'd been caught with Harry Witherspoon on the porch swing back home. She'd been fourteen and insatiably curious about certain aspects of life that her brother had begun to hint about. The Witherspoons had never been invited back to their house after that day.

The memory brought a brief smile, but it faded immediately as she began preparing a tray of foods that she thought might tempt Parker's appetite—a bright red apple, some cheeses, tea biscuits. Mattie put a steaming bowl of soup in the middle of it all and Amelia started off toward the parlor.

Parker was in the same position in front of the fire where she had left him hours ago, but he gave her a wan smile when she entered. "They told me you were sleeping," he said.

She nodded, hoping that the scrapes from Gabe's whiskers were no longer noticeable on her face. "Gabe made me take a nap." Parker looked back at the fire. He didn't seem affected by the mention of Gabe's name. "Will you take some supper?"

"I'm not too hungry."

She set the tray down on the sofa table and knelt beside him, taking his hands in hers. "Parker, you've got to eat. You're going to get sick yourself if you don't."

He leaned back in his chair and closed his eyes. "It just doesn't seem to matter anymore—any of it."

"Don't I matter anymore?" she asked, putting a touch of anger in the question.

His eyes popped open. "Of course, sis. You'll always matter, but..."

"Then eat something for me. If you don't want to do it for yourself, fine. Do it for me." She pulled the end of the table over so that he could reach the food from his chair.

"I'll try," he said without much spirit.

"Do you want me to sit with you?"

He shook his head. She waited while he picked up a piece of cheese and lifted it to his mouth, then she turned and left the room. Mattie was just taking off her apron in the kitchen. Amelia had the strangest urge to wrap her arms around the little woman and cry, but, of course, she did no such thing.

"Come on," Mattie said, picking up a tray laden with fried chicken and whipped potatoes. "I dare say you could do with a heartier meal than just soup, my dear."

"Shouldn't we check on the girls first?"

"They're all fed and resting comfortably. Delia's the worst, poor thing. Her face and hands are covered. But the other cases are going to turn out to be mild, thank God."

Amelia followed her into the dining room. Mattie had been right. Meals had been erratic and interrupted throughout the week, and the hearty food tasted wonderful. The supper and the nap she had had were making her feel almost normal. And now Parker was starting to come out of his worrisome trancelike state, which gave her the liberty of putting her mind back on Gabe and on the words he had almost said. *Maybe we'll find a way,* he had told her. It was only a crack in the door, but perhaps it was starting to open after all.

"Your whole face changes when you're thinking about him," Mattie said, watching her from across the table.

Amelia blushed. "About whom?"

Mattie cocked her head with a look of reproof. "Do you know what you're getting into with Gabe, my dear?" she asked gently.

Amelia took some time answering. A few weeks ago she would never have dreamed that she would be confiding her feelings and hopes to a woman like Mattie Smith. But now it seemed the most natural choice in the world. "I had thought I wasn't getting into anything with him. If it hadn't been for the epidemic, Parker and I would be on our way back to New York by now."

"But something has changed your mind?"

"I'm not sure. I don't want to get my hopes up, but...it was something he said today. When we were...talking earlier in your room."

A look of relief washed over Mattie's face. "So he *did* explain to you!" she said. "I told him that it simply wasn't fair that you didn't know. A woman has the right to all the facts before she gives her heart out—"

"Explain what?" Amelia interrupted.

Mattie went suddenly white. "Perhaps I'm m-mistaken," she stammered. "I just thought..."

Amelia reached across the table and clutched at Mattie's hand, a terrible, sinking feeling in her stomach. "What didn't I know, Mattie? Please! You have to tell me."

"Talk to Gabe, child," Mattie said, her eyes distressed.

"A woman has the right to the facts, Mattie. You just said so."

Mattie pulled her hands from Amelia's and dug nervously with her fingernails into the lace tablecloth. "Gabe has a wife, my dear. He's married."

Amelia's hand slipped slowly back across the table and fell into her lap. She stared straight ahead of her without seeing a thing.

"You're sure?" she asked in a hoarse whisper.

Mattie averted her eyes. "I'm afraid so."

Gabe concentrated on putting one foot in front of the other as he and Nels walked back to the Willard. The meeting with Driscoll had ended with no resolution. Nels had lost much of his assertiveness after the threats to his hotel business and Gabe had been thrown by the presence of Samantha, as Driscoll had no doubt intended. Finally Gabe had laid the commission's ultimatum on Driscoll's desk and, reminding Samantha that he would expect her in the morning, they had left.

He asked Nels to take care of reporting back to the other commissioners about the meeting. Then he hurriedly made his way down the street to Mattie's. Obviously, Driscoll intended to make sure that the entire town knew about his marriage. He had to tell Amelia about Samantha before she heard it from someone else.

His brisk step slowed as he entered Mattie's front hall. In his concern over reaching Amelia, he'd forgotten for a moment that this was a house recently visited by death and that the specter's hulking presence still threatened here.

With a sober face he walked into the parlor. Parker was in the chair by the fire where he'd been for over a day. Gabe hesitated, then went over to put a hand on his shoulder. "How are you doing, my friend?"

Parker looked up with surprise. "Oh, it's you, Gabe," was his only answer.

Gabe didn't know if he'd be able to get through to his partner or not, but he decided to make the attempt. "I need to talk to your sister. Where is she?"

There was finally a touch of life in Parker's voice as he answered, "Why don't you leave her the hell alone? Haven't you done enough to her already?"

Gabe withdrew his hand. "That's just the point. I'm trying to remedy the mistakes I've made." Parker didn't turn around, so Gabe squatted down beside him to be able to see his face. "She deserves to hear from me about my wife. And she deserves to know that I'm going to do my damnedest to try to make this whole thing come out right."

"Amelia already knows about your wife."

"What are you talking about?"

Parker gave him a disgusted glance. "Mattie told her that you're married. She's locked herself up in Claire's room and won't speak to anyone."

He felt a wave of fury over the stupidity of the mistake. How could Mattie have done such a thing? And why hadn't he told Amelia himself long ago? She had a right to be angry with him. "Well, she *has* to speak with me," he said. "I've got to explain to her . . ." He ran a hand back through his hair in agitation.

Parker's face had glazed over again. "I don't think she'll see you."

Gabe puffed his cheeks and blew out an exasperated huff. "She'll see me, all right."

Parker stared at the fire and shook his head slowly. "Give her some time, Gabe."

"Time to get herself so worked up that she talks herself into hating me? Not likely." He turned on his heel and half ran up the stairs, arriving at the door to Claire's room out of breath. He paused a minute, then knocked and softly called her name.

There was no sound. He tried the knob, but the door was locked. He knocked more forcefully. "Open the door, Amelia. I have to talk with you." He kept his voice low but urgent.

His words were met with more silence. He threw back his head in exasperation. He couldn't yell at her. There were sick girls in the other rooms up the hall. "We can't talk through a closed door, sweetheart. I'm sorry I didn't tell you myself, but you've got to let me in to explain."

"Go away." Her voice didn't sound normal.

"Are you going to make me yell my explanations so everyone in the house can hear them?" he asked angrily.

She had come closer to the door. "I don't want to hear your explanations, Gabe. I just want you to leave me alone."

"That's the one thing I won't do, tenderfoot. Now open that door and hear me out, or, I swear, I'll break it down."

There was a long moment during which Gabe had started to examine the brass hinges of the door, figuring that he was going to have to carry out his threat. Then finally he heard the sound of the lock. He waited, and when the door stayed closed, he reached for the handle and went in.

Chapter Fifteen

Her eyes and nose were red and her cheeks blotchy. Gabe flushed with guilt. "I'm sorry..." he began.

She held up her hand. "I told you, I don't want to hear it. I just opened the door so you wouldn't wake up Delia in the next room."

She'd returned to sit on the bed. He crossed over to stand in front of her, but he didn't touch her. "I didn't tell you that I'd been married because I didn't want to hurt you," he said bluntly. "I thought my wife had died nine years ago."

Evidently Mattie had neglected to provide the details, because Amelia looked up in surprise at his words. But then she turned her face away again, her chin lifted in that stubborn way he'd seen before.

His explanations tumbled out like spilled matches. "We married young. I thought I loved her. But when she ran off with another man..." There was another slight hint of surprise in her eyes. "She left me for someone else," he repeated, "and they disappeared. I spent the next ten months looking for her, only to be told, finally, that she'd died in a landslide in Colter Canyon. I didn't know she was alive until last week when she turned up at Driscoll's."

Her head remained averted. "We all make mistakes, Amelia," he said with just a touch of bitterness. "Perhaps you'll even make one yourself some day."

She looked up at him then, her eyes dark and hostile. "I already have," she said.

He gave an audible sigh. "No, you didn't. The mistake was mine, entirely. For the first time in nine years I found something I wanted so much I was willing to risk reaching out and taking it, in spite of my past."

"And just what was it that you were risking, Gabe?"

He ran his hand across his mouth, then gestured toward her. "This. You. I risked having you end up hating me. I risked breaking both our hearts and having to live with that knowledge the rest of my life."

"Spare me your self-pity, please. You told me from the beginning that you had no intention of establishing any kind of lasting relationship with me. *My* heart was the one at risk, Gabe. And, for that matter, my body. I could have ended up with child, perhaps still will, in spite of the remedies supplied by your disreputable friends."

She was good and angry now, which was easier to take than the crushing sadness he'd seen on her face when he first came in. "There's nothing I would like more in this life than to have a child with you, tenderfoot."

She seemed to note his change in manner, but her voice stayed stiff. "A fine thing that would be. You'd have no way to give it your name."

"That's something I intend to remedy," he said firmly.

She looked confused.

"I'm going to ask my wife for a divorce."

Amelia was silent for a long time. Gabe could see a battle taking place behind those lively dark eyes. But, at least for now, the cautious New Yorker won out over the free spirit he had made love to in the mountains. "Congratulations," she said. "But what you do or don't do with your wife is no longer of any concern to me."

She held her neck so stiffly that he longed to put his hands underneath her thick hair and massage her there. Instead he took a step back from the bed. "I'm going to see her tomorrow morning. And after I've made arrangements we'll talk again."

"Where is she staying?" Amelia asked, her curiosity winning out over her resolve to stay indifferent.

"She's at the Lucky Horseshoe."

At her questioning look he added, "I believe Driscoll thinks he can use her against me in some way."

Amelia took in the implications of what he was saying. "I . . . I'm sorry. It couldn't be easy for you."

Gabe's spirits rose. She was definitely softening. He fought off the urge to lean down and kiss her. "We're going to be all right, tenderfoot," he said firmly. "You may not believe it yet, but I hope now you'll come out of this room. Your brother needs you, and Mattie needs you. And whether you want to hear it or not, I need you more than any of them."

Without waiting for her reply he turned and walked out of the room, leaving the door wide open behind him. Amelia stared at his broad back until he disappeared down the stairs. She felt as if her whole body had been passed through a clothes wringer since her supper with Mattie. Her world had turned on its axis. Gabe had always been so confident, so sure of himself, so carefree, the last person to need anything or anybody. Now she'd discovered that he'd lied to her, that he had a past full of secrets, that he suffered doubts and remorse.

Slowly she got to her feet. He'd been right about one thing. It was selfish to sit here feeling sorry for herself when Parker and the sick girls needed her. She picked up a brush from the dresser to smooth her hair into place. Claire's initials were etched into the tortoiseshell handle. Amelia bit her lip. There were people in this house suffering worse than she. She'd think about Gabe later.

Gabe's head was pounding, and for once he couldn't blame it on overindulgence. Now that he'd started thinking about freeing himself from Samantha, he could hardly wait to get the process started. It had been all he could think about during a long, sleepless night. But first he would have to get through the commission meeting this morning. The men of this town needed the backbone he seemed able to provide them with. He wasn't worried that Samantha would arrive before the meeting was over. Even back in St. Louis she rarely awoke before ten.

The commissioners were meeting in a back room at the Willard. Nels, who had been outspoken and confident before talking to Driscoll yesterday, was not saying much, though Gabe sensed that he had at least opened his mouth enough to inform the entire board of the untimely appearance of a wife that no one knew Gabe had. They'd all looked at him uncomfortably when he'd walked into the room this morning, as if someone close to him had died and they didn't quite know what to say.

They seemed to be waiting for him to reassure them that Driscoll would now give in to their demands so they could all go about their business without any trouble. He was discovering, however, that trouble was one of the things Big Jim liked best, and Gabe just wasn't about to make any guarantees that there wouldn't be more of it in store for all of them if they continued to go up against him.

Peter Stuber was the only one to show a sign of spirit. The squat little merchant raised his voice and said, "We've given him a chance. If he won't go along with us, we'll just burn those shacks down under his nose."

There were several nods of agreement, but Gabe didn't notice anyone volunteering to be the one to light the torch to Big Jim's property. He, himself, just wanted the meeting to be over, so he could go up to his room, take a powder for his headache and wait for Samantha.

After a few more items of business, the meeting adjourned. Gabe walked back to the lobby to the foot of the stairs.

"We had a date this morning, Gabe, remember?"

He turned slowly. Almost every eye in the lobby was on her. The few people who weren't watching her were looking at him. It evidently hadn't taken long for word to spread that Gabe Hatch's wife was in town. "Yes," he said gruffly.

"Well, here I am." She put her arms out in a pretty little gesture. She was wearing an orange ruffled dress that was just this side of decent. Back in St. Louis Samantha wouldn't have been caught dead in a dress like that.

He hesitated a minute, took another look around at the curious faces, then said, "Come up to my room where we can have some privacy."

She lifted an eyebrow, but followed him without comment up to his second-floor suite. "Nice place," she said breezily as he closed the door behind them. She did a little twirl as she untied the ribbons to her bonnet and flung it on his sofa. "This is much nicer than the room Big Jim's given me. Perhaps I'll just move on over here."

"And perhaps not," he said firmly.

She fluttered her eyelashes and shaped her perfect mouth into a pout. Her eyes were fixed on him coquettishly, and for the briefest moment he was a boy of seventeen again, lost in those green depths. "You haven't given me a very nice welcome after all these years, Gabe."

He shrugged out of his coat. It was hot in the room, and her presence made it feel stifling. "Why should I welcome you? You're the one who ran out on me, remember? You were the one who was perfectly content to let me think you were dead and buried—for nine long years."

She sat daintily on the edge of the sofa, ankles crossed. Her smile faltered. "There've been times when I've regretted leaving you, Gabe."

For the first time her voice sounded sincere, and Gabe felt an unwanted prick of pity. What had her life been like since she left so long ago? How many men had there been?

He walked over to his armchair and sat down heavily. "I want a divorce, Samantha, and I assume you do, too. I'll make whatever kind of settlement you wish, but I want it to be fast and discreet. That is, if you know the meaning of that word anymore."

She smiled her cat's smile. "But I want nothing of the sort, Gabe, darling."

"Don't be foolish. There's nothing left between us. You know that as well as I do."

Slowly she curled up her legs, hugging the arm of the couch. "That doesn't mean there couldn't be something between us again . . . right now, in fact, if you've a mind."

Now his head was pounding in earnest. He had a most ungentlemanly urge to pick her up bodily and throw her out in the hall. But he knew Samantha. He wouldn't get what he wanted from her by bullying. "I'm sorry, Samantha. I'm just not interested anymore. We've both drifted too far downstream to even think about trying to paddle our way back up."

He could see that she was beginning to get angry, but her voice stayed sugar sweet. "You'd be better off welcoming me back, darling. I promise I can make you forget our past troubles."

His eyes darkened. "I don't want to forget them, Sam. They've brought me where I am today, which is a sight better off than I was with you in St. Louis."

She abandoned her seductive pose and sat up straight. "I'm warning you, Gabe. You'll regret turning me away. I came here to give you one last chance before I take Big Jim up on his offer."

"His offer?"

She smiled. "Of . . . protection."

"Protection," Gabe repeated dryly. "I'm beyond caring what you do with your life, Samantha, but I'd advise you against having anything to do with Driscoll. He's bad news."

"You're jealous."

"No, Sam." He gave a deep sigh. "I'm not. You can sleep with the devil himself, if you want. I'm just trying to give you a friendly warning."

"Big Jim brought me here. He paid off my debts in Colorado."

Something in her voice made Gabe suspect that she was not entirely comfortable about her obligation to Driscoll. "If you need some money, I'd be willing to give you a settlement in the divorce."

The features looked suddenly harsher, older, as she turned on him. "And then what? I'm cast off to make my own way again. No, thank you. At least with Big Jim I have a future. He wants me to stay here with him."

Gabe shook his head. "He's not a man I'd bank my future on, but it's your choice. Just as long as we get the divorce taken care of."

Samantha's angry look was replaced by a nasty smile. "You're not getting a divorce from me, Gabe. Not ever. So put it out of your mind."

Gabe felt the throbbing behind his temples. "What do you mean?" he half shouted.

Samantha stood and reached for her bonnet. "It's part of my deal with Big Jim. He prefers to have me married to you—it gives us a certain degree of... control."

So that was Driscoll's plan. Bring his wife to town, parade her around as his mistress in front of all the respectable citizens of Deadwood and hope that that would make Gabe do whatever he said. But Gabe wasn't buying into the program. He didn't give a damn who knew about Samantha or what she did with herself. If she wouldn't consent to a divorce, he'd find some way to get one without her consent. It was frustrating—he'd have to ask Amelia to wait that much longer. But somehow it would get done.

"Neither you nor Driscoll will ever have a hold on me, Sam. Go to him, if you must. It makes no difference to me."

Her expression softened. "All things considered, Gabe, I'd rather stay here with you than cast my lot with Driscoll." She walked toward him, tying on her bonnet, her body swaying, then she sat down in his lap. "We could be good together again, Gabe," she said in that husky voice of hers that could still send a chill down his spine. "Let me prove it to you."

His body responded automatically to the deliberate movement of her little bottom against him, but his head would have no part of it. "Don't do this, Sam. It's over. I'd like to be able to at least end it with some dignity."

There was a flicker of something like fear in her eyes, but it disappeared so quickly that he couldn't be sure he had seen it. "Don't send me back to Driscoll, Gabe," she said. She entwined her slender arms around his neck.

He removed them gently. "I'm not sending you back to anyone. I have a little money—not a lot—but enough to see that you get back to St. Louis. Maybe you can go to your family and get a fresh start."

"You'd like that, wouldn't you? To have me out of your hair again so you can marry that fancy-schmanzy banker's daughter Big Jim says you've been panting after for weeks."

"Don't do this, Sam," he said again.

She whirled off his lap and looked down at him. "It *is* her, isn't it? That's why you won't have anything to do with me."

Gabe shook his head. "This is just between us, Samantha."

She tossed her head. "Well, it's going to stay between us, my dear *husband*. Because you'll never be free of me."

"There's more than one way—" He stopped as her smile turned to pure malice.

"If you so much as lift a finger toward a divorce, Gabe, I'll make you regret it to the end of your days."

He got to his feet. "And just how would you do that?"

Her voice became soft and deadly. "The child, Gabe. *Our* child. There was no miscarriage."

He grabbed her shoulders. "You're lying!"

She shook her head. "We have a son, husband."

He let her go. "A son," he breathed, falling back down into his chair. Tiny demons exploded inside his aching head.

Samantha took the opportunity to move away from him toward the door. "If you try to free yourself from me, Gabe, I swear you'll never so much as lay an eye on him."

Before he could react further she was out the door, slamming it behind her, leaving him looking after her in stunned disbelief.

He didn't dare take the chance that she was lying. Samantha had been at least five months with child when she had run away, and it was likely that a baby had been born. A son, she had said. He had a son. He'd be almost nine years old. Where was he? Her words implied that she at least knew where he was, even if she had given him into the keeping of someone else. He knew that she hadn't left him with her family in St. Louis, since he'd kept in periodic touch with her brother there.

The knowledge that he was a father had driven every other thought out of his head, but as he walked across the street toward Mattie's he began to think once again of Amelia. He had hoped to be able to come to her today with news of his imminent divorce. He had hoped to take her away from all the sickbeds for a drive in the country where he would ask her to marry him, ask her properly as she deserved. Now he wasn't sure what he would say to her or what her reaction to his news would be.

He was longing for more details about the boy. He didn't even know the lad's name. Did he have his own blond hair and blue eyes? Or were his eyes the vixen green of his mother? But Samantha was the only one who could give him the answers, and he was afraid if he saw her right now he would throttle her.

He was surprised to see Parker coming out of Mattie's. He had finally left his chair by the fire. It was a good sign. For a moment Gabe put aside his own problems. "Hey, there, partner. How are you doing?"

There was no life in the younger man's eyes, but he stopped at the bottom of the stairs to talk. "Hello, Gabe. I don't know what you said to Amelia yesterday, but she's some better."

"I'm glad to hear it." He certainly had no news to cheer her today. "The last thing I want is for her to be hurt by all this."

Parker nodded. "I know. We don't set out to hurt the people we love, but sometimes that's the way it works out. Life just hauls back and hammers you one," he said bitterly.

Parker looked as though he'd been thoroughly hammered over the past few days. "Are you going to be all right?" Gabe asked.

"I'm going to be just fine after about five stiff ones over at the Horseshoe."

"That's not the solution, Parker," Gabe said, putting a hand on his shoulder. "Believe me, I've been there."

"I'm not looking for any solutions, partner. I'm just looking for a way out. And right now a bottle of whiskey seems like the quickest way to oblivion."

"Is there anything I can say to talk you out of it?"

"Nope." He shoved Gabe's hand off his shoulder and walked away.

Gabe let out a long breath and looked up at Mattie's door. Amelia was inside, likely unhappy if she knew where her brother was heading. Now he would arrive to add to her gloom with this new complication in his life. He kicked the bottom of the stairs. Maybe Parker had the right idea after all. Oblivion was sounding kind of good right about now. He did an about-face and followed his partner down the street.

Delia took a last spoonful of hot milk and bread, then sat tiredly back against the pillows. Amelia removed the tray from her lap and the girl gave her a wan smile of thanks. "You've been mighty good to us, Amelia," she said. "I know if Claire were still here she'd be so proud of the kind of sister-in-law she'd be getting."

Amelia had never thought about Claire as a possible sister-in-law, but she supposed she should have. Parker had been convinced that she was going to be his one truelove forever. And the idea of a former prostitute in the family didn't shock Amelia anymore, as it would have a few weeks ago. Hadn't she herself been thinking about giving Parker a professional gambler for a brother-in-law? In fact, she'd thought of little else since her last meeting with Gabe. But now she was beginning to have doubts once again. Gabe hadn't come. She'd expected that he would come back to report on his meeting with his wife, but she hadn't seen anything of him since the night before last when he had met with her up in Claire's room. She shook off her thoughts and turned her attention back to the sick girl. "I'm very sorry about Claire, Delia. Were you two good friends?"

"We're all friends here, but Claire was never quite like the rest of us. She lived a bit in her own world until your brother came along."

"He loved her very much."

"They loved each other—as fierce a love as I've ever seen. It's just a shame, a rotten shame."

Amelia felt much the same. Parker hadn't come back to Mattie's last night. She'd sent Morgan to find him this morning, hoping he'd gone back out to the cabin to be alone. But the Welshman had reported back that he was at the Pink Lady, one of the lower-class saloons in what they were calling the Badlands on the west side of the gulch. He'd been in a game of penny ante poker and had told Morgan that he would come home when he was too broke to play or too drunk to sit upright. When Amelia had offered to go talk to him, Morgan had for once put his foot down and told her he'd hog-tie her before he'd let her set foot in a place like that.

"I know," she answered Delia. "I wish there was something I could do to make it easier for my brother, but I can't think what it would be. I guess it would be best for us to go back to New York and try to forget about Deadwood." And Deadwood gamblers, she added silently.

"You might be right," Delia said. The sides of her pretty, round face were marked with the distinctive red pox, but she hadn't suffered much, and it looked as if the worst of the sickness had passed. "You look like too much of a proper lady to be cut out for a life out here."

Amelia gave a grim nod of agreement. "You might be right about that."

After asking Delia if there was anything more she could do for her, she carried the tray down to Mattie in the kitchen. Morgan was waiting for her there. "Parker's gone out to the cabin, Missy," he told her.

"Is he all right?"

"He's too drunk to know if he's all right or not."

Amelia looked at Mattie. "I should go to him."

"Of course." The older woman gave her a sympathetic smile. "You've been wonderful these past few days—a savior. But the worst is over now and it's time you started concentrating on yourself and your brother instead of the rest of the town."

"I'm going to tell him that we should follow our original plans and start home."

Mattie came over and embraced her. "That's probably the wisest course."

Amelia looked down at her and felt a sudden wave of affection. "I'll miss you, Mattie," she said, surprised to realize that it was true.

"And I you, my dear. Is there anything...do you want me to give Gabe any message for you?"

Amelia shook her head and said with a sigh, "Evidently Gabe has too many of his own problems right now to have time to think about me."

"I'm sending you and Morgan home, sis, and I won't have any argument about it."

Amelia continued peeling the potatoes she had brought with her from town yesterday. It was fortunate she'd decided to stop for supplies before coming out, because they had left no food in the house and she didn't know when Parker had last had a decent meal. He'd spent the entire night getting sick to his stomach after his two-day drinking binge. Of course, it served him right. But his drawn face had begun to worry her.

"You can leave in the morning," Parker went on. "Amelia! Are you listening to me?"

"I refuse to listen to idiocies. I'm not about to leave you in your current state."

"My current state is fine, thank you very much. I just can't face going home now." He got up from his chair and moved around to her side of the table. "Please, sis. I'll come home before too long, I promise. I simply need a little more time. I can't leave . . . I can't leave her yet."

"Claire's not here anymore, Parker."

"I don't need you to tell me that," he said angrily.

"Well, you're acting like you do."

He crouched down next to her chair and used a cajoling tone. "I want some time to myself, sis."

Amelia was not to be swayed. "So you can drain dry the rest of the saloons along the gulch?"

He stiffened. "That's not my intention."

"Well, I think I'll just stay on and be sure it doesn't become your intention."

"You're not my guardian."

They glared at each other, but each felt the other's pain, and Amelia softened first. "I can't leave you like this, Parker. Don't ask me. It would break my heart."

Parker straightened and went over to tend the fire. He was quiet for a long moment, then he said, "You may have even more heartbreak staying here, sis."

"You mean Gabe?"

He nodded. "You know that his wife is living with Big Jim Driscoll?"

Amelia got a sick taste in her mouth. "Living with him? You mean . . . ?"

"She's become his mistress."

Amelia sighed. "Poor Gabe."

"You'd be better off getting out of here and forgetting him."

She threw the last potato into the basin and stood, wiping her hands on her apron. "Until you're ready to leave behind the ghost of your lost love and come home with me, I'm staying here."

Chapter Sixteen

His name was Jeremy. Samantha had had the grace at least to give him a family name—her grandfather's. Jeremy Winthrop had been a respected builder back in Virginia, and his son, Samantha's father, had continued the trade in St. Louis until his death just at the time of his daughter's marriage. Gabe wondered what the remaining Winthrops would think if they could see Samantha now.

She sat on Driscoll's bed in a silk robe that looked as if it belonged to the saloon owner. Driscoll was dressed, eating his breakfast from a tray. Gabe was sure that he'd been brought up here deliberately to leave no doubt about the fact that his wife was now Big Jim's property.

But it wasn't Samantha he had come to learn about. "Where is he, Sam?" he asked her.

"Wouldn't you like to know?" It seemed to be too early in the morning to drink, but he would swear that her words were slurred.

"I've a right to know. He's my son."

Driscoll shoved the tray aside and stood. "We all have rights in this world, Hatch. For example, I have

the right as an honest businessman to build houses and
rent them out at a reasonable price.''

"To build shacks and charge exorbitant rents, you
mean.''

Driscoll smiled and continued as if Gabe had not
spoken. "I have a right to carry out my business without interference from busybody citizens who don't have
enough to occupy themselves.''

"The commission is only trying to make Deadwood
into a safe and lawful town. It's serving everyone's interests.''

Driscoll leaned over and smoothed back Samantha's
hair. "Your wife and I don't happen to agree,'' he said,
still pleasantly. "And I would imagine that until you
start to see things our way, Samantha's not going to be
very interested in talking with you about any...common
interests you might have.''

"A son is a bit more than a common interest,'' Gabe
said. He looked at Samantha. "I want to speak to you
alone.''

She stayed silent, waiting for Driscoll to answer.
"Samantha is under my protection now, Hatch. Which
means she doesn't have to see anyone she doesn't want
to.''

Gabe shook his head in disbelief. "It won't work,
Driscoll. You think that by withholding information
about my son I'm going to go tell the commission to
back off and let you continue running this town the way
you want?''

"That sounds like a nice summary to me.''

"Samantha?'' He turned to his wife, hoping that she
would demonstrate a little of the spirit he knew she
possessed. Driscoll's hand was still in her hair.

"You made your position about us pretty clear two days ago, Gabe," she said bitterly. "You left me with no other choice."

He ignored Driscoll and looked straight at her. "I'll find our son with or without your help, Samantha, and I'll find a way to get a divorce. If you want it all to be done the hard way, then it's on your head."

"You better go on downstairs for a drink on the house, Gabe—think things over a bit," Driscoll said in a congenial tone. "Your so-called commission is not worth making a mess of your life. And there's not a man on it who'll as much as thank you for doing so after it's all over."

"You're wrong there, Driscoll. Just because they're law-abiding citizens doesn't make them lesser men than you."

Driscoll laughed. "They're a bunch of namby-pamby clerks who'll hide behind their store counters at the first sign of trouble, and you know it."

"I don't think so."

"Fine. You just go on back and tell your fellow *commissioners* that the only way they're going to get changes in the shantytown is to burn it down."

"That would be no great loss."

Driscoll crossed over to Gabe and opened the door. "But don't forget that old saying, Gabe, when you tell them. How does it go? People who play with fire often get burned?" He gestured with his arm for Gabe to leave. "The offer of a free drink is still good. Just tell Roscoe when you get downstairs."

It was Stuber, Harrington and Nelson again, a repeat of the first meeting they had had when he'd agreed to join their cause. But this time the expressions on their faces were uncomfortable, almost embarrassed. Gabe was in his armchair facing the three, who sat lined up together on his hotel room sofa.

"Personally we'd like to see you stay on, Gabe," Stuber said, looking as if he meant it.

"Of course." David Harrington's assurance was less sincere. Gabe suspected the banker had been one of the ones who had voted him out.

"I thought you said you needed someone like me to be able to fight Driscoll on his terms?" Gabe asked. "And I have to tell you, I think that assessment is right. Driscoll plays dirtier than probably any of you know."

Nels was the only one of the three with real regret in his voice. "That's exactly what I told them. We need Gabe. Driscoll has no scruples, which gives him an automatic advantage over everyone who does have them."

"But not over me?" Gabe asked dryly. He supposed that it was logical that these men would put a gambler in the same category with a snake like Driscoll. Perhaps that's where he belonged after all. And, hell, why should he care? If he was off their bloody commission, he'd be free to go to Samantha and demand the details of his son's whereabouts. Driscoll would have no more reason to force her to withhold the information. It just galled him to have to give up on something that he'd started and that he'd believed in. All because the misguided moral guardians on the commission found it scandalous that he had a wife who was living in sin with the town's richest saloon owner.

Nels looked down at the floor. "I believe that you're a good man, Gabe," he said.

Harrington interrupted. "We want to thank you for your efforts thus far, of course, Hatch. And we hope you won't take this personally."

Gabe ran his hand over his face. He'd not thought about shaving since his drinking bout with Parker. "Of course not," he said with a fixed smile. He stood. "Now, I'd not want to keep you gentlemen from your important duties."

The three shuffled to their feet and left the room with more apologies and overly cordial goodbyes. Gabe shut the door after them and stood a moment, trying to do a quick review of his life in the past few hours, days. The commission was behind him, and good riddance. He needed to talk to Samantha alone, with or without Driscoll's permission, and force her to tell him about their son. But first things first. Like a drunk needing a shot of red-eye, he felt an ache in his gut. He wanted to see Amelia. His life was still too much in disarray to have much to offer, but he had to be sure she was still willing to wait for him. He had a sudden, awful thought. What if she and Parker had already left for New York? Without stopping to collect his hat, he slammed out the door of his room and ran down the hotel stairs two at a time.

This time Amelia knew even before she saw his horse coming across the valley. She'd been sitting on the bridge as she had so often these past few days, dangling her feet over the edge, aimlessly watching the water. There were things she could do around the cabin. Mattie had showed her how to make bread and she'd brought the ingredients out with her. But she couldn't seem to muster up the energy.

After their talk yesterday she and Parker had spent the rest of the day tiptoeing around each other like different species of birds defining territories. She knew that he still wanted her to leave him and go home. He knew that she would not do so, and that she would fight every step he took in the direction of self-destruction. But after an awkward supper he'd finally told her that he was going into town whether she liked it or not. And that he had no idea when he would return. When she'd protested, he'd told her she could wait for him till doomsday for all he cared, and he'd left. She'd told Morgan to go with him. He'd been torn, not wanting to leave her by herself, but she had insisted. The thought of a night alone in the valley did not daunt her as it would have once. She had made friends with the trees, the mountain jays and the little ground squirrels that had taken to coming right up to her door for the biscuit crumbs she tossed them.

And maybe she'd sensed that he would come, after all, today. She felt it in the accelerated thrum of her heart and the tingle in her arms. She watched as he approached on his big bay horse. He rode straight and easily. He was hatless, his blond curls blowing in the wind. She stayed where she was on the bridge, gripping the edge with palms that had suddenly become moist.

"I was afraid you'd gone," were his first words as he jumped off his horse and stalked toward her across the wooden planks.

He sounded so urgent that at first she was afraid he had come to tell her that something had happened to Parker, but his next actions corrected that impression. He bent over and lifted her from the bridge, bringing her against him to give her a hard kiss on the mouth. "I thought you and your brother might have already started home," he repeated, more calmly this time.

His eyes matched the deep blue autumn sky. Her throat tightened just looking at him. "Parker wouldn't leave," she said distractedly.

"And you wouldn't leave him," he confirmed.

She nodded her head. They stared at each other for a long moment. "I'm sorry for kissing you," he said. "I know I haven't the right."

With a sad smile she said, "After...what we had, I guess it's silly to worry about just a kiss, isn't it?"

"No." His voice was surprisingly firm. "Because I'm not going to kiss you again until I *do* have the right."

Her face brightened. "Then you've spoken with... with your wife?"

"I've spoken with her," he said, but his voice was grim. When she looked at him questioningly, he said, "I was hoping we could ride up to my cabin...to *our* cabin...so we could talk without interruptions." He looked around as if expecting to see Parker or Morgan.

"My brother and Morgan are in town. Parker said he didn't know when he'd be back."

"Oh. Well, good. We'll talk here, then." He took her hand and started toward the cabin, glancing down to take in the way her worn gingham dress molded to her figure. "It's probably safer if we stay around here," he added ruefully.

Gabe suggested that they put off their talk until after supper, so they worked together mostly in silence to heat up some leftover stew and johnnycake. Just being around him again was making Amelia feel more alive than she had in days.

Neither was very hungry, but they picked at their food and exchanged what information they had about the receding smallpox epidemic. Talk of Gabe's wife was put off by unspoken mutual consent.

After they finished eating Amelia insisted on cleaning up by herself. Gabe sat in the rocker smoking a cigar and enjoying the sight of her quiet efficiency as she neatly banked the fire, then lifted off a heavy kettle of boiling water to soak the dishes.

"You've come a long way since the first night I sat watching you in this room, tenderfoot," he observed.

She smiled. "They'd never know me back home. Matilda always shooed us out of the kitchen if I so much as buttered a piece of bread."

"You won't be the same when you go back."

A shadow crossed her face. "No."

Gabe realized that she was thinking about another way that she wouldn't be the same. It was time he talked to her about his wife.

"I told you I had talked to Samantha."

"Is that her name?" She tucked her hair back behind her ears and turned to face him as if she were a soldier preparing for battle.

"Yes, Samantha. She's staying with Driscoll at the Lucky Horseshoe."

Amelia's stiff posture softened a little as if she wished she could go to him. "I know. Parker told me. I'm . . . I'm sorry."

"Under normal circumstances, I wouldn't give a damn who she was with. But I've found out some news that will alter every aspect of my life from now on."

Amelia's eyes widened. "Something about your wife?"

"Indirectly." He stood and motioned to the rocker. "Why don't you sit down here if you're finished?" She did as he suggested and when he had pulled up a small chair to sit beside her, he continued. "Amelia, Samantha has told me that I have a son."

The gentle motion of the rocker stopped. "A . . . son?"

The words started pouring out as if he had to make her understand all at once, quickly, before she had time to make any kind of judgment against him. He told her of the months he had searched, hoping to find a wife and child, willing to forgive, to start over to build a family. He told her of the despair he had felt as one lead after another proved futile until finally a sheriff in Center City had told him that his wife had been killed along with five others in a landslide.

"I hardly remember the entire next year," he said, staring into the fire. "My head was such a jumble of feelings—grief for the lost love of my youth, but my overwhelming feeling was guilt."

"Guilt?"

He didn't turn to look at her. "Guilt for not being able to give her what she needed, for driving her away, I suppose. I thought I was spending all my time working in order to build a future for us both, but later I could see that by leaving her alone with her fears and her insecurities, I was destroying the only chance we ever had for a future."

"Most women would feel lucky to have a husband who was working hard to develop a career in order to provide for his family."

"I think Samantha thought that part would come automatically. She never understood that sometimes it was necessary to work hard in order to live well. Then, when she found out she was going to have a baby, it was almost as if she went a little crazy. She said she wasn't about to struggle all her life on my paltry salary and raise a bunch of squalling brats."

Amelia shuddered. "Your Samantha sounds like a real prize."

Gabe finally turned his gaze back to her from the fire. "She needed to grow up, and I didn't give her the chance. So she took what she thought was the easy way—ran off with a fellow who seemed to have a lot of ready cash and was willing to make life seem like a party again."

"I'm surprised you even bothered to go after her."

"She was my wife. I was promised to her for better or worse. I believed in those things back then." His smile was twisted. "And then there was the child . . ."

"So when you heard she was dead, you thought your baby had died along with her."

He nodded, remembering. "As I said before, the next year or so was pretty rough. I woke up one morning in Seattle getting sick to my stomach into a horse trough on Skid Road, and I realized that Samantha had not just destroyed herself and my baby—she'd destroyed me, too. The thought made me so damn mad that I went out that day and got a job in a logging camp. I was a high rigger, the most dangerous work they had to offer, but I didn't care. I started making good money and at night I started winning even better money. It wasn't hard. Most of the shantyboys in the camps weren't very good at numbers, and numbers had been my life. Card playing just came natural."

He paused. Amelia hadn't moved a muscle during his entire recital. "So you gave up on the logging and went to just gambling?" she prompted.

"I stuck with the logging for a couple years, then there didn't seem much point to it anymore. I drifted down to the gold camps—California, Colorado."

"With Miss Lotta Crabtree," Amelia put in a bit testily.

Gabe threw back his head and laughed. It was a welcome break from the intensity of his tale. "Why, Miss Prescott, I do believe you're jealous."

Amelia blushed. "I just remember that you had mentioned her."

"And I thought you were half-asleep that first night when I was telling Parker and Morgan about those days. I didn't think you were paying the least bit of attention to me."

"I was paying attention," she said, her eyes intense. His confession had changed something between them, moved them from carefree lovers to a more complex level, one where shared pain soldered the bond.

Gabe sat back in his tiny chair and studied her. "I'm going to break the promise I made you earlier this afternoon, tenderfoot. I'm going to kiss you." His voice had grown suddenly hoarse. He cleared it and tried to lighten the mood. "One kiss—just because you had the gumption to admit that you were attracted to my charming demeanor and baby blue eyes from the moment you set eyes on me."

"I said no such thing, Gabe Hatch." She pushed her rocker back away from him.

"That's what it sounded like to me."

"Well, you're wrong."

"All right." He sat his chair upright again. "I won't kiss you, then."

"I should hope not." She put her hands primly on her knees and started her rocker in motion again.

Gabe watched as her body swayed back and forth in natural rhythm with the movement of the chair. Desire smoldered deep in his belly. He tried to keep it at bay by returning to the subject of his past. "So now you know the story of my life. It's not such a pretty picture, especially when you consider that all these years I've had a son who's never even seen his father."

"But that wasn't your fault," Amelia said gently.

He shrugged. "Whose fault it was doesn't change the result for the boy. He's still been without a father."

"But now, surely, you can find him and explain."

Gabe stretched his neck and looked up at the ceiling. "It might not be that easy." He told her about Big Jim and Samantha's threats to keep the boy's whereabouts a secret. "Driscoll seems to think that as long as he has control of Samantha, he can control me."

"I can't imagine *anyone* thinking that they can control you," she said fervently.

Gabe smiled at her disarming confidence in him. "I can think of only one person I might let control me, and it's definitely not Driscoll." He made a little nod in her direction. "But it doesn't make any difference now, because the good townspeople of Deadwood have pre-empted Driscoll's plans."

"What do you mean?"

"They've booted me off the commission. Seems they're too respectable to be associated with someone whose wife is the current town scandal."

Amelia huffed with indignation. "They're a bunch of fools!"

"I tend to agree. But, nevertheless, it was done. And the good thing is that it leaves me free to search for Jeremy."

"He's called Jeremy?"

"Yes." He stood and walked over to the fireplace. "That's all I know about him. I don't know what color hair he has or what kind of food he likes to eat. I don't know if he plays with a hoop in the streets of some city or rides a horse in the countryside. I don't know if he paints or studies or has bad dreams at night. The only thing I know about my son is that he's called Jeremy."

His voice broke and Amelia felt tears rise in her own throat. "You'll know all those things soon, Gabe. I'm sure of it. And you'll make a wonderful father for him."

He walked back to her chair and picked her up, then reseated himself in the rocker with her in his lap, as they had sat so often together in the oversize chair up in his cabin. He dropped his head to her breast. "I don't know anything about being a father," he said in a muffled voice. "I don't even know how to go about finding my only child."

She held him against her for a long moment. The fire had burned low, and it was almost dark in the room. Through the thin fabric of her dress she felt moisture from his cheeks. "Oh, Gabe," she said in a trembling voice. Then she put her hands on either side of his head and pulled him toward her. Under the soft hair of his mustache she found his mouth. He seemed to hardly respond, but she continued to kiss him, tugging his lower lip between hers. Suddenly he clutched her tightly and pulled back. "I've said I wouldn't kiss you again, Amelia, until I have the right."

She leaned up so that she could whisper directly in his ear. "I'm giving you the right, Gabe."

He turned his face to claim her mouth in a long kiss that left each of them out of breath. Involuntarily her body squirmed against him in the chair. He stood with her in his arms to move to the bed. The first time they had been together in her bed they'd been surprised by her brother, but both were beyond caring about that now. Their parting, the life-and-death scenes they had both witnessed over the past few days, the uncertainty over the future all combined to put a desperation into their lovemaking that they'd never before experienced.

He stripped her clothes off her roughly, then made up for it by gently sucking at her breasts and the tender skin at the base of her neck.

She responded by helping him off with his own clothes and running her hands along the washboard hardness of his chest and stomach, then lower to his fully aroused manhood. He drew in a tight breath as she encircled him with her hands. And after just two or three strokes he reached down to brush her hands aside and guide himself inside her. They stayed joined and quiet for a long moment, satisfied just to be part of each other again as if the world had suddenly shifted into rightness.

But the exigencies of their bodies wouldn't let them savor the sensation. He started to move within her, reaching deep until she dug her fingers into his naked back and arched like a drawn bow. Gabe had shed tears only once before in his life, but he felt them flow now as she joined him in an increasingly frantic natural rhythm that seemed to take all the emotions of the past few days and center them in an incredible explosion of sensation. He cried out her name as they climaxed together, and she sealed his lips with an openmouthed kiss that went on and on, even as the flush of lovemaking began to recede from their bodies.

Gabe was heavy and sated on top of her. She held him tightly as if that way she could keep him there forever. But as the moments passed, his breathing returned to normal, and he shivered. He pushed himself up with his arms, allowing their moist skin to unstick itself. Then he rolled over and out of the bed. "I'd best build the fire back up," he said. "It's grown chilly."

Amelia's heart sank at his distant tone and words. "We can go underneath the blankets," she said. "We'll be warm enough."

But he'd already reached to pull on his pants. Without answering her he went over to the fire, stirred the coals with a small log, then added it and two others to the pile.

Amelia began to feel self-conscious lying naked by herself on the bed. She slid under the covers, then held them open as he turned back to the bed. "Aren't you coming back?"

He walked slowly over to her. Backlit by the fire, his wide shoulders and narrow waist looked even more powerful than usual. The expression on his face was hidden in the darkness. When he reached the bed, he tucked the covers around her and sat down on top of them. "I'll not have your brother walk in on us again, tenderfoot," he said lightly.

She tried to make out the features of his face. "My brother's not the reason you're leaving," she said. There was a strange pain in her chest as if she'd run uphill too hard.

He picked up her hand and kissed it. "I hadn't planned for this to happen tonight," he said.

"You're sorry it happened?" Her tone was defensive. Her body felt as if it had cooled down fifty degrees in the space of minutes. Now she shivered under the sheet.

"My foolish, beautiful girl. How could I possibly be sorry about what we just shared? It's just that..."

He paused and rubbed the back of her hand where he held it against his leg.

"Just that what?"

"I guess too much has happened this past week—my wife awakening from the dead, discovering that I have a son, the smallpox taking away an ethereal young girl like Claire." He shook his head. "Maybe even the rejection by the commission has affected me more than I would have thought. Somehow I feel like I need to start to put my life in order."

A tremendous coldness settled over her. "Which means that you don't want to be with me anymore."

"No." The denial didn't sound convincing. "It means that I have to start doing things the right way, in the right order. And being with you like this when I'm still married to Sam is somehow not the right way."

The part of Amelia she had inherited from her mother wanted to cheer his sentiments. A lost soul is saved. A sinner repents. She'd been steeped in the concept since she was a babe. But the other part of her wanted to rail out at him for leaving her behind as he embarked on this new life redemption of his. Couldn't they work together to put his life back in place—fight Driscoll and his wife, find his son—together? But he seemed to be saying that he didn't want her involvement in his life, at least for now. He didn't even want to make love to her anymore.

"Perhaps you're right. Parker and Morgan could be back any time. You'd better leave." Her tone was colder than she had intended.

"How can I make you understand?" There was a crack in his voice again, and for a moment Amelia could hardly believe that this was the same cocky, self-confident man she had met when she had first arrived in Deadwood.

Her own hurt eased as she absorbed some of his. "I do understand, Gabe. Honestly. I hope you find the new life you seek, and I hope you find your son."

Gabe stood and made a gesture of impatience with his hands. "You sound as if you're saying goodbye."

"Isn't that what you're trying to say to me?"

"I'm just saying that the time isn't right for us. One of these days I'm going to have my life back in order, and then I'm going to ride up to that big banker's mansion of yours in New York City—"

"We don't live in a mansion," she interrupted in protest.

But he continued. "Ride up to your house and demand that your father give me the hand of his daughter in marriage."

She felt a glow of pleasure at the word, but the feeling faded quickly. It was all a nice fantasy, perhaps one deliberately voiced to make it easier for Gabe to walk out that door and leave her now. "And if my father's daughter has already chosen another from her many suitors back home?" she asked carefully.

She could see the white of his teeth in the darkness. "I'd steal her back from under his nose and challenge the blackguard to a duel."

"They don't fight duels anymore in New York, Gabe." She gave a little chuckle at the notion, in spite of the heaviness in her heart. "Besides, you're going to be reformed, remember?"

"Ah, yes. Well, then, I'd not hurt the fellow, I'd just scare the bejesus out of him and be sure he never set eyes on you again."

She smiled sadly. "So I'm to wait for you?"

He leaned down and kissed her. "If you know what's good for you, madam."

Without another word he stood and walked quickly out of the room. She turned around, propped her head on her hands and stared at the fire. Two months ago she had had no idea life could get so complicated. Suddenly she had found herself wildly in love with a man who said he could not love her back—at least not yet— but who wanted her to wait until some unspecified time when he would be free to seek her out. As her father would say, it did not sound like the most promising of propositions. But her father dealt in income statements and profits and balance sheets. She couldn't remember him ever teaching his daughter how to make those kinds of judgments when the proposition was one of the heart.

Chapter Seventeen

Amelia walked out of the telegraph office, a satisfied smile on her face. It felt good to be doing something positive for a change—acting rather than reacting. She had gotten the idea the night before when she had begun thinking about her father. One of the things both her parents had taught their children was that every person had the power to shape his or her life for the better. So Amelia had decided to start doing a little shaping for herself, and the wire she had just sent was the beginning.

The next order of business was to find her brother. Parker and Morgan had not come home again last night, and she was worried. She would have thought that Morgan would have sent word out to let her know that they were all right.

She squared her shoulders and headed down the street toward the Lucky Horseshoe. She had no desire to run into the disagreeable Mr. Driscoll, nor to run into Gabe, for that matter, but she figured that the saloon was the likeliest place to look for Parker. Before leaving she had slipped her little revolver into her reticule. She had absolutely no intention of using it, nor any illusions that it would do the least good if she did. Her lessons with

Gabe had not progressed far enough—at least the *shooting* lessons. But the heavy bump of the gun against her thigh was somehow reassuring.

She reached the saloon and, with a little quiver of misgiving, pulled open the door. She had calculated that it would not be too crowded at this early hour, and it appeared that she had been correct. In fact, as she looked around, she could see that the place was empty except for one table of cardplayers in the rear of the room and two people near the bar. One was a short, bewhiskered man who stood behind the bar polishing glasses. He was talking to a woman on a barstool in front of him. The cardplayers ignored Amelia's entrance, but the two at the bar noticed her entry at once.

"Can I help you, ma'am?" the bartender called. "Do you need directions somewhere?"

Amelia took a step into the room, squinting to see if any of the players were Parker or Morgan. They were not. Then she looked around the room. In the midst of her discomfort at being in such a place, she felt a prick of curiosity. There were paintings over the bar, just as she had heard described in the crusades she had attended with her mother. The ladies in them were quite lovely, and quite naked, draped in sheets that seemed to hit at just the wrong spots to provide decency.

She turned to the man who had spoken to her. "I'm not lost. I was just looking for my brother, Parker Prescott. Perhaps you could tell me if you've seen him here."

When Amelia said her brother's name there was a quick gasp from the woman on the stool. She jumped down and sauntered across the room. "You're the Prescott girl?" she asked, assessing Amelia with hostile green eyes.

Amelia blinked in surprise. "I'm Amelia Prescott," she answered.

The woman drew nearer. "So *you're* the little birdie who's currently feathering Gabe's nest."

Suddenly Amelia understood who the woman must be, and she drew back, horrified. She had thought her one of the bar girls, a pathetic kind of creature waiting around in whore's clothing for the next man who would buy her a drink. Amelia's first impulse was to turn and run, but her inquisitiveness got the better of her. "Are you Samantha?" she asked.

The woman smiled slyly. "I see that darling Gabe has told you about me."

"I . . . yes, he's told me about you."

"Oh, that's right. When I left him in his room at the Willard yesterday, I believe he was about to ride out to see you."

This woman had been in Gabe's *room?* But then, why not? She was, after all, his lawful wife. Suddenly she felt a surge of compassion for him. No wonder he felt as if he needed to find a fresh life for himself. Not for one minute did she believe that Samantha had been at Gabe's hotel for the purpose she was trying to imply. She had an unkind urge to puncture the woman's arrogance. "Yes, Gabe was at my place most of the day yesterday, and well into the night."

Samantha's large breasts puffed out noticeably. "Gabe always was one to have his toys on the side," she said. Her smile no longer reached her eyes. "Of course, if I snapped my fingers, he'd always come running back to me."

Her description of their marriage was nothing like the one Gabe had given her, and Amelia felt Gabe's account to be the more credible. She decided all at once that she couldn't stand the sight of the woman's smiling, painted face. "Snap away, Samantha," she said with a satisfyingly catty smile of her own. "I think you'll find that he's not coming back anymore."

Samantha's whole body tensed. Her arm came up, and for a moment Amelia thought the woman was going to slap her. But suddenly a loud voice called from the top of the stairs. "What's this? We have a visitor, I see."

Both women turned to see Big Jim trotting down the stairs toward them, his belly flopping with each step. "Miss Prescott," he said in his booming voice. "To what do we owe the honor?"

Amelia wished she had turned and left the minute she had seen that Parker was not in the bar. But it was too late now. She drew herself up and fingered the heavy reticule dangling at her side. "I was about to leave, Mr. Driscoll. I just came in looking for my brother."

He came over to her and took her elbow, bringing her farther into the room. The onion scent of his breath brought back their other disagreeable encounter out at the cabin. She pulled out of his grasp. "Now, your brother's an unfortunate case, Miss Prescott," Driscoll said in a concerned tone.

At his words she stopped pulling away. "What do you mean?"

"He was here two days ago and lost just about everything but his long johns, begging your ladies' pardon, in a friendly game." He leaned so close she could see the flash of his gold tooth. "Thing is, your brother's a might sore-tempered. He accused Deuce Connors—who's as honest Injun as they come—of stacking the cards. Then he started ranting against me and my fine establishment. Saying crazy things like I was responsible for starting up the smallpox that killed his sweetheart. Crazy things. I do believe your brother was the worse for drink that night, Miss Prescott.''

Amelia felt sick to her stomach. She glanced over at Samantha, who was watching the exchange with a grim smile of satisfaction. "What happened?" she asked.

"Why, my boys had to throw him out. They had to work him up a little to do it, too. It wasn't their fault. The fracas was entirely your brother's doing.''

Amelia backed up to the door, grasping for the handle. "Where is he?" she managed.

Driscoll shrugged and walked toward her, putting his hand roughly around her upper arm. "I think you'd better come over here and have a drink of water. You're looking a bit peaked, Miss Prescott.''

His grip tightened painfully as he tried to pull her back into the room. She pushed against his soft chest with her free hand and wrenched herself away, then fled out the door, her heart beating overtime. She took no time to reflect on her escape. Fear over what had become of Parker rose in her throat. What had Driscoll's men done to him? Where was he? She started running down the street, not knowing where she was heading. Suddenly arms grabbed her and twirled her around, and she was being held against Gabe's solid, comforting chest.

"They've beaten up Parker," she panted. "Driscoll's men. The night before last. And I've heard nothing of him. I don't even know where he is.''

Gabe put his arms around her and spoke calmly. "I know. I've just heard about it myself. He's over at Mattie's, Amelia. He's all right.''

"I have to go to him.''

"Of course, but get your breath first. It won't help him to have you fly in there all hysterical."

Her heart started to slow and she realized that Gabe's advice was sound. She straightened her dress and her hair and took a couple of deep breaths to compose herself. "I'm all right now," she said.

"I'll go with you."

Gabe's hand on her arm steadied her as they quickly made their way down to Mattie's. The little madam met them at the door, her words tumbling out. "I wanted to send for you, Amelia, but your brother absolutely forbade it. He wouldn't even let Morgan ride out to you—said he didn't want you to see him like this because it had been his own blamed fault again. And he was right about that much of it, I reckon. The idea of trying to go up single-handed against Big Jim, why, it makes my hair stand on end just thinking about it."

Amelia was interested in only one thing. "Is he all right?"

Mattie smiled, and Amelia felt a rush of relief. "Well, now, he could pass as an old coon with those pretty shiners he got himself, and he just might have a rib or two broke, but he's going to be fine. I was going to come out and tell you about it today whether he was ready to let me or not."

Amelia took off her bonnet and set it on the hall table. "Where is he?" she asked, anger beginning to replace her fear.

"He's up in Claire's room. He asked to stay there."

The mention of Claire's name made Amelia hesitate. No matter how riled she might be at her brother for getting himself into yet another scrape with Big Jim and, especially, for not letting her know about it when he was badly hurt, she had to remember that he was still suffering from the effects of grief. He wasn't his normal cheerful, sensible self.

"Thank you for taking care of him," she said to Mattie, then she turned to climb the stairs, with Gabe following close behind her. When they reached the second floor, she stopped. Now that she knew Parker was all right, there was something she wanted to say to Gabe.

"I met your wife," she told him.

Gabe looked taken aback. "You met Samantha?"

"Yes. This morning at the Lucky Horseshoe, when I went to look for Parker. It wasn't the most pleasant encounter."

"Encounters with Samantha these days usually aren't."

She wanted to tell Gabe about the feeling of sympathy for him that had come over her when she'd realized that he was legally tied to such a person. But something in the stiff way he held himself when he'd said his wife's name made her reluctant to speak. She didn't think he would welcome her pity.

She paused a moment more, then said, "Things got even worse when Big Jim showed up."

Now Gabe looked irritated. "What in thunderation made you go to a place like that, tenderfoot? Have your brains leaked plumb out of your head?"

"I just thought it was the most logical place to look for my brother."

"Did Driscoll bother you?"

"No." She betrayed herself with a flicker of her eyes.

"What did he do to you?" Gabe's voice became deadly calm.

"Nothing, really. He just sort of pulled on my arm...." She rubbed the spot which, now that she thought about it, still ached.

Gabe clamped his jaw. Without a word he unfastened the buttons at her wrist and pushed the sleeve up her slender arm, revealing red, finger-sized welts that were beginning to turn purplish. He stared at them a long moment, then pulled the sleeve back down and carefully buttoned it again. The look in his eyes gave her the same kind of panic she had felt back in the saloon when she had first heard about Parker's fight. "Forget about it, Gabe," she urged. "I'm all right now. And I want to go in and see my brother."

She stepped around him and walked down the hall to Claire's room. Gabe followed her without a word.

Parker was sleeping when they opened the door, but he awoke and sat up as they entered. Amelia had thought she was prepared after Mattie's comment about the raccoon, but she gave a little gasp at the sight of him. Gabe's hand came up to rest reassuringly on her shoulder.

Parker grinned ruefully. "Sorry, sis. Now you can see why I didn't want them to send for you to hover over me until I started to look a little better. If you think this is bad, you should have seen me night before last."

"Yes, I should have," she replied indignantly. "I should have been here with you, no matter what you looked like."

"Well, it's over now. I'm going to live, more's the pity."

She walked over and sat next to him on the bed, putting her arms around him. "Don't talk like that, Parker. I wouldn't know what to do if anything happened to you."

He winced as her arms brushed his sore ribs. "Ah! It's look, but don't touch, sis. Nickel a peek."

Perhaps the beating had restored some of his natural humor. He actually sounded better than he had since before Claire's death. She pulled back from him. "Are you truly all right?" she asked.

He winked at her. "Truly. But I do have a matter I'd like to discuss with Gabe, if you wouldn't mind leaving us alone for a few minutes."

He shot a straight glance over at the gambler, who stood by the door, and his look was answered by a nod of understanding from Gabe. Amelia felt excluded by some kind of peculiar male communication. Excluded and uneasy. "As a matter of fact, I would mind," she said, chin up. "I want to hear just exactly what you're going to discuss."

Gabe spoke soothingly, as if to a child. "Why don't you go fix your brother some tea, sweetheart? I'm sure Mattie would like to fill you in on how all your patients here are doing."

She looked from Gabe back to her brother as they both waited expectantly for her to leave. Then she bounced backward on the bed to a more comfortable seat and crossed her arms. "I'm not going anywhere. Not until you two tell me what you're up to."

Gabe looked at Parker, who lifted his eyebrows and shook his head in resignation. "She hasn't listened to me for twenty-one years," he said. "I don't know why I should expect that she'd start now."

Gabe cleared his throat. "Well, then..."

"I'm going after Driscoll," Parker said bluntly.

Amelia dropped her arms in surprise, making her skirts flounce up around her, but Gabe looked as if he had anticipated Parker's remark.

"No one can go after Driscoll alone. That's why the commission was a good idea. When everyone stands together—"

"Your precious commission!" Parker exploded. "You weren't in town yesterday, were you?"

Amelia thought she detected a flush on Gabe's face and wondered if he was remembering that yesterday he had been in her bed.

"No, I wasn't here."

"You missed the great showdown," Parker went on, flinging his hands around. "The townspeople up against Big Bad Jim. Fix up your shacks, Jim, or we'll burn them. That was the idea, right?"

Gabe nodded. "We drew up a resolution."

"Which was not worth the damn paper it was written on. Your commissioners backed off—to a man. They stood together, all right, and Driscoll was given free rein to build more of his filthy dumps."

"What do you mean, they backed off?"

"Oh, they went up to the shantytown to burn it down. Had their torches ready and everything." Parker gave a snort of disgust. "A bunch of pantywaist merchants against Driscoll's hired guns. Who do you think won out? All it took was a few threats and the commissioners turned tail and ran."

Gabe slapped his thigh as if reaching for an imaginary gun and let out an exasperated sigh. "They should have anticipated that. They should have had a plan worked out before they ever started up there."

"Yeah, well. They didn't. So now we're just supposed to sit around and wait until the next disease comes along to kill off more young women like Claire."

"Take it easy, partner. If you want to go against Driscoll, you can't work yourself up into a frenzy.

You'll fare no better than the commissioners did. We need to plan how to go about this."

"Are you saying you'll help me?"

Gabe glanced at Amelia's arm. "It turns out I've more than one score to settle with Driscoll, too."

Amelia bounced off the bed and stood with her hands on her hips, glaring at them. "You're idiots, both of you. Do you want to end up with the rest of your ribs broken, Parker? Or maybe dead? That would certainly make everything better, wouldn't it?"

They both gave her a kind of "women-don't-understand-these-things" look, which only added to her fury. "Isn't there some sort of territorial law you could send for to bring order to this town? To stop the crooked card games? To make sure innocent people don't get beat up by a bunch of hired thugs?"

"We tried the lawful way with the commission. It didn't seem to work," Gabe said. "The only thing a man like Driscoll understands is a show of power to match his own."

"Oh, fine. And you and Parker going up against him would be a show of power equal to all the gunmen he's got working for him."

Gabe looked over to Parker with a grin. "We'd be a good start, wouldn't we, partner?"

Parker grinned back, and Amelia stamped her foot in frustration.

"You may not know it, tenderfoot," Gabe continued, "but your brother's a natural. He can drill an eagle's eye at three hundred yards."

She rolled her eyes. "All right. I give up. If you two are going to play wild West, so am I. If you go to confront Driscoll, I'm going with you."

In unison the two men protested. "You'd just be in the way, sis," Parker said, which was not the first time in her life she'd heard such a statement from her older brother.

"We'll lock you up in here," Gabe threatened.

She smiled calmly. "Mattie and the girls will let me out."

The argument went on for several minutes. Gabe was the first to weaken. "I suppose you might provide a kind of distraction that would be to our advantage. But you'll do exactly as you're told and not take any chances."

"That's fine with me."

"You'll carry a gun," he continued, "and under no circumstances will you fire it."

She looked as if she was about to object, but he warded her off with a raised hand. "Unlike your brother, tenderfoot, you couldn't plug an eagle's eye if the bird were sitting on your toe. I don't want you to shoot one of us by mistake."

"What's all this talk of shooting, anyway?" Amelia asked impatiently. "It would be suicide for the three of us to walk into a gunfight with Driscoll's men."

"Morgan will help," Parker put in.

"So that makes three, four with me, against how many? A dozen professional gunslingers?"

"Not more than half a dozen, unless you count Roscoe and Fingers, the piano player," Gabe answered nonchalantly.

"I don't think we need to worry about either one of them," Parker observed.

"You're insane, both of you," Amelia said.

Gabe walked over to her and took her hand. "It's like I told you, tenderfoot. There comes a time when you either start to take your life in hand or let it all go to hell. Same's true of this town. The commissioners were on the right track. And in spite of everything, I still think that they are good men. They just need a little bit of steel to stiffen those spines of theirs." He turned to Parker on the bed. "I'll be back shortly, partner. You find Morgan and make sure your guns are oiled up." He bent and gave Amelia a kiss on the cheek, then added over his shoulder to Parker, "And try to keep this sister of yours under control."

"Keep *me* under control," Amelia sputtered, but Gabe was already out the door and halfway down the hall.

Four Fingers had started up on the piano getting ready for the evening rush. Samantha sat at the bar, tapping her foot absently. She lifted a shot glass and drank half the contents in one gulp. Suddenly Driscoll came up behind her and pulled the glass out of her hand.

"Take it easy on that stuff. You've been downing it pretty steady since your tête-à-tête with your husband's lover this morning. She kind of got under your skin, didn't she?"

"Leave it to Gabe to fall for a priggish little schoolmarm like that."

"Nothing schoolmarmish about her," Driscoll said. "She's quite a looker."

"He'd drop her cold if I'd have him back."

Driscoll sat on the stool next to her. "Yeah, of course he would. And I'm the queen of England." He gave a harsh laugh.

"I could get him back any time I wanted," she said. Her words were beginning to run together.

"What use does Hatch have for a stinking drunk like you?" he asked, pushing her arm away from him. "Or me, either, for that matter. I've just about decided to send you back to whoring in the gold camps where you belong."

She reached out and clawed the side of his face, leaving red trails with her nails. He grabbed her wrist and twisted it viciously. "I'll break your arm if you try anything like that again."

She backed off the stool and retreated to the end of the bar, rubbing her bruised wrist. "You're a cold-hearted bastard, Jim," she said fiercely.

"Yeah, well, tell it to someone who gives a damn." He turned to Roscoe, who had been listening uncomfortably to their exchange. "No more for her tonight," he told the bartender. Roscoe nodded and collected Samantha's glass.

Driscoll turned to leave, then stopped as the piano playing abruptly ceased. Just inside the doorway a group of newcomers was assembling—several of the town merchants, Harrington, the banker, Nels Nelson from over at the Willard. At the front of the group stood Gabe Hatch, both Prescotts and their Welsh companion. Driscoll sat back down on the barstool and faced them, leaning his elbows back up against the bar. His eyes darted to find his men stationed around the room, and he gave them almost imperceptible nods.

"Come in, gentlemen, and Miss Prescott," he added with a little bow to Amelia. "The games are hot tonight and the beer is cheap."

"We're not here to drink or play," Gabe said calmly.

"We only offer one other commodity in this saloon. But I assume you gentlemen didn't come to buy a whore. Even a pretty one like Miss Samantha, here."

He tipped his head toward the end of the bar where Samantha stood gripping the polished wood with white knuckles.

Gabe's face tightened at Driscoll's words, and his eyes went to Samantha for just a minute, but he continued as if the insult had not been spoken. "We've come for three things, Driscoll. Once we get them, we'll leave, all peaceful-like, and everyone will be happy."

Driscoll gave him an oily smile. "I'm a peaceable man, Hatch. What did you have in mind?"

Gabe took a few steps closer, allowing the men with him to move into the room. Amelia stayed where she was next to Parker, fingering her revolver, which she held hidden in her skirts. Morgan stood a little distant from the rest, his eyes wary.

"First, we need an apology to Mr. Prescott here and repayment of funds illegally won from him two nights ago by Deuce Connors."

"Illegally?" Big Jim asked mildly.

"The game was crooked. And if we square up this time, we won't try to go back and collect for all the other crooked games Connors has run for you in the past. Second, we need to have you sign an agreement saying that if your shantytown properties are not cleaned up within the next thirty days, you agree to have the matter submitted to the jurisdiction of the territorial courts in Yankton."

"Some of these gentlemen and I came to a different arrangement yesterday, Gabe. I don't believe you were around."

"These gentlemen have changed their minds, Driscoll. That arrangement's been canceled. This is the new one." He held up a legal-looking paper.

Driscoll didn't even give the document a glance. "You said there were three things."

Gabe looked down the bar again at his wife. "I want to know where my boy is. We can settle up that part in private, if you prefer."

There was a sound of movement across the room. One of Driscoll's henchmen had pulled out his gun and was pointing it at Gabe. "Should I just go ahead and plug him, boss?" he said.

Out of sheer instinct Amelia found herself tightening her fingers on her revolver, but before she or anyone else could make a move, Morgan loomed up behind the gunman and enveloped him in a bear hug that knocked the gun out of his hand and sent it clattering across the floor. Then the big Welshman picked up the man from the neck and the seat of his pants and hurled him toward the thick frosted glass of the front door. He went sailing through with a tremendous shattering of glass. Through the broken shards they could see him drag himself down the steps and off into the dust of the street, leaving a trail of red behind him.

Gabe hadn't moved a muscle.

"Now, how about if we let Gabe and Mr. Driscoll continue their discussion?" Morgan asked calmly.

The room was quiet. Driscoll's flabby cheeks had taken on blotches of red. "I don't care how many baboons you bring in here, Hatch," he said with a glance at Morgan. "There's no way you can fight me." He moved heavily off the stool. "Look, I'm a reasonable man. Let's make a deal. Forget about the shantytown. If the people up there want to live like animals, that's their problem. I just build the shacks and charge the rent. So we'll let it be. And, in return, I'll see you get your son back." He nodded his head toward Samantha. "This piece of baggage you're married to isn't worth any more problems."

As he spoke, his eyes gave subtle signals to the rest of his men, stationed around the room. "We all want to live in peace together in this town," Driscoll continued, his voice even. Suddenly he gave a quick nod of his head. Four men who had been sitting at a corner table, apparently in a peaceful game of cards, leapt to their feet. Before anyone could react, two of them jumped on top of Morgan, knocking him to the ground, two more grabbed Gabe's arms and twisted them painfully behind them. Deuce Connors, who had been standing just down the bar from Driscoll, drew his gun and took a step closer to Parker. "Make a move, New York," he growled, "and you're dead."

Fear surged through Amelia's arms and legs. Her eyes on Connors, she started to raise her gun. All at once she was wrenched backward by a strong arm around her neck. The barrel of a revolver was shoved up against the side of her head. She couldn't see the man who held her.

Driscoll leaned back against the wall. "Well, now, that's better. I knew we'd find a peaceable way to have this discussion." He glanced over to where two of his men were now kneeling on top of Morgan. One held a gun at the back of his neck. "If he moves so much as an eyelash, pull the trigger," he told them.

Ignoring Gabe, who had ceased to struggle against his captors, Driscoll addressed the other commissioners. "Now, I'm disappointed in you gentlemen. I thought we had this all settled yesterday. But I'm a very patient fellow, and once again I'm going to overlook our little disagreement. I've come to the conclusion that Mr. Hatch here is the real problem, so if you all will just head out that door, I'll see that his days of disrupting our town's harmony are at an end."

Harrington lowered his hands and turned toward the door. The others appeared more reluctant. "None of this has to be settled with violence," Nels Nelson said, his voice higher than normal.

Driscoll nodded. "You're right. That's why I'm giving you folks a chance to leave peaceful-like. Prescott, you can leave, too. Take your sister. My business is only with Hatch."

"Take her out of here, partner," Gabe said to Parker in a low voice.

The man holding Amelia pulled her gun out of her hand, then loosened his hold. Behind them, David Harrington slipped quietly out the door. No one else made a move to leave.

Driscoll gave a snort of impatience. "If you'd all rather watch, it's all right with me." He made a signal with his hand toward Deuce, who shifted his aim from Parker to Gabe. The men holding Gabe took a step away from him.

Amelia gave a cry of alarm that died in the midst of a deafening blast of a gun from the end of the bar. All eyes turned to see Samantha, her eyes wild, holding Roscoe's Colt .45 in both her shaking hands, still pointed at Driscoll. The saloon owner had stiffened at the sound of the shot, then, as if some kind of force was holding his body, fell very slowly off the front of the barstool to the floor. His head lay at an odd angle, and a trickle of blood seeped from a hole at the side of his neck.

Deuce's gun, still trained on Gabe, wavered. Gabe kicked it out of his hand. He and Parker both had their own guns unholstered and were covering Driscoll's men, but they seemed so stunned by what had happened to their employer that none appeared to be a threat. Gabe pushed Amelia behind Parker. Then he walked steadily over and pulled the gun gently from Samantha's frozen hands. The two men on Morgan let him go. He stood and went to kneel beside Big Jim, putting his hand on the saloon owner's neck alongside the wound. Then he looked over at Gabe and confirmed what everyone already knew. "Big Jim's dead."

Chapter Eighteen

The murder of wealthy property owner James W. Driscoll in Deadwood last week created a stir all the way to the territorial government in Yankton. Government representatives decried Deadwood's increasing reputation for lawlessness, which was enhanced earlier this summer when Jack McCall, murderer of James Butler "Wild Bill" Hickok, was acquitted in a vigilante trial. In an effort to avoid a repeat of the McCall debacle, the government sent a marshal to take Mr. Driscoll's accused killer, Mrs. Samantha Hatch, into custody and transport her back to the territorial capital for trial. Mrs. Hatch was accompanied to Yankton by her husband, Gabriel.

Black Hills Pioneer, October 12, 1876

They had waited for two weeks, using the excuse that Parker's ribs needed to heal before the bruising stagecoach ride back across Dakota Territory. But both knew they were really waiting for some word from Gabe.

"I suppose we should start packing tomorrow," Amelia said after supper one night. "You seem to be feeling a lot better, and there's no reason to stay around."

"I should talk to Gabe before I leave," Parker said casually. "About the mine. After all, he's my partner."

"I thought you were just going to give it to him," she answered in the same indifferent tone.

"Well, I should at least talk with him."

It was getting late and Morgan had already gone out to his bed in the lean-to, but Amelia was restless. She'd heard nothing from Gabe and she'd not yet had an answer to the telegram she had sent to her father. Once again, she was beginning to think that the fantasies she had spun for herself about a life with Gabe were never going to come true. She stood, wrapped herself in her shawl and said, "I'm going for some air."

"Don't go out of sight of the cabin." Parker's mood had improved along with his appearance since the showdown at the Lucky Horseshoe. The purple color around his eyes had almost entirely faded.

"I'm just going to the bridge," she said. At the door she stopped and blurted out, "He's already told me that he's going to be busy getting his life back into order. He'll be more occupied than ever now with Samantha's troubles. And he has a son to find...."

Parker stood and walked over to her. "He'll still want to see you, sis. He's in love with you."

She shook her head, then pulled the shawl more closely around her shoulders. It wasn't officially winter yet, but it had certainly grown cold.

The mine was still in operation. Parker and Morgan continued to pan out a few flakes each day, about the same amount as before, just enough to keep the operation going. But the work outside in his beautiful valley seemed to be completing the healing process for

Parker. Each day the moments when his face tightened with grief became fewer. Little by little he was regaining some of his former lightheartedness.

"You know, sis," he said one night as he came in with Morgan for supper, "if it weren't for Father needing help, I'd never leave this place. In spite of everything we've been through—Claire's death, Driscoll's crooked card games—I love it. I love the West. It's intoxicating in a way that liquor never could be."

"And you ought to be a pretty good judge of that by now," Amelia said dryly.

Parker grinned and went over to give her a muddy hug. "I've learned my lesson there. I could give the sermon at one of Mother's temperance rallies."

"You're getting me dirty," she protested, pushing him away, but it gave her a lift to see her brother teasing once again. Though it would take him a long time to recover from losing Claire, it appeared that his good humor would bring him through it in the end. She wished some of it would rub off on her. She might have a harder time forgetting the love she had found and lost in Deadwood. That it was lost had become increasingly obvious as the days drifted by with no word from Gabe, not even a telegram letting them know where he was.

Morgan had followed in behind Parker with an armful of firewood, which he deposited next to the fireplace. "You might love it here, Parker, but I don't think it's going to make you the fortune you hoped for. We've been over your whole claim. You're not going to get much more than what you can pan out of the stream," he said.

"I know. I've come to terms with that. Anyway, I've been thinking that I'd like to move on—see the wide-open spaces that I hear the drovers talk about."

His eyes had that far-off look that made Amelia jumpy. "But you're not going to do that, right?" she asked hastily. "You're coming back home with me."

He gave a great sigh and pulled a chair up to the table. "Yes. I'm going home to sit hunched over columns of figures in a stuffy office at a bank where I'm the boss's son and not really welcomed by anyone, including my own father."

Amelia frowned. After some long hours of talks in the past few days, she was finally realizing the sacrifice it would be for Parker to go back, but she didn't know what to do about it. "Perhaps we can talk Father into retiring soon and finding someone else to run the bank."

"Perhaps," he said gloomily, reaching for the bowl of potatoes.

"I have a surprise for you for dessert," she said brightly. "I've made a pie."

She'd worked most of the day on her creation, but it was worth it. The crust had baked to golden perfection, and she'd picked and picked until her arms were ready to fall off in order to gather a fat heap of berries to make the filling.

"That sounds mighty fine, Missy," Morgan said, looking around the cabin for the promised pastry.

"I put it out in a box in the stream to cool," Amelia explained, proud of her new Western ingenuity.

Morgan and Parker exchanged a look across the table. "Maybe you'd better bring it back in, sis," Parker said carefully.

"It can wait until after dinner."

"You'd better fetch it now, Missy, while it's still out there to fetch," Morgan said in a warning tone.

Amelia jumped to her feet. "What a silly thing to say. Who would steal a pie out here?" But her misgivings increased as she walked quickly out of the cabin and down to the river where she had carefully placed the pie about an hour before supper. She had made sure to anchor the box securely so that it wouldn't come loose and be carried away by the current.

The sun had just set, but the twilight allowed her to clearly see the scene. A big raccoon was sitting up on its haunches, happily dipping its claws in and out of her pie and carrying dripping handfuls of berries to its mouth. She stood stock-still, unable to believe her eyes. Then she yelled and raced down the bank, flapping her skirts. Without much alarm, the fat, furry animal took a last swipe inside the box, then ambled off along the stream.

Amelia knelt in its place and grabbed the box. Only berry-stained fragments of her golden crust remained. She dropped the whole thing heavily back into the water with a wail of frustration.

"Look at it this way, you've made one of God's creatures a very happy little fellow today." She whirled around at the sound of a voice she had begun to think she might never hear again. In her distress over the pie she had not even heard Gabe walk up behind her.

"It was so p-perfect," she mourned.

He knelt beside her and wiped the tears from her cheeks. "You're the darnedest woman I've ever met, tenderfoot. You've traveled halfway across the country, been through a smallpox epidemic, witnessed a murder, all without a tear. But an old coon eats your pie and you cry like a baby."

"I'm not crying," she said, sniffing and running the backs of her hands impatiently over her eyes.

"Oh," Gabe said. He pulled a handkerchief from inside his jacket and handed it to her.

"I'm just mad, is all," she continued. "I was hoping to cheer Parker up with a nice piece of pie. He's gloomy about going back to New York." She dabbed at her face with his handkerchief as she let her eyes go avidly over Gabe's face, making herself realize that he was really here. Suddenly she didn't care a bit about the pie. She was elated and furious all at once. She wanted to shout at him—where have you been? Why haven't you contacted us? For two days she'd been holding on to news that could change his entire life, but she hadn't even known where to find him to tell him about it.

"He's gloomy about going back?" he repeated. "Were you planning on leaving without saying goodbye?"

She pulled herself a little up the bank and sat with her legs out straight in front of her. "We seemed to have no other choice, Mr. Hatch, since we had no idea where you *were.*"

"You knew I went to Yankton with Samantha."

"Yes." She felt suddenly petty, complaining about not hearing from him when his wife was undoubtedly in a fight for her very life. "What has happened to her?"

"The prosecutors aren't interested in hanging a woman, especially when there is evidence that she was abused by Driscoll."

"Abused?"

He nodded grimly. "The bastard. She had marks all over her body. I wish I'd killed him myself."

"Thank God you didn't. *You* they might have hung for it."

"She'll probably have to spend some time in prison. I've contacted her family back in St. Louis, and it looks like they're going to stand by her."

"And you?"

He went from his kneeling position to sit beside her, putting his legs out alongside hers. "She doesn't want me around. I believe Samantha did love me at one time, long ago. But love is a funny thing. It can turn itself inside out and become hate.''

"But in the end she saved your life.''

"Yes.'' His voice sounded brittle and sad. "I asked her why she did it. All she would say is that she owed me.''

Amelia put a hand on his arm. "I'm sorry, Gabe.'' She had some news for him that would no doubt make everything seem brighter, but it was not quite the moment to tell him. They stared at the rushing water for several minutes without speaking. Just being beside him again was making her feel as if the world had shifted back into place. But there was still a lot to be settled. "Does this mean you won't be able to get your divorce?'' she asked finally.

He looked at her, a glint in his eyes. "Remember that I told you I wouldn't kiss you again until I had the right?''

She nodded.

"So maybe this will answer your question.'' He reached for her and his mouth was on hers, teasing, then hungry and demanding. As if the contact was not enough, he hooked her legs with his and tumbled them both back on the bank. She could feel the damp grass beneath her head, hear the stream flowing alongside them, and then she could hear nothing, feel nothing but his lips and tongue drawing the life out of her and putting it back in. He stopped only when both were breathless and had grown hard against each other.

"Parker's up in the cabin?'' he asked with a groan.

"Yes,'' she whispered.

He pushed himself up away from her and said firmly, "Well, I can't offend my future brother-in-law.''

Amelia looked up at him and repeated slowly, "Brother-in-law?"

"That's what they call the brother of one's wife."

She hesitated another minute, looking into his handsome, smiling face. Then she sat up, indignant. "Do you call that a proper proposal, Mr. Hatch?"

He leaned over and grabbed the back of her neck, tilting her head for another long kiss. "No. If I could think of a way we could escape to my cabin without your watchdogs, sweetheart, I would spend the entire night proposing and proposing...." His voice faded as he reached for her again.

"Amelia!" came Parker's shout from the doorway.

They scrambled apart. "I'm down here, Parker. Gabe's come back."

The joy in her voice was unmistakable. Together they got to their feet and walked arm in arm up the little path to the cabin.

"Welcome back, partner," Parker said a little warily, studying his sister's face. "We were starting to think we had seen the last of you."

Gabe adjusted his jacket. "Sorry to disappoint you partner," he joked. "You see, I had made a promise to Amelia that I wouldn't kiss her again until I was free to do so. Trouble is, I discovered it was a mite hard to keep the promise when she was within kissing range."

Amelia's face had turned bright red. "Gabe!" she admonished.

"Your brother's a man now, sweetheart," he said, putting his arm around her shoulders again. "He understands these things. Anyway, I decided to stay on in Yankton until I could be sure that my divorce was progressing smoothly through the courts. It turns out that it's not too difficult to divorce a convicted felon, which is what poor Samantha will be by the end of the month.

I'm not technically free yet, but I figured I'd done enough to keep to the spirit of my promise, if not to the letter.''

Parker looked as if he wasn't completely convinced. "According to Amelia, you're not in the market to get yourself tied up again right away. Something about starting over on a new life."

Gabe reached up with his thumb to smooth it against Amelia's cheek, as if trying to make the red blush disappear. "I've realized that I can't start a new life or have any kind of life at all without your sister, Parker. And if you'd be willing to stand in for your father, I'm asking you formally to give me her hand in marriage."

"It's about time," Morgan grumbled from his seat in the corner.

Parker looked stunned for a minute, then answered, "I'm sorry, Gabe, but I can't do that."

Gabe's face fell, and Amelia looked at her brother in amazement.

Then Parker laughed and continued, "I'm afraid neither I nor my father would dare give away my sister's hand. My mother would hang us out to dry for not respecting her God-given female rights. So I guess you'll just have to take up the matter with Amelia herself."

Gabe took his arm from around her neck and moved in front of her. For a moment Amelia thought he was going to go down on his knees in an old-fashioned manner. But instead he grabbed her under her arms and pulled her up off her feet into a long kiss. It was somewhat more decorous than the ones they had shared on the riverbank, but it was thorough.

"I think the lady's willing," Morgan observed.

Parker turned away to tend the already blazing fire.

When Gabe finally set her down, Amelia's face was shining. "Congratulations, sis," Parker said over his shoulder as he stabbed the poker at the burning logs. There was just the faintest overshadow of unhappiness in his tone.

Amelia walked over to put her arms around him. She whispered in his ear, ''Someday you'll find love again, too, big brother.''

He put down the poker and gave her a hearty squeeze. Then he pulled her arms from his neck and turned to Gabe. ''So, what are your plans? How soon are you intending to rob me of my sister?''

Gabe laughed. ''I'm reforming, remember? I don't intend to rob anyone of anything. But seriously...'' He indicated the four chairs around the table and one by one they sat down. ''The divorce will come through in due time. I've good people working on it. And in the meantime, I'll be doing everything to find my son. And then there's a little matter of employment. I can't very well be a respected family man in New York City and continue gambling.''

''You'd be willing to live in New York?'' Amelia asked. She was trying to be serious, but a smile of sheer happiness kept breaking out on her face.

He reached across the table and took her hand. ''Tenderfoot, you've proven yourself. No one can say you didn't conquer the wild, woolly West. But unlike your vagabond brother here, your heart's back home.''

She knew he was right. She missed her parents, her home, the bustle of the city. She missed restaurant meals and starched clothes. She even missed Matilda's scoldings. ''But what will you do there?'' she asked.

He shrugged. ''There was a time when I was considered a rising young accountant in St. Louis. I imagine one of those Wall Street houses would be happy to hire on a talented fellow like me.''

Morgan had been listening to the conversation mostly in silence, but now he drawled, "Looks to me as if everyone's problems are about to be solved." The three younger people looked at him questioningly. He continued, "Parker hates the bank and doesn't want to live in New York. His pappy needs some good help, but doesn't want to take on anyone who's not in the family. Gabe, on the other hand, *wants* to live in New York with Missy, but doesn't have a job there. His specialty is numbers, and one of these days he's going to be a member of the family. Now, how would you young folks put all that together?"

Amelia grabbed one of Parker's hands in her left hand and one of Gabe's in her right. "Gabe can go to work for Father!" she exclaimed.

Morgan smiled benevolently. Parker and Gabe looked a little uncomfortable. "I don't want your father to think I'm marrying into the family in order to work at his bank," Gabe said.

"I don't want Father to think I don't care about him," Parker said.

"Don't be foolish, either of you. It will take Father and Mother about three minutes to see that Gabe and I are truly in love with each other. And once Father gets used to having someone in the family who really *wants* to work with his precious figures, he'll be so happy he'll wonder what he was thinking of to try to force you into it all those years."

"Are you sure?" Gabe asked.

"Do you really think so?" Parker asked at the same time.

"Of course she's right," Morgan said, his deep voice lending authority to the proposal.

And suddenly everyone was talking at once and laughing and making plans until Amelia stopped the chatter with a little shriek. "I haven't told you yet—the most important thing of all!"

She got up from the table and went over to retrieve a piece of paper from her valise. Then she walked over to Gabe and handed it to him, her dark eyes twinkling with excitement.

He took the paper from her fingers and read it. It was a telegram, addressed to her. "Have found lad at Burnham Academy NYC. Further instructions? When can we expect you home? Love, Father."

Gabe blanched and the paper fell out of his fingers. Amelia picked it up. "It's Jeremy, Gabe. They've found him!"

"But how...? When...?"

She sat down again, then bounced up and down on the seat with excitement as she told her story. "After giving everything away to all their causes over the years, my parents may not be rich, but they have acquired something more valuable—a wide-reaching, wonderful network of influential, good friends. My father can find out just about anything. So I asked him to start looking for your son. I sent the wire the day after you first told me about him."

Gabe was still ghost white. "He's in New York City?"

She nodded, giving another little bounce. "At a boarding school just minutes from my home. Can you believe it? It's a good school, too. Samantha at least did that much for him."

"A new wife and a new son in one fell swoop. You must be reeling, partner." Parker gave Gabe a friendly shove that almost knocked him off the stool.

"I can't believe it," he said, sounding dazed.

"I'll wire my father tomorrow to go check on him,"

Amelia said. "They can take him to live in our house until we arrive, if you like."

Gabe's eyes glazed. "It appears I'll owe a greater debt to the Prescott family than I can ever pay."

Amelia couldn't contain herself on the seat anymore. She jumped up and squirmed between Gabe and the table to deposit herself in his lap. Then she whispered suggestively for his ear only, "I'll think of a few interesting ways to collect on that debt."

Gabe put his arm around her and sighed with happiness. He shook his head and looked at Parker. "You know, partner, it's a lucky thing I came along when I did to keep this incorrigible sister of yours out of trouble."

Parker pushed back his chair and stood. "It looks like it's time for you and me to hit the sack, Morgan." He grabbed the Welshman by the arm and started dragging him out the door. Amelia had once again wrapped her arms around Gabe, and he had bent over her for a long, sweet kiss.

"But what about that pie?" Morgan protested.

Parker glanced back at the couple, who no longer seemed to notice their presence. "Sorry, Morgan. I'm afraid if you want pie, you're just going to have to go back home and sweet-talk Matilda."

*   *   *   *   *

Author Note

Shortly after the smallpox epidemic in the fall of 1876, the Deadwood Board of Health and Street Commissioners made themselves into a real city council and began the process of turning the town into a diverse community that, through the years, has retained the flavor of those early wild West days. A visit to this beautiful area today will take you right back to the time when gunfights were daily fare, and prospectors, gamblers, "ladies of the evening" and settlers were colorful actors in real-life Western dramas.

As for my drama, though Gabe and his lady are destined for a life of happy-ever-after in New York, we leave Parker heading west alone, still mourning his lost love. He has given up drinking and gambling and has resolved to guard his heart more closely in the future. This last resolution is sorely tried, however, when he ends up spending a long winter in Wyoming Territory on the Lucky Stars cattle ranch, which just happens to be owned by three beautiful sisters. Watch for his story in *Lucky Bride,* coming in January 1997.

presents
award-winning author

DALLAS SCHULZE

with her new Western

SHORT STRAW
BRIDE

A heartwarming tale
you won't want to miss!

Coming this November

REBECCA

43 LIGHT STREET

YORK

FACE TO FACE

*Bestselling author Rebecca York returns to "43 Light Street"
for an original story of past secrets, deadly deceptions—and
the most intimate betrayal.*

She woke in a hospital—with amnesia...and with child.
According to her rescuer, whose striking face is the last
image she remembers, she's Justine Hollingsworth. But
nothing about her life seems to fit, except for the baby
inside her and Mike Lancer's arms around her. Consumed
by forbidden passion and racked by nameless fear, she
must discover if she is Justine...or the victim of some mind
game. Her life—and her unborn child's—depends on it....

Don't miss *Face To Face*—Available in October, wherever
Harlequin books are sold.

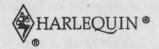

HARLEQUIN ®

®

43FTF

HARLEQUIN ®

Scandals

A passionate story of romance, where bold, daring characters set out to defy their world of propriety and strict social codes.

"Scandals—a story that will make your heart race and your pulse pound. Spectacular!"   —Suzanne Forster

"Devon is daring, dangerous and altogether delicious."
                                                        —Amanda Quick

Don't miss this wonderful full-length novel from Regency favorite Georgina Devon.

Available in December, wherever Harlequin books are sold.

SCAN

You are cordially invited to a

HOMETOWN REUNION

September 1996—August 1997

Bad boys, cowboys, babies. Feuding families,
arson, mistaken identity, a mom on the run...
Where can you find romance and adventure?
Tyler, Wisconsin, that's where!

So join us in this not-so-sleepy little town and
experience the love, the laughter and the
tears of those who call it home.

WELCOME TO A
HOMETOWN REUNION

The Murphys and the Stirlings have been
feuding for fifty years—ever since Magdalena
left Clarence at the altar, or vice versa.
Two generations later, Sandy Murphy and
Drew Stirling are unwilling partners in an
advertising campaign, and sparks fly. Everyone
in Tyler is wondering if history will repeat itself.

***Love and War* by Peg Sutherland,**
Available in November 1996
at your favorite retail store.

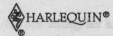

HARLEQUIN®